"Your innocent look makes me sick!"

Nathan's words were explosive and startled Kristin.

"I don't know what you're talking about!" she cried.

"No? What about this?" And from the pages of her book he held up the newspaper clipping with the photograph.

All color drained from Kristin's face; she looked the picture of guilt. Appalled, she blurted, "I only—"

But Nathan interrupted her. "You only hid it! It's a pity you didn't find a better place. Your little masquerade could have gone on forever."

"It wasn't like that!" she protested.

"Oh, you were planning to tell me about it, were you?" he said silkily. "What were you going to say? 'Oh, by the way Nathan, you have a wife and son.' Is that what you planned to do?" he shouted. "Answer me!"

JAN MACLEAN

an island loving

Harlequin Books

TORONTO • LONDON • LOS ANGELES • AMSTERDAM
SYDNEY • HAMBURG • PARIS • STOCKHOLM • ATHENS • TOKYO

Harlequin Presents first edition September 1982
ISBN 0-373-10529-0

Original hardcover edition published in 1980
by Mills & Boon Limited

CHAPTER ONE

LESS than an hour after her father had left, Kristin MacKenzie heard the chug-chug of a boat through the roll and crash of the Pacific swell. Her keen ears instantly discerned that it was not her father's boat returning, nor was it the deeper rhythm of Luther's gill netter. But who else would be coming to visit her?

She had been weeding the vegetable garden, and now she got to her feet, stripping off mud-caked gloves and dropping them on the ground beside her trowel. She walked across the neatly cropped emerald-green grass, past the tool shed and the radio shack, out on to the bluff. The lighthouse stood there, solid and sturdy, painted in wide bands of white and red, its thick glass eye staring endlessly out to sea. Leaning against the fence, Kristin gazed down into the inlet, which was sheltered from the worst of the wind by jagged outcrops of rock. A skiff was nosing into the mooring place at the head of the inlet. A bright blue skiff with a red-haired man at the wheel ... Del Clarke.

The soft curve of Kristin's mouth tightened. He hadn't waited long to arrive, she thought crossly, certain that the timing of his visit was no coincidence. Someone at the Landing must have told him that her father, Dugald MacKenzie, had left today for his biannual visit to Port Alberni. Del would not have come otherwise. Dugald might be nearing sixty, but his massive frame still moved as lightly as a cougar's and his fierce old eyes had frightened away more than one of the would-be suitors for his daughter. Not that Kristin had minded in the case of Del Clarke.

Now she watched Del tie up the skiff and leap on to the wharf. He began slowly climbing the steep wooden steps anchored up the cliffside; apparently he had not seen her watching him.

Kristin dodged behind the bulk of the lighthouse. Since her childhood, when she and Dugald had first come to live on

5

Sitka Island, it had been to her a symbol of safety and security, the flash of its blinding light the very heartbeat of the island. She steadied herself with one slim hand against its shingles, biting her lips with indecision. She could hide in the woods until Del had gone, or she could call Alice on the radio and ask her to send Luther over ... but then her innate courage stiffened her spine and her grey eyes grew pugnacious. It was *her* island, wasn't it? Why should she hide from Del Clarke? She could handle him without anybody's help! After all, her father would be gone at least two weeks, and she couldn't spend all her time running away from the red-haired fisherman. She squared her shoulders, took a deep breath, and stepped out into the open.

'Looking for someone, Del?'

He spun on his heel and Kristin was delighted to see she had startled him. Pursuing her advantage, she went on, 'I'm afraid Dugald's not here, so you've come all this way for nothing.'

He gave a short laugh. 'You know damn well I didn't come to see your father, Kristin MacKenzie. It's you I came to see.'

She widened her eyes in feigned surprise. 'Oh? Why me?'

His pale blue eyes stared at her in bafflement, for he had never known how to deal with her mockery. He was a heavy-set man in his early thirties, ruddy-complexioned, with a crop of red-blond curls; he had the doubtful reputation of being the meanest fighter along the Sound. He was still wearing hip waders and oilskins over dungarees and a checked woollen shirt, so Kristin knew he must have come straight to the island from tending his nets.

Finally he spoke. 'Well, aren't you going to ask me in?'

She hesitated, not wanting to, yet not really having any option. There were unwritten codes of hospitality on the isolated western shore, and no visitor was ever turned away. 'All right,' she said grudgingly.

She preceded him across the grass to the house, blind to the vista of forest and sea, not even hearing the lonely screaming of a gull that drifted overhead. Ushering Del into the kitchen, she filled the kettle and put it on the stove. 'Have you eaten?'

'Not since five o'clock this morning.'

She hadn't stopped for lunch either, so she might as well eat with him. With a brisk efficiency that masked her discomfort, she began preparing an omelette. Del seated himself at the kitchen table and lit a cigarette, not even bothering to ask her permission, she noticed resentfully.

'Dugald gone for long?'

'I'm not sure,' she answered coolly. Del would probably find out anyway, but there was no need to make it easy for him.

'I don't see why you're not staying at the Landing while he's away.'

'The animals have to be looked after, and someone has to keep an eye on all the equipment.'

'He could hire someone for that.'

'What would be the point when I'm already here?' she asked, cracking an egg sharply against the side of the bowl. 'Just because I'm a woman it doesn't mean I'm totally helpless.'

'I wasn't sure you knew you were a woman,' Del drawled.

Something in his voice made her glance at him sharply, and she couldn't suppress a little shiver of nervousness at the way his eyes ranged over her figure; she was glad she was wearing her oldest clothes, faded loose-fitting cords and a blouson top. 'What do you want on your omelette, cheese or mushrooms or both?' she said prosaically, hoping to sidetrack him.

'Both. The way your father keeps you hidden away here, I didn't think you'd had the chance to find out you're a woman. It's no life for a young girl, living miles from anywhere. At your age, you should be out having fun.'

'I'm perfectly happy as I am.'

'How do you know? You've nothing to compare it with. You don't miss what you've never had.'

An angry flush of colour on her high cheekbones, she slapped a plate in front of him and poured him a mug of coffee, then sat down across from him. The omelette steamed fragrantly, but she barely noticed what she ate; the sooner he'd eaten his meal, the sooner he'd be gone.

When he had finished, he pushed his plate away and lit another cigarette. 'You'll make someone a fine wife, Kristin.'

'Thanks,' she said sarcastically.

'Aren't you going to ask why I came?'

'All right—why did you come?'

'They're showing a couple of movies in the hall at the Landing tonight.'

In spite of herself, her eyes brightened, for movies were a rare treat.

'If you come back with me now, we could go together.'

'And then what, Del Clarke?' she said tartly.

He had the grace to look slightly shamefaced. 'Well, you could stay at Alice's, couldn't you?'

For a moment she was tempted. She was almost sure Del would be on his best behaviour, and he was right, she could stay with Alice and see all her friends at the Landing. Topping it all was the lure of the movies: the thrill of viewing strange countries and cities, of admiring the glamorous women and sophisticated men who almost seemed to speak another language, so alien were they to her way of life. Surely there couldn't be any harm in her going?

Almost as though he had read her thoughts, Del said, 'You'd be better off at the Landing anyway. A storm's on the way—didn't you hear the latest met report? There was a special bulletin an hour ago.'

Kristin shook her head; she had been weeding in the garden. If there was to be a storm, it would be far more pleasant to spend the time with Alice and Luther than here alone.

But then some instinct of caution came to her rescue, and she remembered her father's casual remark yesterday that the supply plane from Tofino would be a couple of days late; there'd been engine trouble. So if the plane hadn't come, how could there be a movie? She glanced swiftly at Del, catching a look of smug certainty on his face; he had known what an enticement the film would be to her.

'When did the plane get in?' she asked smoothly.

'Oh, late yesterday afternoon.'

'That's funny. Dad said it wasn't coming yesterday.'

Del was plainly disconcerted and took a moment to recover. 'Your dad isn't always right about everything,' he muttered.

'There isn't any movie at the Landing tonight, is there, Del?'

'Okay, okay, so there's no movie. We could still spend the evening together. There's always a card game going somewhere.'

'No, thanks,' she retorted, angry at herself for having so

nearly agreed to go to the mainland with him.

'Oh, come on, Kristin. When are you going to start living a bit?'

'My idea of living isn't a card game with your drunken friends,' she snapped tactlessly.

He got up from the table, his cheeks mottled an angry red, and she regretted her hasty remark. Del could be as mean and unpredictable as a grizzly; she knew that from the few other occasions when she had been in his company—occasions, however, when she had been with a crowd. Not alone with him, as she was now.

'You little snob!' he sneered. 'Your precious father's done a good job on you. You think you're a step above the likes of me, don't you?'

She made a protesting gesture, but he grabbed her fingers in his calloused palm and jerked her upright. 'Do you know what'll happen to you? You'll end up an old maid, with no one but your father to look after. And all because you're too damned particular.'

'I'm not!' she retorted vehemently, even though deep in her heart she knew there was a grain of truth in his words. More than once her father had said to her, 'I won't let you marry anyone from around here, my dear. Someone will come for you, someone from far away, I feel it in my bones. And until then you'll keep to yourself.'

Something of her thoughts must have shown in her face, for Del said thickly, 'I'll show you I'm good enough for you, Kristin.' He pulled her against him, and with brutal directness fastened his mouth on hers.

His clothing smelled of fish, his breath of stale beer. His unshaven chin rasped her skin, and in a crescendo of panic she felt one of his hands fumbling with the softness of her breast. Her heart pounding frantically, she tried to break free, but he had her pinioned. Unable to breathe, filled with a nameless revulsion, she felt her senses begin to swim. In desperation, she did the only thing possible; she allowed her knees to buckle, her body to sag limply in his hold. His grip shifted as her full weight fell on him, and she had the precious minute she needed. Filling her parched lungs with air, she jabbed him as hard as she could in the stomach with her fist, then pulled away from him.

He gave a grunt of pain. 'You'll pay for that!'

'Stay away from me!'

His eyes, hot with an animal-like hunger, raked her from head to foot, and she shuddered uncontrollably, pressing her fingers against her thighs to still their trembling. Striving to keep her voice even, she said, 'You'd better go. And don't come back.'

'I'll go when I'm good and ready.'

She went on as if she had not heard him, sounding as convincing as she could. 'Perhaps you're not aware of the arrangement Alice and I always have when Dad's away. If I don't contact her on the radio at certain times of the day, then she and Luther come over here in their boat right away. I'm already ten minutes late. Do you want them to come and find you here?'

He glared at her, his features a mingling of rage and frustration. 'You think of everything, don't you? You're too damned clever by half. Okay, I'll go. But I'll be back, Kristin.'

She paled at the menace in his tone, wondering how much longer she could maintain her self-control. Not looking at her again, Del strode across the kitchen, slamming the door behind him. From the window she watched him head for the steps that led down the cliff. Not until he was out of sight did she release her pent-up breath in a long, quivering sigh. Thank God he had believed her story about the radio message—a story she had made up on the spur of the moment. As she stepped out of the house, from below she heard the deep roar of his motor; never had anything sounded so welcome. Stumbling to the fence, she watched the skiff edge down the narrow inlet to the open water. There Del revved up the engine, so that the bow sliced through the restless waves of the channel. Within minutes he was out of sight.

Bonelessly Kristin collapsed on the grass. The wind had freshened. Gusting unimpeded across the vastness of the Pacific, it flattened her blouse against her figure and tugged at the silken weight of her hair, hair that was the lustrous dark brown of an osprey's plumage. Her face was heart-shaped, her features delicately sculpted. The dark wings of her brows emphasised her eyes' grey beauty; they could be as turbulent as a stormy sky or as serene as the silver surface of a lake. But now they were bleak with remembered fear. Relieved though she was that Del was gone, she was suddenly intensely aware of her isolation. There was not another human being on the island. And seven miles of turbulent ocean separated her from the little settlement at Sitka Landing . . .

She found herself gazing at her surroundings almost as though she had never seen them before, as though they were not as familiar to her as life itself. In front of her stretched the Pacific, now grey and wind-tossed. Her father had instilled in her a healthy respect for its vagaries, for it was as untamed and untrustworthy as any wild creature. Yet she had grown up on its shores, and fallen asleep to the rhythm of its breakers most of the nights of her life. She knew and loved its every mood.

Nearer at hand lay an untidy cluster of islands, one or two with a meagre growth of shrubs and stunted trees; they bore the brunt of the first breakers, and white foam surged over treacherous shelves of rock just beneath the ocean's surface. It was a warning against these that the lighthouse stood firm against the wind and shone its beacon.

Behind her lay the outbuildings, the barn, and the house, all white-painted and red-roofed, and to her left the pasture. Because she loved flowers, she had planted old-fashioned rose bushes on the seaward side of the house, while in the back delphiniums and lupins were already in bloom. Later in the summer fuchsias and hydrangeas would add their perfume to the ever-present ocean tang. The clearing in which the buildings stood held at bay a tangled forest of cedar, hemlock, and the tall Sitka spruce from which the island got its name.

A trail wound through the forest to the far side of the island, which was one of Kristin's favourite haunts, for there the woods gave way to open fields sprinkled with wild flowers. A long-abandoned farmhouse overlooked the cove, and instead of rugged cliffs, there was a long curve of pale sand and the gentle ripple of wavelets. From the beach on a clear day could be seen the snow-capped mountains of Vancouver Island and the tree-clad hills of its western shore, split by the fjord on whose banks nestled the fishing village of Sitka Landing.

It was a small world in which Kristin had grown up, for she had never lived in a city, never driven a car, never attended a regular school or university. Yet her father's house boasted a library many a more formally educated man might have envied, and a record collection spanning five centuries of music, with both of which Kristin was thoroughly conversant. As a result of this unconventional upbringing, she was a curious blend of knowledge and ignorance, of wisdom and innocence. Although her friends in Sitka Landing were few, and often weeks would go by without her seeing them, she cherished them nevertheless, for they shared the honesty, humour, and mutual independence so essential to any isolated community. Del Clarke, she thought ruefully, was the only exception.

She could not have said whether she was lonely. She was sure her father loved her, although it was an inarticulate love; his wife's death years ago had driven Dugald MacKenzie into a self-sufficient shell, one which his daughter had never quite succeeded in penetrating, no matter how hard she tried. Punctiliously he had taught her all he knew about the ways of the ocean and wilderness; he had never censored her reading, or restricted her wanderings on the island. But she could never share with him her joy over the beauty of a sunrise, or her sorrow over the death of a fledgling seabird. She had struggled alone through the emotional upheavals that beset any teenager. So, quite unconsciously, she wore an air of apartness and had learned to keep her own counsel. Her father's presence, the visits with her friends, the freedom to roam where she pleased on her beloved island; they were companionship enough.

But lately this had changed, although why Kristin could not have said. Within the past few months, since she had turned twenty, she had experienced more than once a sharp longing for someone nearer her own age with whom she could clamber over the rocks at low tide, and swim from the beach in summer ... someone with whom she could share her fantasies, her laughter, and her occasional tears ... someone who—loved her? But here her scarcely formed dreams seemed to run into a blank wall and she would chide herself for such foolish thoughts.

Del Clarke's boat had long since disappeared from view.

Kristin shivered suddenly in the wind's bite. Almost she wished that in spite of his behaviour she had gone with him, for she suddenly craved the sound of another human voice, the comfort of another person's company. She gave herself a mental shake and got to her feet, knowing that the best cure for her malaise was to do the chores.

That there was a storm on the way was soon confirmed by a weather report on the radio. Ignoring the little chill of foreboding in the pit of her stomach, Kristin set to work. After collecting the eggs, she herded the chickens into the shed and checked their feed. Then she milked the cow and put down fresh straw in its stall, firmly latching all the doors on the barn. By the time she had finished it was late afternoon and the light was beginning to fade. Massed purple clouds had advanced from the horizon and hung over the island, heavy with rain. The wind keened through the trees. It was an evening for drawing all the curtains and staying indoors, the girl decided wryly; she would treat herself to a broiled steak for supper, and a piece of hot apple pie.

Afterwards, she never knew what it was that drew her to the cliff's edge for one last look at the ocean before she went indoors. As she stood there, her slender form buffeted by the wind, she was awed by the gathering fury of the storm. The horizon had vanished, smudged out by an advancing curtain of rain. Giant waves threw themselves at the outer islands, only to shatter on the rocks into turbulent foam that the gale seized and flung towards the shore. In the channels betweeen the reefs the water rolled and churned. The driven spray moistened her face, salty on her tongue; the cacophony of the breakers deafened her ears.

About to turn away, she stopped, a puzzled frown on her brows. Almost subconsciously she had noticed something that should not be there . . . a piece of driftwood? Her gaze travelled slowly over the outer islands to the largest of them, one she and her father had nicknamed Whale Island for its humpbacked shape. There—behind that outcrop of rock—her heart began to thud in her breast, for it looked like the pointed prow of a boat. Her mouth dry, she wheeled and raced to the house, returning seconds later with the binoculars. Oh God, it was a boat!

She ran over to the cliff steps, where the different angle of vision gave her a clearer view. A small yacht was wrecked on the reef. Its mast had snapped, and tattered remnants of the sails snapped in the wind. One side was completely stove in, and even as she watched a wave swept over the stern and the yacht lurched unsteadily. Another wave like that one, she thought grimly, would free the boat from the rocks and it would sink like a stone.

Suddenly she gasped with horror. What was that dark shape by the cabin? With shaking fingers she cleaned the salt spray from the lenses of the binoculars and trained them on the deck. A huddle of clothing—and were those boots? There was someone on the yacht.

For a moment she panicked at the full realisation of her predicament. She was totally alone on the island, and in this weather no one could reach her for help. Only she could save the person on the boat.

She forced down her mounting terror and began to think, as her father's years of training for just such an emergency asserted themselves. Dashing back to the house, she donned rubber boots, a heavy sweater and a waterproof poncho, and shrugged one of the emergency haversacks on to her back. Snapping a flashlight and a small hatchet to her belt, she ran outside again, head down against the wind's force. She took the stairs at a reckless pace, jumping the last five steps to land with a thud on the wharf. Thank goodness she hadn't locked the boathouse—it saved a precious few seconds.

Inside the boathouse the chorus of wind and water was muted. The two skiffs, *Seawind* and *Ellen*, bobbed gently on the swell.

The smaller boat, *Seawind*, would be easier to handle alone. Her brain clicked automatically over its contents: lifejackets, lifebelt, oars, ration pack. She tied the haversack to the thwarts, then opened the outside door of the boathouse, trying not to notice how frighteningly rough even the inlet was. The motor started instantly, and Kristin breathed a quick prayer of thanks for her father's never-ceasing vigilance for his equipment. Seated at the stern, she nosed the craft out of the boathouse.

She knew these waters like the back of her hand, and had been on them in all seasons of the year. But never had she ventured forth alone in weather like this. Her mouth thinned grimly. Concentrating all her energies on a narrow world of rocks and heaving water, she steered along the northern cliff of the inlet. Once she left its shelter, she would have to navigate a fifty-foot stretch of open water to reach the lee side of the first island. She revved up the motor, gripping the tiller firmly.

There was a terrifying moment when *Seawind* reached the open water and Kristin thought she had lost control. The tiller was wrenched from her hand and the skiff swung to port. A wave broke against the gunwales, drenching her in its spray. Choking for air, she seized the tiller by instinct alone, and swung into the wind again, knowing that her life depended on the steady beat of the motor. The prow surged upwards to the crest of a wave, then lurched down into its trough. Up—down. Another sheet of spray lashed her face, plastering her hair against her head.

Not daring to let go of the tiller, she blinked her eyes frantically—only ten feet to go, five—she was safe, at least temporarily.

But even in the shelter of the rocks, she dared not slow her pace, because always at the back of her mind was the image of the yacht so precariously balanced on the reef, and of the dark shape by the cabin. She drove *Seawind* through the channel, mentally plotting her course; the most direct route would have been around Gull Cove and then straight to the yacht, but she did not dare brave the open waters over the ledge in a sea like this. So she would have to edge past the Gull Rocks, tie up the skiff in the western split of Whale Island, and walk across the island to the yacht. She must hurry ...

Her arms tense with strain, she navigated the wicked currents. To add to her worries it was becoming rapidly darker, and the scene that would be forever imprinted on her brain was a monochrome of black rocks, grey water, white foam. As she rounded the last of the Gull Rocks she could see the bulk of Whale Island ahead of her. Beyond its reef lay the open sea, its gigantic waves striking terror into her heart. Let the yacht still be there, she prayed frantically. Please God, don't let me be too late!

Desperate with anxiety, she headed *Seawind* into the tiny

harbour in the split. The skiff was steering with increasing sluggishness, for it was awash with water, and it took all her strength to hold it into the wind.

The split was about ten feet wide and thirty long; her father had drilled an iron rung into the cliff and to this Kristin tied *Seawind*'s hawser, thankful that the sides of the boat were protected by old rubber tyres from being smashed against the rocks. She pulled on the haversack and with the ration pack in one hand hauled herself up the roughly hewn steps on to the island. The rock was slippery with spray and once she fell, scraping her hand on its barnacle-encrusted surface. Not even noticing the pain, she scrambled up the cliff and with deep thankfulness felt the springy island grass underfoot.

The first drops of rain struck her face, driven like bullets by the wind. That would lessen the visibility even more, she thought despairingly.

Bending low to avoid the wind, she staggered across the grass, skirting the shoulder-high undergrowth that covered the centre of the island in an almost impenetrable tangle. Finally she reached the windward side of the island. Carefully noting her position, she dropped the two packs and the hatchet on the grass and shrugged out of the poncho; it would only hamper her from now on. A flashlight and a coil of rope in one hand, she began the steep descent from the grassy slope to the rocks.

The yacht was still there. Its deck was now tilted seaward at a dangerous angle and it shuddered visibly with every fresh onslaught of the sea. Time was running out. With exquisite care Kristin inched across the rocks towards it. She could not afford to fall now . . .

She drew level with the smashed timbers of the yacht. Straining her eyes in the gloom, she gazed in disbelief at the deck by the cabin. The figure was gone. She gave a sob of sheer terror. Had he been washed overboard? Had he drowned in the whirlpool of foam that sucked greedily at the battered yacht?

Then, through the raging of wind and ocean, she heard a different sound, and her head swung round. Switching on the flashlight, she turned the beam towards the prow. The man— for it was a man—had dragged himself forward. In the yellow beam of her torch she saw him trying to haul himself to his knees.

A wave broke against the yacht, and the deck shifted, throwing him against the narrow brass railing. Through the storm's roar she heard his moan of pain.

She cupped her hands around her mouth. 'Don't move!' she yelled. 'I'm coming!'

For a moment she hesitated, her brain racing. But there was really no choice. She had to climb aboard the yacht, and hope that the extra weight would not be enough to loosen it from the rocks. She took a deep breath and resolutely swung her leg over the rail. The deck was slippery with rain, and she inched towards the prow, clutching the railing with her free hand. With dramatic suddenness the yacht shifted again, its timbers creaking, and Kristin would have been flung against the mast but for her grasp on the side. There was not a second to waste . . .

She fell on her knees beside the still figure. He was a big man, she saw with a sinking heart, far too big for her to move alone. His black hair was soaked through, his face paper-white, his eyes closed. She shook him urgently by the shoulder. 'You must help me! We've got to get off the boat before it sinks.'

For a moment she thought he had not heard her. But then, with visible effort, he heaved himself up on one elbow and, looking straight at her, opened his eyes. They were of a startlingly brilliant blue. Even hazed with pain, they bespoke a formidable intelligence and an innate authority, so that insensibly she gave a tiny sob of relief. She was no longer alone in her battle against the storm; she had an ally.

'I've got a rope,' she said clearly. 'I'll make a harness around your shoulders. We'll have to go over the railing to the rocks and then up the cliff. Where are you hurt?'

'A bang on the head. I keep passing out,' he muttered, and for the first time she noticed an ugly wound, matted with blood, on his scalp. 'And a couple of cracked ribs, I think. Help me to sit up.'

She put her arms in his armpits and dragged him half upright, so that he was leaning against the railing. His features contorted with pain.

'I'm sorry,' she faltered.

'It's okay. Let's get out of here.'

Her fingers awkward with cold, she looped the rope around

his shoulders and across his chest and back, knotting it as
Dugald had taught her. Then she started to tie the other end
around her waist.

'Don't do that!'

'I have to. It's the only way I can get enough leverage——'

'If I slip, that means you follow me into the sea.'

Incredibly her lips quirked into a smile. 'Then please don't
slip.'

'Look, this is no joking matter,' he said, his eyes hard with
anger. 'I've got a knife in my pocket, and if I slip, I'll cut the
rope.'

'Don't you dare!'

'What the hell else do you expect me to do?'

She glared at him. 'So I'll have come all the way out here
for nothing.'

'Maybe instead of arguing about it, we'd better see if we're
even going to get off the boat.'

He was right, of course. Chagrined, she took a grip on herself. 'The best place to get ashore is up by the cabin.'

'Okay.' He began to crawl along the slanted deck, Kristin
helping as best she could. Their progress was awkward and
agonisingly slow, but finally they reached the spot where an
outcrop of rock was level with the deck.

'You've got to get over the rail,' she gasped.

'You go first.'

It seemed quite natural that he had taken command, and she
did as she was told. From the corner of her eye she saw a vast
wave rear up out of the blackness and roll inexorably towards
the yacht. 'Hurry!' she cried. 'Or we'll be too late.'

He got to his knees. She grabbed the rope around his chest
and pulled with all her might, careless of how much she was
hurting him, her fear giving her added strength. He got one
leg over the railing just as the wave crashed against the stern.
There was an ugly rasp of wood against stone as the yacht
tilted further away from the rocks. The man flung himself
forward and Kristin seized him frantically. He fell across her,
knocking her backwards; she cried out as her back struck the
cliff.

CHAPTER TWO

FOR a long moment they lay entangled on the rock, the rain pelting them mercilessly. Then she felt him shift his weight. She groped for the flashlight, which was tied to her belt, and flicked it on. 'Are you all right?'

'Yeah. We only just made it, didn't we?'

'Much too close for comfort.'

There was a ghost of laughter in his voice. 'What happens now?'

She felt an almost hysterical urge to laugh as well, and tamped it down. They weren't safe yet . . .

'I have a skiff anchored on the other side of the island. But there's no way we can make it to the shore in the dark. We'll have to camp here overnight. If you can get up the hill, I can rig up some kind of a shelter in the bushes. There's food as well.'

Again that thread of laughter. 'You're a marvel! Let's go.'

Bracing herself against the rock face, Kristin supported him as best she could. She was a tall girl, but even in the dark she could tell he was inches taller than she. 'I'll go ahead and pull you up if I can,' she said, injecting more confidence in her voice than she felt. 'The rocks are slippery, so be careful.'

As she spoke, another huge wave bludgeoned the yacht, and helplessly she saw it settle deeper in the water. It was only a matter of time before it sank . . . a curtain of spray was flung at them by the gale, and she buried her face in his chest, feeling his big body curve protectingly over hers. For one of those split seconds that are timeless she felt utterly safe. She closed her eyes.

He bent his head to hers, his lips brushing her cheek. 'Are you okay?' She nodded dumbly. 'Let's go, then,' he repeated.

Again she had the odd—and not unwelcome—sensation that the leadership had moved from her shoulders to his. Strangely heartened, she sensed a new confidence seep into her limbs, and for the first time since she had sighted the yacht, she dared

19

to hope that they both might get out of this alive.

Shining the torch over the rocks, she picked out the easiest incline up the cliff, and a few steps at a time they began to climb. The next few minutes rapidly turned into a nightmare. Exposed as they were on the cliff face, the wind could attack them in all its fury, and in spite of her exertions, Kristin was soon shivering with cold. Blinded by the rain, she struggled on, the man's arm over her shoulders, her arm about his waist.

She could hear him gasping for breath, and knew his injured ribs must be stabbing him with pain every step he took. Once he stumbled and fell heavily to his knees, unable to suppress a harsh exclamation of agony.

Unaware that tears were mingling with the raindrops that streaked her cheeks, Kristin knelt beside him. 'We're nearly there. Can you manage just a little further?'

His reply was inaudible, but with dogged courage he got to his feet and they staggered on.

The soft turf under their feet was like a miracle. Shining the torch over the stunted trees, Kristin soon found a patch where the thickly growing branches arched over the ground like a roof. It would keep the worst of the rain off until she could rig up a shelter. She guided the man towards it and eased him to the ground. 'I'll have to take the torch and get the haversacks,' she shouted. 'But I'll be right back.'

When she returned, he was leaning against a gnarled tree trunk, his eyes shut, looking utterly exhausted. Remembering all her lessons in wilderness survival, she knew he needed food and warmth and dry clothing. Working as quickly as she could, she spread the rubberised poncho over their heads, tying it firmly at each corner. The emergency kit yielded a thick sheet of plastic, which she spread on the ground over bits of spruce bough which she had hacked off the nearby trees. The stranger seemed to have sunk into a semi-conscious daze; she tugged at his sleeve. 'Come in out of the rain. Oh, please, I can't move you on my own!'

Her voice finally penetrated. 'Sorry,' he mumbled, and she was frightened to hear how weak he sounded. She must heat up some food ... a hollow in the rocks yielded almost pure rainwater, and she lit the tiny paraffin stove, setting the billy-can on top. The steady blue flame cast an eerie light over their surroundings; the undergrowth rustled continuously and somewhere two twigs rubbed against each other with a high-pitched squeak. She was glad she was not alone ...

'Don't tell me you're afraid of the dark?'

She glanced up, deeply relieved to hear his voice. A gamine grin eased the strain from her delicate features. 'Terrified of it,' she said firmly.

'What you did this evening was the most courageous thing I've ever seen,' he said quietly. 'I would have drowned if it hadn't been for you.'

She gave a reminiscent shudder, wondering if the yacht was still clinging to the rock. 'Thank you,' she said in a low voice. 'But I didn't really think of it as brave. I just—did it.'

'That's the best kind of bravery there is.'

She could feel hot colour flooding her cheeks, and lowered her eyes in embarrassment from his steady gaze. His words of praise curled warm fingers around her heart.

The water was steaming in the pot. Glad of the diversion, she opened the ration pack and mixed two packages of de-hydrated soup in plastic mugs. But when she passed one to him, she realised his hands were shaking uncontrollably. Quite unselfconsciously she lifted his palm to her cheek.

'You're freezing!' she exclaimed. 'Here, let me help you.' Sitting close beside him, she guided the cup to his mouth so he could drink, not satisfied until he had drained the mug. Only then did she drink her own. Afterwards, she lit the kerosene lamp that came with the emergency kit, and blew out the stove.

'I'm going down to the skiff,' she announced matter-of-factly. 'There are blankets stored there, and maybe an old jacket of my father's. I shouldn't be more than fifteen minutes. Will you be all right?'

She thought she had successfully concealed her dread of venturing into the dark and rain again, but as she looked at him, she knew that with uncanny perception he had sensed her fears. He made a grimace of intense frustration, and she guessed he was not a man who liked being helpless.

'I have to go,' she said reasonably. 'I don't have any choice. You're soaked to the skin, and I'm pretty wet myself.'

'Yeah, I guess you're right.' He stretched out his hand and

grasped her wrist, his eyes intent. 'Be careful.'

The lamplight cast mysterious shadows over her face, darkening her eyes to a smoky grey. Warmed by his concern, she smiled at him, her mouth curving. 'I will be.'

'You're very beautiful,' he said abruptly. 'But of course you know that.'

She blinked at him. 'Oh no,' she said with complete sincerity. 'My mother was the beautiful one in the family. I can't remember her, but I've seen pictures of her. I don't look a bit like her—my father's said so.'

'Maybe you don't look like her. Why should you, after all? You're yourself. But you *are* beautiful.'

A small part of Kristin's mind registered what a strange conversation this was after the violence and terror of the past hour. But deep within her she was conscious of the easing of a long-held pain. She had never felt she could measure up to her father's memories of the lovely woman who had been his wife; now this stranger was telling her it didn't matter. She, Kristin, was a woman in her own right—a beautiful woman. Her features softened, a shy pink colouring her cheeks, so that she did indeed look very beautiful. 'Thank you,' she said softly.

The note of command was back in his voice. 'Go as quickly as you can, but don't take any unnecessary risks.'

She nodded her compliance. Before she could change her mind, she ducked out of the shelter and loped across the grass; knowing that he was waiting for her made the trip less arduous. The skiff was still anchored in the split, its scuppers awash with rain. She slithered down to it, jumped aboard, and wrenched open the locker in the prow. They were in luck: four blankets. But no jacket . . . her father must have left it in the boathouse. She bundled the blankets up in an old piece of oilskin, and arrived breathless back at the shelter five minutes later.

The stranger was sitting where she had left him, his head slumped forward on his knees. As she squeezed through the narrow opening in the trees, he looked up, greeting her with a smile that twisted her heart. He was still shivering uncontrollably and all the horror stories she had ever heard about death from hypothermia flitted through her mind.

She lit the little stove again and heated a can of thick stew, which he insisted on feeding himself. It seemed to revive him; after the last mouthfuls he said with a certain deliberation, 'It looks as though we're going to spend the night together, and I don't even know your name.'

'Kristin. Kristin MacKenzie.'

'That's an unusual name ... pretty.'

'It was my mother's second name.'

He stared at her sombrely. 'It's time I asked a few obvious questions. Won't you be missed tonight? Where do you live?'

'I live on Sitka Island—a half mile to the east. My father is the lightkeeper there. And no, I won't be missed—he went away this morning for two weeks.'

'There's no one else on the island?'

'No.'

'You mean he left you all alone? You're too young to be left by yourself like that.'

'I'm twenty,' she said with considerable dignity. 'And it's not that bad being on my own. Anyway, someone has to look after the animals and see that the equipment's running smoothly. And I contact my friends at the Landing at least every couple of days by radio.'

'I see.'

There was a grimness about his mouth that Kristin could not understand. She waited for him to volunteer information about himself, and finally said tentatively, 'What's your name?'

He closed his eyes and she saw a look of bitter frustration score his features. 'I ... I don't know.'

'You don't know?' she repeated incredibly. 'What do you mean?'

'Just what I say.' He stared down at his hands, his voice taut. 'I can't remember my name or where I come from or where I was going. I can't remember what I was doing on a yacht miles from anywhere, or how I got banged on the head.'

'But that's dreadful.'

He gave a short laugh totally devoid of humour. 'Yes. It's inconvenient to say the least. Where are we, by the way?'

'On the west coast of Vancouver Island. Fifty miles north of Tofino,' she answered blankly. 'You mean, you've got amnesia?'

'I suppose that's what I mean. Somehow I got a hell of a

blow on the head,' he touched his scalp ruefully, 'and I must have been out cold for quite a while to have ended up on those rocks.'

Trying to be practical, she said, 'Don't you have a wallet in your pocket? Or any other means of identification?'

She saw hope flare in his eyes. He fumbled in the pockets of his jeans and then of his jacket. 'No—nothing.'

'Well, look, there's no sense worrying about it right now. Once we get home, we can listen to the marine radio. They have a missing persons list, and you'll probably recognise your name——'

'You didn't notice the name of the yacht?' he rapped.

'No—no, I didn't. Sorry,' she said miserably.

'God, don't apologise, child. You had plenty on your mind as it was.'

'Really, it'll be all right,' she reassured him gently. 'And now I think you should get out of your wet clothes. I found blankets on the skiff.'

'What about you?'

'I'll be fine.'

Before she could guess his intention, he reached out and felt her jeans and sweater. 'You're as wet as I am. So you needn't think I'm taking all the blankets.'

She scowled at him. 'You're being very difficult.' He needn't think she was going to undress in front of him, she thought irritably, even though she was longing to be rid of the clammy dampness of her jeans.

'This is no time for false modesty, Kristin,' he told her.

'I wasn't——'

'Yes, you were. We'll share the blankets—and that's an order. Believe me, you don't have a thing to worry about. I'm as weak as a kitten and in no state to make a nuisance of myself.'

She flushed scarlet, fumbling with the hem of her sweater, her dark lashes hiding her eyes. Then she felt his fingers lifting her chin until she could no longer avoid his gaze. Feeling gauche, and desperately unsure of herself, she stared at him unhappily.

'Trust me, Kristin,' he said softly.

'I—I've never spent the night with a man before,' she stammered.

'I know you haven't,' he answered gently. 'Tell you what—why don't you arrange the blankets, and then you can put out the lamp before you undress.'

Grateful that he had not made fun of her fears, she did as he suggested. Spreading the thinnest blanket over the plastic sheet for them to lie on, she put the other three over it. Pulling her wet sweater over her head, she folded it neatly and put it under the plastic as a pillow. 'Give me your jacket and I'll do the same for you.'

He shrugged out of the jacket and she made his pillow in the same way.

'You'll have to help me out of my sweater.'

'Okay. Should I do anything with that gash on your scalp?'

'I don't think so.' He touched it gingerly. 'It's stopped bleeding, so let's leave well enough alone. I can manage now—so why don't you blow out the lamp?'

In the darkness she peeled off her wet blouse and jeans, hanging them over a nearby branch. She was wearing only a lacy bra and panties which covered her scarcely at all. If only they could have lit a fire—but everything was too wet.

She fumbled for the blankets, touched his bare skin by mistake and recoiled with an audible gasp of dismay.

'Settle down, Kristin,' he said curtly. 'I've already told you that you don't have a thing to worry about.'

She slid under the blankets, edging as far away from him as she could. Deliberately she turned her back, curling up for warmth, for the blankets were scant protection against the cold. She sensed, rather than heard, him lie down beside her. 'Goodnight,' she said in a small voice.

'Goodnight, Kristin. Sleep well. And—thanks again.'

She lay still. She felt damp and chilled and thoroughly wide awake. A twig snapped, and she jumped. Above them the poncho flapped in the wind; somewhere rain was dripping steadily into a puddle.

Ten minutes later she was still staring up into the blackness. Beside her, the man—if only she knew his name!—seemed to be already asleep, although his breathing was shallow and uneven. He muttered something unintelligible, shifted abruptly, and gave a harsh cry of pain, just as sharply bitten off.

With sudden insight, Kristin saw her behaviour of the past

half hour as both foolish and naïve. She was no longer a child
... but she had been acting like one, she thought, ashamed of
herself. This man, whoever he was, was no Del Clarke, who
would force himself upon her. And although he had been
shipwrecked and injured, and had lost his memory, he had
never once lost his self-control. He had made amazingly light
of what must have been—and still was—a horrifying experience.

That smothered cry in the dark awoke all her womanly
compassion, and overcame the last of her silly fears. With a
calm sureness she rolled over to face him, and stretched out
her hand. She touched what felt like his shoulder and only
then did she realise he was shivering with cold. Without even
thinking what she was doing, she moved her body to lie near
his, pressing her legs against him and curving her arm over his
chest.

'You should have told me you were cold,' she chided.

'You feel lovely and warm,' he mumbled.

'Thank you,' she answered demurely.

'Here—sit up a minute.'

Mystified, she raised herself on one elbow.

'Okay, lie down again.'

He had changed position in the dark and as she lay back, his
arm curved around her body, his hand cupping her shoulder.
Pressing her nearer, he murmured, 'Mmm—nice.'

She could feel the hard arch of his ribcage against her
breasts, and said in quick alarm, 'Won't I hurt you?'

'Other side,' he muttered economically.

She lay still. The tremors shaking his frame seemed to be
subsiding, she thought thankfully, and sensed that his breathing was becoming quieter and deeper.

Slowly there seeped into her consciousness a host of sensations, all new to her ... her cheek was resting in the hollow of
his shoulder; his skin was smooth and smelled cleanly of soap,
an aroma somehow indefinably masculine. Her left arm was
lying over his chest; she could feel the roughness of hair
against her elbow, and the slow rise and fall of his breathing.

A sense of wonder filled her that she should be lying so
intimately with a man who was virtually a stranger to her, and
yet feel no fear. But it was more positive than a simple lack of

fear, she thought, her mind fumbling around these unaccustomed concepts. She trusted him—was that it?

With an inward shock of discovery, she knew that she could not even stop there. For she was honest enough to admit to herself that the deeply pleasurable sensations welling within her were rooted in her body, and not in her emotions. The hand that lay across his torso longed to run itself through the tangled mat of hair on his chest, and to explore the muscled contours of his throat. Her lips ached to press themselves into the curve of his shoulder. She closed her eyes in panic, horrified to find herself swept by such alien desires.

Because her father's library had always been open to her, and because she was a voracious reader, she had at least an intellectual knowledge of the power of sexual desire. But in terms of experience she was innocent. A few kisses from the Landing boys after a dance, Del's rough embrace—that was all. How could she be so attracted to this man, this unknown visitor whom the sea had brought her? A quiver of dismay ran through her.

'Are you cold?'

For a moment she was silent; she had thought he was asleep. 'N—no,' she stuttered.

'What's wrong?'

'Nothing.'

'Kristin,' he said quietly, but with that undertone of steel that she had noticed before in his voice, 'I may not know who I am or where I come from, but I do know I dislike prevarication. Something's bothering you, isn't it?'

Shaken as much by his discernment as by his tone of command, she whispered, 'Please—it's nothing.'

'Come on, Kristin, tell me what's wrong. I certainly won't go to sleep until you do.'

Her mind raced. She could not tell him the truth—what would he think of her? Easy, wanton, promiscuous—all the ugly words danced in front of her eyes. She did not pause to consider why his opinion of her should be so important. Taking courage, she spoke what was at least partly the truth. 'You do believe me that I've never done this before—slept with a man, I mean?'

He began to chuckle, then bit it off with an exclamation of pain. 'Hell! I can't even laugh.'

'I don't think it's funny,' she said mutinously.

There was still a glimmer of amusement in his tone. 'Of course I didn't think you were in the habit of sleeping with men. Why should I?'

'Well, I don't know,' she faltered.

He changed tactics. 'Kristin, do you like us lying here together like this?' He gave her a little squeeze with his arm, bringing her even closer.

The blanket of darkness gave her the courage to be honest. 'Yes.'

'Good. So do I.' His voice was very gentle. 'And there's nothing wrong with that. It's nothing to be ashamed of. In fact, it's perfectly natural. So why don't you stop worrying about it and go to sleep?'

'You really do understand, don't you?' she said, in a little voice in which wonderment and delight were equally mixed.

'I guess so,' he replied, plainly mystified. 'You sound as though no one's ever taken the trouble to try and understand you before.'

'Well, I suppose they haven't.'

'Not your father? Or your boy-friends?'

'I could never talk to my father about emotional things. And I haven't any boy-friends.'

'The men around here must be crazy!'

She giggled. 'You're very good for the ego.'

If he thought her life had been singularly bare of compliments and even simple attention, he forebore to say so. For a few minutes they remained silent, Kristin ever more conscious of a delicious lassitude creeping through her limbs from the closeness of his body.

'Goodnight, Kristin.'

'Goodnight.'

He shifted in the darkness and with a pang of anticipation she knew he wanted to kiss her goodnight. She turned her face towards him. His lips brushed her cheek and drifted towards her mouth. It began gently, that first kiss, so gently that she relaxed into pure enjoyment of a pleasure hitherto unknown. A tremor rippled through her slender frame when the pressure of his mouth became more insistent. Her lips parted under his, and she gave a tiny moan of pure delight, and without conscious thought propped herself on one elbow, so that she was half lying over him. His hand slid from her shoulder along the curve of her spine, and she arched her body fiercely against his. Then his fingers moved from her waist to the softness of her breast. The pleasure was so intense that for a moment she went rigid with shock.

As though that were a signal, he wrenched his mouth from hers and turned his head away, fighting for control. His chest was heaving, and the heavy pounding of his heart reverberated against her flesh.

'What's wrong?' she whispered.

'This is just what I didn't want to happen,' he grated.

'But——'

'Kristin, you're very young and very innocent. You're also very desirable. I should never have kissed you in the first place —it's my fault.'

'But you wanted to kiss me, didn't you?'

'I'm only human.'

She lay back on the rough blanket, her mind and body in a turmoil. Had she made herself cheap in his eyes? Should she not have responded to him? But how could she have helped it? The sensations that had swept over her from the touch of his lips and hands had been as irrevocable as the waves of the sea.

'Go to sleep,' he ordered harshly. 'It won't happen again.'

A shaft of pain ripped through her. So he didn't want it to happen again—was she that repugnant to him? Deeply hurt, she took refuge in anger. 'It certainly won't,' she said coldly. Turning her back, she composed herself for sleep, certain that she would remain wide awake all night . . .

She was dreaming . . . time and again she headed her skiff for the yacht, only to be driven back by the maelstrom of wind and water. On the deck she could see the man's huddled shape slide closer and closer to the railing. A wave surged towards the yacht, its foam washing over the deck, and she knew he would be swept overboard before she could reach him. She cried out, but the wind seized her call and flung it away contemptuously.

'Kristin! Wake up!'

Struggling to the surface of a nightmare depth of sleep, she clutched him with frantic fingers. 'You were drowning!' she sobbed. 'And I knew I couldn't reach you in time. All I could do was watch——' The tears were streaming down her cheeks, as all the accumulated tensions of the past few hours erupted in a storm of weeping. He held her close, murmuring soothing bits of nonsense into her ear until gradually she grew calmer.

'Oh dear,' she sniffed finally, 'I'm sorry.'

'You needed to do that—don't apologise.'

She sniffed again. Amused, he said, 'Where's the flashlight? I think there's a handkerchief in the pocket of my jeans.'

She fumbled for the torch and switched it on. 'I must look a fright,' she said with a watery grin.

'Typical woman!'

'The jeans are on your side of the bed,' she teased hopefully, yet ready to leap out of bed if he should start to get up.

'But I don't need the handkerchief,' he retorted.

She pulled a rude face at him and slid from under the blankets. Giving her nose a hearty blow, she got back into their makeshift bed as quickly as she could. About to switch the torch off, for the first time she noticed a narrow chain around his neck with a tiny silver amulet, shaped like a fish, dangling from it. 'What's that?' she asked, intrigued.

His blue eyes puzzled, he fingered it. 'I don't know,' he said uncertainly. A frown scored his forehead. 'I feel as though I should remember. But I don't.'

She reached over and held the delicate little fish in her hand; it was exquisitely carved, and she said slowly, 'It looks very expensive.' Her voice suddenly quickened with excitement. 'The other side feels different.' She turned it over, shining the torch directly on it. 'There's writing on it.' She strained her eyes spelling out the letters. 'It says "Nathan". That's all —just "Nathan". That must be your name!'

His eyes met hers but they showed none of her enthusiasm. His voice flat, he said, 'I suppose so. Nathan ... but Nathan who? God! Why can't I remember?'

It was the first time his iron self-control had slipped. Wanting very much to comfort him, she said, 'A first name's better than nothing. And I'm sure it's only a matter of time until your memory comes back.'

'I hope you're right.' Wearily he rubbed his forehead with the back of his hand.

'Have you got a headache?'

'Yeah—the devil of a one.'

She switched off the torch so that they were again cocooned in darkness, and lay quietly wakeful until she was sure that he had fallen asleep.

When next Kristin opened her eyes, a dim grey light was filtering through the branches overhead. Rain still dripped steadily into the undergrowth, and she could hear the smothered howling of the wind. She pulled the blankets closer, glad of Nathan's warmth beside her. But with quick concern she realised it was more than warmth: his body was afire with fever, and he was stirring restlessly in his sleep—perhaps that was what had woken her. She glanced up at him. His forehead was beaded with sweat. Patches of colour marked his cheek-bones, visible even through the weathered tan of a man whose life was spent outdoors. Who was he? she wondered. And where had he come from? What had driven him to sail alone in the treacherous waters of the Pacific?

She lay still, letting her eyes wander over his features. His hair had dried in a cluster of untidy curls that were the iridescent black of a raven's wing. His profile was strongly marked, with a disconcertingly firm chin. He would be older than she by at least ten years, she guessed, for fine lines scored his cheeks. Her eyes lingered on the chiselled mouth—even in sleep it hinted both at self-discipline and an underlying sensuousness. A remembered warmth flooded her as she re-called the questing passion of his kiss.

But her disturbing memories were soon routed by a host of worries. If he was ill—really ill—what would she do? The storm seemed unabated, and the mere contemplation of the nightmare crossing in the skiff was enough to make her shudder. Yet how could they stay here, without warmth or dry clothes and with only the minimum of food? Her forehead creased with anxiety.

'Kristin——'

'You're awake!' She twisted on her side, propping her head on her elbow, quite unaware of the heavy fall of her hair across his shoulder, silken on his skin.

'Kristin, we've got to get out of here,' he muttered, his voice hoarse with effort. 'This storm could go on for days.'

'But you're ill——'

He brushed aside her protest. 'If I am, now's the time to go, before I get worse.'

Kristin knew that he was right, but her spirit quailed at the thought of getting him to the boat. And what if the skiff got swamped, or overturned in the channel? She would never be able to save him then.

'Can't I go back alone and radio for help?'

'You know as well as I do that no one can reach us in this weather. Go check on the skiff, and come back as quickly as you can.' He closed his eyes. For him the discussion was closed.

That was fine for him, she thought crossly, knowing how illogical she was being, yet driven to anger by her intense anxiety. She sat up and reached for her clothes. They were still wet, the damp fabric making her shiver. She struggled into her jeans, which seemed to have shrunk overnight, then awkwardly pulled the sweater over her head, trying not to brush against the wet branches overhead. Accidentally she tipped one corner of the poncho, and a stream of cold water trickled down her neck.

'Oh damn!' she muttered.

'You're even prettier when you're in a temper,' Nathan drawled, his blurred blue eyes watching her sardonically.

'I am not in a temper!'

'No? Looks mighty like it to me.'

'Oh, shut up!'

'If I were well, you wouldn't get away with speaking to me like that.'

His threat was quietly spoken, but instinctively she retreated from his reach. 'So you win the argument by brute force— how very clever of you!' she said sarcastically, aware even as she spoke of how appallingly badly she was behaving. Just because her nerves were stretched tight, she didn't have to sound like a harridan.

Because she was basically a straightforward and even-tempered girl, she opened her mouth to apologise. But he had clearly lost interest; his eyes had closed and his face was half turned away from her. Biting her lip in frustration, she pulled on her boots—they at least were dry—and bent double, edged out of the shelter.

One swift glance confirmed all her fears. The waves were still throwing themselves at the rocks, the wind flinging the spray high in the air. The channel was a seething cauldron of grey-white foam. She began to run across the grass, her mouth suddenly dry. What if the skiff had worked free of its moorings? Then they would be truly stranded——

But the skiff was there. Straining at the hawser, it rocked up and down on the swell. Her relief was such that she forgot her annoyance with Nathan and eagerly ran back to the shelter. 'It's there!' she announced unceremoniously.

He had dressed himself while she was gone. 'Good,' he grunted, not even looking at her. 'Pack up the stuff and let's get out of here.'

She was hurt by his distant manner, for always at the back of her mind hovered the memory of that searing kiss. Trying to sound as cool as he, she said, 'I'll make a trip with all the gear, then come back for you.'

When she got back, he had crawled out of the shelter and pulled himself upright, although she noticed how heavily he was leaning on the stunted tree branches for support. Without saying a word, she looped his arm over her shoulder and put her own arm around his waist, and they set off across the grass. She braced herself to bear as much of his weight as she could, and they made more or less steady progress to the rocks, although they were both rain-soaked and breathless by the time they reached them. Kristin eyed the steep, rain-washed steps to the skiff with misgiving. 'I'd better go first.'

'No! Let me——'

Ignoring his protest, she slithered down the bank. But her toe, reaching for the second step, hit a piece of seaweed and skidded from under her. With a sharp cry of fear she lost her balance. She fell on her side, her fingers grabbing for a hold on the rocks, her hip bumping down the steps. Eyes tight shut in total panic, she waited for the cold grey waters to close over her.

A hand grasped her wrist and halted her fall. Quivering with fear, she cowered against the rockface.

'Kristin!'

Slowly she looked up. His face was barely a foot from hers, his features taut with strain. 'Put your right foot on that ledge,' he gasped.

With sickening suddenness she realised he was bearing all her weight on his left arm—the arm on his injured side. Her foot fumbled for the ledge.

'Okay, there's one more step, then you can reach the skiff. You may have to jump, so be careful.'

She felt for the last step. Glancing over her shoulder, she judged the distance to the skiff, and not giving herself time to think, she jumped. The deck swayed beneath her. With a thud Nathan landed beside her. He pushed her down on the thwart. 'Put your head between your knees,' he ordered curtly.

As she did so, the sick dizziness gradually left her. She lifted her head, taking a deep shaking breath. 'It's my turn to say thank you.'

She had not expected to see anger blazing in his blue eyes. 'You little idiot! You could have been drowned! Didn't you hear me telling you to wait?'

Dumbstruck, she quailed under the lash of his tongue. He muttered an oath under his breath and turned away. By an intense effort of will, he seemed to have overcome his illness.

With the efficiency of an experienced sailor, he untied the hawser, and then stepping around her, started the motor. Hugging her knees to stop their trembling, Kristin trained her eyes on the fog-shrouded cliffs of Sitka Island ... the cliffs of home. The skiff swung clear of the split and with a strange sense of inevitability, she realised how completely she had put her trust in Nathan's ability to handle a strange boat in unknown waters. As he veered among the reefs and shoals, skilfully compensating for the vagaries of wind and current, she found herself wondering how he could ever have been shipwrecked. Even though he was ill, it was obvious that he was a man attuned to the sea, and she felt a mounting respect for him as he finally reached the haven of the inlet and headed for the boathouse.

CHAPTER THREE

THE motor sputtered into silence, and Kristin slowly stood up, fastening the hawser to its ring. She climbed stiffly on to the wharf and waited for him to join her. Without speaking, he motioned for her to precede him, so she began to climb up the wooden stairs, her limbs leaden, her mind a blank from exhaustion and the final release of strain. They crossed the grass, and Kristin opened the back door. As she stepped into the kitchen, she saw it with a new clarity: the homely details of checkered tablecloth, crisp gingham curtains, and delicate-leaved ivy twined around the window. The brass ornaments seemed to twinkle welcome. A lump rose in her throat.

Nathan closed the door behind him. As if drawn by some force greater than herself she turned to face him, this tall, arrogant stranger whom the sea had brought her. His eyes were caverns of blue in a face drained of vitality and he was swaying on his feet. But he was safe. She felt herself begin to shake with reaction, and pressed the back of her hand against her mouth to stifle the sobs that crowded her throat. But she could not. Helplessly she began to cry. Through a haze of tears she saw him reach her in two quick strides, and felt his arms go around her, pulling her close to the hard bulk of his body. She buried her face in his sweater, her body shuddering as she wept. He held her quietly, one hand stroking the wet hair back from her face, his voice murmuring soothingly in her ear. It was an embrace that made no demands on her, offering simple comfort, security. He could have been her brother.

Gradually her sobs subsided. Nathan reached for the package of tissues on the table, and passed her a handful. 'Blow,' he ordered.

She gave him a shaky smile. 'I seem to be making a habit of this. Believe it or not, I hardly ever cry.'

'You don't expect me to believe that,' he said, his grin easing the lines of pain and weariness about his mouth.

Convulsively she clung to him again, her voice muffled in

35

his sweater. 'Oh, Nathan, we're safe! I was so frightened.'

With a hand under her chin, he lifted her face to his.

'I know you were. But you did what had to be done just the same, didn't you? And—as I said to you once before—that's the mark of true courage.'

She blushed. His words of praise awoke a new pride in herself; commendation of any kind had been rare from her self-absorbed father. Furthermore, Nathan had spoken to her without any patronage, as an equal, and she stood tall in front of him, a glow of pleasure in her grey eyes. 'Thank you,' she said seriously, intuitively knowing how wrong would be any attempt to brush aside his words, or deny them.

'You're welcome. And now, do you have a first aid kit?'

'Yes, of course, but——'

'You've got a nasty graze on your face.'

Subconsciously she had been aware of a burning sensation on one cheek. She walked over to the mirror hanging by the refrigerator and looked at herself, aghast. Her long hair was tangled about her head. Dark circles of weariness lay under her eyes, and an ugly scrape, caked with dried blood and dirt, disfigured her cheek. 'I look awful!' she groaned.

He came up behind her, his reflection topping hers. 'If you're starting to worry about how you look, there's nothing seriously wrong with you!'

'I can't say the same of you, Nathan. You look ill,' she said bluntly, for a hectic flush stained his cheeks, although the rest of his face was drained of colour. 'You must get to bed.'

'After I've fixed up that scrape.'

Knowing there was no sense in arguing, she brought out the first aid kit and put some water in a bowl, perching on the counter-top so he would not have to stoop. Neat-fingered as a doctor, he cleaned away the tiny particles of dirt and rock. Once she winced, and he stopped instantly. 'Sorry—did I hurt you?'

She nodded, suddenly breathless. His face was a scant six inches from hers, so close that she could see tiny flecks of rust in his pupils. His lashes were as long and thick as a woman's, yet there was nothing remotely effeminate about him. The exact opposite, she thought wryly. The pull of his intense masculinity was acting on her like a magnet; she longed to lean forward and touch his mouth with her lips.

No longer able to meet his gaze, she lowered her eyes, only to see a heavy pulse throbbing at the base of his throat. With a surge of primitive triumph she knew he was as affected by her nearness as she was by his.

He spoke with husky deliberation. 'You want me to kiss you, don't you?'

Kristin had never learned to be coy. 'Yes, I do.'

'I want to kiss you too.'

His face moved closer until she felt herself drowning in the blue depths of his eyes. Then his lips met hers with exquisite gentleness, a gentleness that was in itself a torment. With deliberate sensuality he took the fullness of her lower lip between his teeth, nibbling it provocatively. Without conscious volition her hands cupped his face between them, stroking the corded muscles of his throat, running themselves through his thick hair. His kiss became more demanding, his lips more insistent. She slid down from the counter, and he moulded her slim form against him.

In the living-room the old grandfather clock chimed the hour, its bell-like tones echoing sonorously. As though he had been shot, Nathan pushed her away, turning his head intently to the sound, a look of desperate enquiry on his face. 'What was that?' he demanded.

'The grandfather clock.'

He raked his fingers through his hair, his eyes closed in fierce concentration. 'I remembered it—the chimes. I must own a clock like that. For a moment I thought I was home.'

Kristin sensed the bitter struggle he was waging, as he tried to push away the mists that shrouded his memory, and held her breath, aching with her inability to help him.

Finally he shook his head in frustration. 'It's no good,' he said dully, 'it's gone. God, why can't I remember?'

The pallor beneath his tan had intensified; he looked in the last throes of exhaustion. Kristin said with calm confidence, 'You will remember in time, I know you will. But you're worn out. You must rest, Nathan. The bathroom is through there, and I'll make up the bed for you.'

It was a measure of his weakness that he accepted her instructions without demur. She gave him towels and a dressing-gown of dark blue wool she had just finished making for her father, and as she went into the bedroom, heard the hiss of the shower.

The guest room had a wide picture window that overlooked the Pacific. Having no desire to see its storm-tossed expanse, Kristin drew the moss green curtains, which like the bedspread was made of a shiny silk. The charmingly patterned wallpaper was an attractive foil for them; the rug was thick cream-coloured wool. Deftly she took out clean sheets from the lavender-scented drawer and made the bed. Despite her concern for Nathan's condition, she was conscious of a deep happiness welling within her as she heard him moving about in the bathroom. She switched on the small bedside lamp, for the curtains had artificially darkened the room, then looked up with a smile as he walked in.

'I'm about ready for that,' he groaned, indicating the bed.

The wool robe was slightly too small for him. With a quiver of her nerve ends she knew he was naked beneath it, for in the V of its neckline she could see the dark tangle of hair on his chest, and the gleam of the little silver amulet. Flustered, she said abruptly, 'I'm going to get you something to eat,' and edged round the bed to the door. He made no attempt to stop her and she heard the creaking of the bedsprings as he sat down.

When she returned in a few minutes with a bowl of thick soup on a tray, Nathan was already asleep. He was lying on his back, the lamp throwing his strong profile in relief. She stood quietly in the doorway, watching him, a puzzled frown on her brow. What was it about this man that so stirred her senses? Handsome, rugged, masculine, he was all of those. His toughness, his arrogance, his self-confidence, were those what appealed to her? Unable to answer her own question, and oddly frightened by her lack of understanding, she left the room.

It was early evening before Kristin was ready for bed, for all the usual chores had needed doing. Afterwards she had enjoyed a luxuriously hot shower, which eased the soreness from her muscles. Already bruises had darkened down her side and she found a number of scrapes which she could not account for. After towelling her hair dry so it fell in soft waves to her shoulders, she satisfied herself that Nathan was sleeping quietly, then went to her own room. Falling into bed, she sank almost immediately into sleep.

It was pitch dark when she woke up. Outside the gale whistled round the house and the rain still beat a furious tattoo on the roof; but she knew neither of these would have awoken her. She sat up and heard it again: Nathan's voice, calling something in the dark. She leaped out of bed and hurried across the hall, pulling the white nylon gown around her as she went. Carefully setting the bedside lamp on the floor, so it would not shine in his eyes, she switched it on.

He was tossing restlessly in his sleep, the blankets tangled about his waist. An ugly bruise disfigured his rib cage, and when she laid her palm on his forehead, it was burning hot. Murmuring something inaudible, he shrugged away from her touch. Trying to be practical, she went into the bathroom and wrung out a facecloth with cool water. Sitting on the edge of the bed, she smoothed it over his face and neck. For a moment he lay still, before he pushed her hand aside. 'No—no,' he muttered fitfully, and then more strongly, 'I'll cut the rope.'

Thoroughly frightened, she seized his shoulders. 'Wake up, Nathan, wake up!'

His eyes opened and stared up at her without any recognition. 'I told you—I'll cut the rope.'

'Nathan, you're dreaming.' She shook him again, her eyes dark with anxiety. 'Don't you know who I am?'

Focusing on her face with difficulty, he said thickly, 'You look like an angel.'

She was in no mood to find this either complimentary or remotely funny. 'It's me, Kristin.'

'Kristin?' He repeated her name as though he had never heard it before.

'I rescued you from the yacht—don't you remember?'

He extended an unsteady hand and stroked the shining fall of her hair. 'Beautiful . . .' Before she guessed his intention, he pulled her down on top of him, his mouth finding hers with a desperate hunger. His kiss devoured her; his hands roamed her body with the urgency of a starving man. The strap of her nightgown snapped and his fingers found the curving fullness of her breast, teasing its tip to hardness. His ruthless handling awoke a hunger in her as great as his own; her body ached and pulsed with a sensual need she had not known even existed. The heat of his skin burned through her thin nightdress as his searching hands swept her ever deeper into a tumult as wild as the ocean. Intoxicated by the hardness of his chest against her swollen breasts, she was beyond caring that her nightgown had fallen almost to her waist.

His lips left her mouth to bury themselves in the hollow of her throat; his fingers pushed away the curtain of her hair, exposing to his view the shadowed valley between her breasts. And then his body stilled.

Lifting a strand of glossy brown hair, he fastened glazed blue eyes on the girl's face. 'Carla, is it you? But you're not Carla.' His head fell back on the pillow, his mouth grim with strain. 'Oh, God, where am I?' he muttered deliriously. 'She doesn't have long hair, I know she doesn't——'

Kristin froze to the stillness of a statue. To her horror she was ripped by a primitive stab of jealousy. Carla—who was she? The name burned into her brain, for whoever Carla was, she had most certainly shared Nathan's bed. At the thought, Kristin's fingernails bit into her palm.

Although her rejected body cried out for assuagement, she managed to stand up, rearranging her nightdress with shaking hands and pulling her gown over her bare shoulders. She fled to the bathroom, where she stood staring at herself in the mirror, her eyes huge in her white face. He had not even known who she was, she thought brokenly. He had made love to her with a mindless animal hunger—she could have been anyone. Or—and this seemed even worse—had he thought all along she was Carla? If so, then she, Kristin, had just been a substitute for someone else ... a thought which sickened her, making her feel cheap and ashamed.

She turned on the tap and vigorously splashed cold water on her face. Stealing herself, she went back into Nathan's room. His fever had mounted, sweat trickled across his forehead so that his hair clung damply to his skin, while his fingers plucked restlessly at the bedclothes. Praying that there would be no repetition of his violent lovemaking, she straightened the disordered bed as best she could, and started sponging his face and chest with cool water in an effort to reduce his fever. At times he fretfully pushed her away, and from his broken comments she knew he was reliving the nightmare of the shipwreck.

Time passed slowly—one o'clock, two, three. She was almost ready to give up, when she thought she detected faint signs of improvement in his condition. Her nerves stretched to breaking point, Kristin rested for a few minutes in the bathroom, then picked up the cloth once more and went back into the bedroom.

'Kristin . . .'

She gave a gasp of relief, for his blue eyes were clear and lucid. Her knees weak, she sank on to the edge of the bed. 'Oh, thank goodness.'

'What's wrong?' he asked.

She stared at him disbelievingly. 'Nathan, you've been ill for half the night. I've been so worried!'

He frowned in perplexity. 'You've been up for a while?'

She glanced at the bedside clock, which said ten past three.

'Since midnight.'

'God, I'm sorry. You must be worn out.'

'Mmm—I am. I was scared for a while—you kept having nightmares about being back on the yacht, and then you'd wake up, but you didn't recognise me.' This was as near as she dared to get to talking about his lovemaking. She held her breath, wondering if he would recall it, wondering what she'd say if he did.

His forehead creased in bewilderment. 'I don't remember that at all.' He took her hand in his. 'You'd better get to bed, Kristin, and get some sleep. I'll be okay now. I think the fever's broken.'

Gently he pulled her down towards him and she felt a shiver of superstitious fear at this uncanny sense of repetition. Even though his mood was different now, and he was kissing her presumably out of gratitude, she was tense in his embrace, fighting back the desire to surrender to the tenderness of his lips.

He released her suddenly, sparks of anger burning in his eyes.

'Go to bed, Kristin.'

'I——'

'I've never yet been reduced to kissing an unwilling woman and I don't see why I should start now.'

'But, Nathan——'

'You were responsive enough last night and on the Island. What's happened? Or do you make a habit of turning it on and off like a tap?'

The blatant unfairness of this made her flinch. 'No! Of course not.' She sought for an explanation that would satisfy him, and said weakly, 'But you've been ill, and we both need to get some sleep.'

'If that's what's more important to you, then go to bed— your own bed.'

Too tired to argue any further, she said stiffly, 'Goodnight,' leaving the room before he could discern the telltale sheen of tears in her eyes. Only she knew how much will-power it had taken to seem cold and unmoved in his arms. And it was equally obvious that only she remembered the passion they had shared in that very bed less than three hours ago.

Overwrought emotionally, and physically exhausted, she lay awake for a long time and the first grey glimmer of light was brightening her room before she finally slept. Even then, it was a fitful sleep, punctuated by unsettling snatches of dreams and periods of wakefulness. Finally at about nine-thirty she gave up, and got out of bed. She slipped on her long white house-coat, grateful for the warmth of its softly woven woollen fabric. A cup of strong black coffee was what she needed, she thought decisively, and headed for the kitchen. She peeped into Nathan's room on the way, relieved to find him peacefully asleep, his breathing deep and even. For a moment she allowed her eyes to linger on the dark strength of his features, the muscled breadth of his shoulders—how handsome he was, this stranger from the sea! And what devastation he had wrought in so short a time in her quiet and ordered life. With a strange sense of perception she felt that his arrival signified the end of one chapter of her life, and the beginning of a new one—who was to tell where it would lead her? Strangely frightened, she stood a moment longer, then with a sharp sigh, threw off her momentary depression and went into the kitchen, partly clos-ing the door behind her.

Very soon the comforting aroma of coffee filled the kitchen. Searching in the refrigerator for the cream—why did it always seem to be tucked away at the back?—she suddenly heard over the bubble of the percolator the creak of the back door hinges. She whirled in fright just as the inner door opened. Del was standing there.

'Oh,' she gasped, closing the refrigerator and leaning against it for a moment to get her breath, 'you scared me! I didn't hear you coming.'

His eyes wandered over her lazily and abruptly she realised how her breasts were thrown into profile by the way she was standing. She moved to the sink, wishing she had dressed when she got out of bed.

'Close the door,' she said sharply. 'There's an awful draught.'

He did as she asked, advancing into the kitchen. 'You don't seem very pleased to see me.'

'Well, it's a bit early in the day for a social call, isn't it? I've only just got up.'

'I see that.' And again he leisurely surveyed the curving lines of her figure in the long, clinging gown.

'Stop it, Del!' she said crossly.

'Stop what? I wasn't doing anything.'

She glared at him in frustration. 'Oh yes, you were. Well, now that you're here, sit down and I'll get you a coffee.'

She joined him at the table, spooning sugar into her mug and stirring in the cream. 'Mmm—that tastes good,' she murmured.

'You look tired,' he said.

She glanced at him in surprise, for it was not like Del to pay much attention to other people's feelings. 'Yes, I am,' she said slowly, knowing he had given her the perfect opening to tell him about the shipwreck and Nathan's presence in the house. But somehow she found herself reluctant to do so.

'I was worried about you during the storm,' Del blurted, his big hands awkward on his coffee mug. 'So I thought I'd better get over here and see how you made out.'

She looked at him keenly, knowing that for once she could take his words at face value. Touched by his uncharacteristic concern, she said softly, 'That was nice of you, Del. Thanks.'

'You shouldn't be alone here like this.'

It was on the tip of her tongue to tell him she wasn't alone, but again something held her back.

'We've been into all that before,' she said drily.

'You're as stubborn as your old man!'

'Well, at least I come by it honestly,' she laughed, wanting to keep him in good humour, 'and I'm sorry I bit your head off when you came in the door, but you did scare me.' Wanting a change of subject, she asked, 'What's the weather like? I haven't even looked outside.'

'There's still a fair swell running, but the wind's dropped.'

'I must let the chickens out, and the cow too—they hate being cooped up for long.' She got up and went over to the window, pushing back the curtains so she could see out. 'There's a bit of blue sky over there,' she said with great satisfaction.

'Can I have another coffee?'

He had spoken from right behind her. As she turned he rested one hand on either side of her on the counter top, so that she was trapped in the circle of his arms. 'Del——'

'I really was worried about you, Kristin.'

His rough voice was unquestionably sincere, and when she thought how he had braved ten miles of open water to tell her so, she couldn't help feeling grateful. Unwisely she reached up one hand and lightly touched his cheek. 'I know you were— and it was nice of you to come and make sure that I was all right.'

His pale eyes took fire. His hands moved to encircle her waist and his mouth seized hers. Although instantaneously all her senses shrank from his touch, for a shocked instant she was immobile in his embrace.

'I guess I'm interrupting something.'

She felt the shock run through Del's body at the sound of another male voice. He wrenched free of her. 'Who the hell are you?'

Kristin felt hot colour surge to her cheeks as she met Nathan's hard blue eyes. 'You're up,' she said inanely.

'I would have thought that was obvious. And as I said, I'm sorry if I've interrupted something.'

Del seized Kristin by the arm, dragging her attention back to him. 'Just who is this guy?' He gave an ugly laugh. 'I've been underestimating you, little Kristin. It sure didn't take you long after your dad left to find yourself a man, did it?'

'Don't be ridiculous—it's not like that at all,' she sputtered, so angry the words tripped over her tongue.

'Oh?' he sneered, eyeing Nathan's rumpled jeans and naked chest. 'He seems pretty much at home to me. No wonder you look tired this morning, Kristin—you didn't get much sleep, eh?'

His insinuations made her cheeks flame. 'You just listen to me, Del Clarke! I'd never laid eyes on him until the day of the storm——'

'He's a mighty quick worker, then——'

'Shut up!' she snapped, too angry to care what she said. 'Shut up and listen! His yacht was shipwrecked on Whale Island and I had to take the skiff to get him ashore. He's been ill, and that's why I was up half the night.'

'And that happens to be the exact truth,' Nathan said coldly. 'So why don't you introduce me to your friend, Kristin?'

'Oh, I'm sorry,' she stumbled. 'Nathan, this is Del Clarke. He's a fisherman from Sitka Landing.'

'So your yacht was wrecked,' Del said slowly, apparently not noticing Nathan's lack of surname. 'You were on your own?'

'Yes.'

'You must have been blown off course.'

'Why do you say that?'

'Well, where were you heading for?'

There was a momentary hesitation, before Nathan named the settlement to the south of them. 'Tofino.'

'And I suppose your cargo went down with your boat. That's too bad,' Del said meaningfully.

Nathan's eyes narrowed dangerously, but his voice was perfectly under control. 'What are you trying to say, Mr Clarke? Why don't you come right out with it?'

'The name's Del. We don't go for formality on the islands,' Del drawled, obviously enjoying keeping the stranger in suspense.

'Del, then,' Nathan snapped impatiently.

'I would have thought it was obvious what you were up to— or are you trying to shield Kristin from your—er—activities?'

Kristin bit her lip, as the air vibrated with tension between the two men. Neither of them seemed aware of her presence. She was desperately conscious of the sheer physical effort it was costing Nathan to remain upright, for he was haggard beneath his tan. With a casualness that did not deceive her in the least he grasped the doorpost with one hand, his movement revealing the dark purple bruises disfiguring his ribcage. Yet when he spoke it was with a calm authority. 'Get to the point, Del—and give me a coffee, will you, Kristin, please?'

His adversary's calmness obviously infuriated Del. 'Yeah, I'll get to the point,' he said truculently. 'Smuggling, man—dope. That's what I'm talking about.'

Kristin could no longer keep silent. 'You're crazy, Del!'

'Oh, no, I'm not. You know as well as I do about the dope trade from Vancouver to the west coast here. It's a profitable business, isn't it, Nathan? Why don't you tell me your last name?'

'Nathan will do.'

Del laughed. 'I can see why you want to stay incognito. But you don't have to worry, I'm not about to tip off the cops. I haven't always kept my own hands lily-white.' With an air of camaraderie that repelled Kristin, he said jocosely, 'How much did you lose when your yacht sank?'

'I lost my yacht—and that's all. You've got the wrong man, Mr Clarke.'

'You'll have to do better than that to convince me. But let's say you're right—then just what were you doing sailing alone in these waters?'

Only Kristin noticed how Nathan's fingers tightened their grip on the door frame. 'Perhaps I just like sailing,' he replied evenly.

'Don't make me laugh, man. No one sails for pleasure in these waters. The east coast, maybe—but not here.'

Without thinking, Nathan ran his fingers through his hair, then was unable to suppress a grunt of pain as he hit the lacerations on his scalp.

'So you got hit on the head,' Del sneered. 'I wonder who did that? So maybe the cargo didn't go down with your yacht—maybe you'd been relieved of it already. You'd better be a little more careful in future. Drugs are in the big league, and those boys play it rough.'

For a moment Kristin was appalled by the neatness of Del's case. It *was* strange that Nathan should have been sailing alone in these waters, and even stranger that such an experienced sailor as he undoubtedly was would somehow have got himself knocked out and shipwrecked. Had his supposed loss of memory simply been a ruse to deflect her from asking too many awkward questions? Her grey eyes perturbed, she recognised anew his toughness, his air of command, his self-sufficiency. Had he put all those qualities to use in what must surely be the most despicable trade in the world: that of dope trafficking?

Then his gaze met hers, and with a sick certainty she knew that he had read her thoughts. So rapidly that she wondered afterwards if she had imagined it, she saw a flash of pain cross his features. But he had himself in perfect control as he said quietly, 'Whom do you believe, Kristin—Del or me?'

She raised her chin and drawing on some deep inner intuition said, 'I believe you, Nathan.'

A grin briefly erased the strain from his mouth. 'There you are, Del—two against one,' he said lightly.

Del took Kristin by the arm. 'I don't know who the devil this guy is, but he's done a fine job pulling the wool over your eyes. If you've got any sense you'll send him back to the Landing with me.'

'I can't do that, Del—he's not well.'

Del gave a coarse laugh. 'What you mean is, two nights haven't been enough.'

Nathan's voice cut like a whiplash. 'That's enough, Clarke! One more remark like that and you'll be out that door so fast you won't know what hit you.'

'I'd like to see you try!'

Nearly suffocating with fear, Kristin gasped, 'You'd better go, Del. Please——'

'Want him to yourself, eh? Be careful, little Kristin—if you get yourself in hot water, don't say I didn't warn you. If Dugald MacKenzie turned his nose up at a fisherman, how do you think he'll like you sleeping with a dope smuggler?'

Her thin thread of control snapped. 'Get out!'

'I'm going. But I'll be back.' His voice heavy with menace, his eyes trained on Nathan's still figure, he repeated, 'Yeah, I'll be back.'

Kristin closed the door behind him and shoved the bolt into the latch, leaning against the panels as the anger slowly seeped from her body.

'You lied to me,' said Nathan grimly.

Her eyes flew open. 'What did you say?'

'The night before last you told me you didn't have any boy-friends. But Del Clarke sure walked in here this morning and made himself at home. Or do you kiss everyone that comes along?'

The unexpectedness of this attack together with all the tensions of the past hours made Kristin lose her temper completely. 'He's *not* my boy-friend! And I don't give a damn whether you believe me or not. What business is it of yours anyway?' She faced him furiously, her breast heaving, her eyes almost black with anger, her dark hair in startling contrast to the long white robe.

'So you were more kissed against than kissing,' Nathan said cynically.

He was right, of course, but she was damned if she would admit it. She stalked over to the sink, her gown swirling about her legs. 'Oh, I have at least a dozen boy-friends, so I can change every month,' she snapped childishly, banging her mug down in the sink with unnecessary violence.

She never knew what his reply might have been, for from the little room off the kitchen came the call signal from the radio.

'Oh—excuse me,' she muttered with automatic politeness.

Flipping on the switch, she heard Alice's voice reaching across the stretch of ocean. 'Kristin? I've been worrying about you—did you weather the storm all right?'

'Yes, I'm fine. How about you?'

'Luther lost a net, but that's all. Would you like us to drop over for a while this afternoon? It'll only be a short visit, but we'd like to come.'

Alice's serene friendliness suddenly seemed just what she needed. 'I'd love that,' she said more warmly than she intended.

'Are you sure you're all right?'

'Yes, really. I'll put the teapot on. Will Luther bring you?'

'Yes, it's still too rough to fish, but after two days in the house he's as cross as a bear. He needs to get out!'

Kristin laughed, for she could not imagine Luther being as cross as a bear: he was the most fun-loving, even-tempered person she knew.

'I'll see you in a while,' she chuckled, and signed off.

Her good humour restored, she went back into the kitchen. 'That was my friend Alice Matthews from the Landing,' she explained to Nathan. 'She and her son Luther are coming over for a short visit in a couple of hours. I must get dressed.' She paused, her eyes glinting wickedly. 'Perhaps I'd better get something straight right now. Luther never has been, is not, and never will be my boy-friend.'

Nathan grinned, if a trifle reluctantly. 'Oh?'

Kristin's face softened. 'Alice has been like a mother to me ever since we came to the Island and I love her dearly. And Luther is just like the brother I never had. You'll like him, I'm sure.'

'How will you explain my presence?'

Puzzled, she said, 'Well, I'll tell them the truth.'

While she had been talking on the radio, Nathan had sat down on one of the kitchen chairs, his body slumped with weariness. Now he stared down at his hands, and she found herself admiring their latent strength.

'Kristin, I don't like to ask you to deceive your friends, but do you think we can keep my loss of memory a secret between us?'

'We could if you like,' she answered slowly. 'But why, Nathan?'

He looked up, his blue eyes tormented with doubts, doubts he had not allowed Del Clarke to see. 'Maybe Del was right, Kristin. Maybe I am a smuggler.'

'Of course you're not!'

As though he had not heard her vehement denial, Nathan went on, 'It certainly fits the facts, you have to admit that. Why else was I sailing a yacht up this coast by myself? And how did I get knocked out?'

The fact that she herself had shared these very doubts earlier made it doubly important to her that she should reassure him. She sat down beside him. 'Nathan, listen to me. I can't give you a rational reason or explain why I feel this way: but I do know you're not involved in the drug trade. It's a foul business, and I'm convinced you've never had anything to do with it.'

He took her hand in one of his, rubbing her slender fingers with his thumb. 'You're being very trusting.'

'I suppose I am. I'm going by instinct, I guess,' she said, trying to suppress the tiny shiver of delight she felt at his touch.

He laughed shortly. 'Well, let's just hope your instincts don't let us down. Now, how about that coffee?'

'I'd better get you something to eat as well. How about scrambled eggs on toast?'

'Sounds great.'

As she busied herself at the stove, she said thoughtfully, 'We can't keep it a secret indefinitely, Nathan. And wouldn't it be better to get in touch with the police? Surely they can find out who you are, then?'

'I've thought of all that, Kristin. But for now I just want to keep it quiet. As you suggested earlier, we can keep an eye out for any reports of missing persons. I'd surely recognise my own name ...'

'Well, if you think that's best ...' her voice trailed away uncertainly as she put the food in front of him.

'Thanks, Kristin, that looks good. Once I've eaten I'll go back to bed.' He grinned ruefully. 'Partly because I don't feel that good, and partly because it'll get us out of answering a whole lot of questions from your friends.'

By the time Luther's boat chugged into the inlet, Kristin had dressed, washed the dishes and looked after the animals. She stood on the cliff waving at the two of them, as they began to climb up the wooden steps. Alice was of medium height, plump and grey-haired; her warm brown eyes twinkled with kindness and an unabashed enthusiasm for life. Her son, apart from a thatch of untidy brown hair, his tallness, and a decidedly masculine cast to his features, was very like her.

Alice finally reached the top step. 'I'm getting too old for these stairs, Kristin,' she panted. 'Now that summer is nearly here, we'll have to have our visits on the wharf. How are you, dear?' She hugged the girl affectionately.

'I'm fine. I've got a lot to tell you, so come on in the house.'

'Was Del over today?' Luther asked, as they walked across the grass.

'Yes.' The girl wrinkled her nose. 'He's been a bit of a nuisance since Dad left.'

'Okay—I'll see what I can do about it,' Luther said matter-of-factly, and Kristin knew he would look after the matter; he was totally dependable.

In the house, as Kristin put on the kettle for tea, Alice asked, 'What was your news?'

'Well, I have a visitor.'

'Who?' the older woman questioned, obviously intrigued.

'His name is Nathan and he was on his way to Tofino in a yacht when he was shipwrecked,' Kristin said quickly, hoping that this would cover the awkward business of Nathan's identity. 'It was on Tuesday—the day Dad left.' She described what had happened from her first sighting of the yacht on the rocks of Whale Island, warming to her tale as she went. 'He's in bed now,' she finished. 'The fever left him rather weak, and he's still groggy from the blow on his head. He gets a bit confused at times, but I'm sure he'll be okay in a couple of days.'

'Shouldn't he see a doctor?' Luther asked.

'He didn't seem to think it was necessary.'

'Goodness, what a terrible time you must have had, getting him to safety,' said Alice with a shudder, for she knew only too well the dangers of the stormy Pacific. 'You deserve a medal.'

'Nonsense,' Kristin replied, looking embarrassed. 'You would have done the same. Look, why don't I go and see if he's awake? If he is, you can at least poke your head in the door and say hello.'

She got up and went down the hall, quietly pushing open the door to Nathan's room. He turned his head and smiled at her drowsily. 'Hi. Did your friends come?'

'Mmm. Alice would like to meet you.' She beckoned Alice in, and went back into the kitchen to chat with Luther. When Alice returned in a few minutes, there was a satisfied smile on her face. 'Frankly, Kristin, I'm glad he's here,' she announced. 'I never did approve of the way Dugald leaves you alone so much; anything could happen to you out here. But Nathan seems a fine man and I'm sure he'll be good company for you until he's well enough to continue his journey. And perhaps by then Dugald will be back.'

Kristin frowned slightly; she had given no thought to the fact that sooner or later Nathan would have to leave.

'Dad'll be gone two weeks this time,' she volunteered.

'Tch, tch,' Alice clucked. 'It's just as well he didn't tell me that the last time I saw him—I'd have given him a piece of my mind.'

'If you've finished your tea, Ma, maybe we should head home,' Luther suggested, winking at Kristin; the long-standing feud between Dugald and Alice was a regular joke between them.

'I suppose you want to get back before dark,' was Alice's rejoinder. 'He doesn't want to miss his date with Jane.'

'You've been going out with her for three months now,' Kristin teased. 'You'd better watch out, Luther, you'll be ending up an old married man.'

'I reckon there might be worse fates. And by the way, just behave yourself, girl. I don't know what the world is coming to, Ma, here we're leaving Kristin alone on the island with this guy Nathan.' He grinned widely, 'Do you think he'll be safe?'

Kristin blushed rosily and gave him a healthy shove. 'Don't judge everybody by yourself!'

His tanned face alight with laughter, he gave her a quick kiss on the cheek. 'Take care, Kristin. Come on over and see us as soon as you can.'

'Make sure you do that,' Alice corroborated, 'and make sure you get some rest in the next couple of days, too. Don't go waiting on Nathan hand and foot the way you do with Dugald.'

'Alice, you're hopeless!' Kristin chuckled. 'You're picking on poor Dad just because he's not here to defend himself.' She hugged her friend. 'I wish you could stay longer—but thanks for coming, it was lovely to see you both.'

CHAPTER FOUR

MORE than once in the next three or four days she found herself recalling Alice's words, for Nathan had been more shaken by the shipwreck than he had let on, and even had a slight relapse of his fever, so that Kristin did indeed spend a fair bit of time waiting on him. He didn't talk much and never touched her. But even so, a current of understanding and sympathy seemed to flow between them and for Kristin they were days of deep contentment.

Gradually his health improved and he spent less and less time in bed. She showed him the study, a charming book-lined room overlooking the ocean, with a huge fireplace fashioned of beach stones, and found to her delight that he was an ardent and thoughtful reader. Shyly at first, but then with increasing assurance as she realised that he took her opinions seriously, she began advancing her own critiques of some of the books she had read; they discovered mutual favourites; and it became their habit to light a fire after supper and spend the evening reading and chatting. It opened a whole new world to Kristin—a world of companionship she had never experienced before. From their friendly arguments and discussions she developed a deep respect for his judgment and for his flashing, rapier-like wit that was never turned against her.

Another discovery of Kristin's in the last few days was her desire to make herself more attractive. Used to roaming the island in jeans and a shirt, she now found her wardrobe sadly lacking in variety. But she was clever with her needle and from the pile of fabrics tucked away in the top of her wardrobe she made herself a long slightly flared skirt of cranberry-red wool, as well as a peasant-style jumper in flowered percale. With a degree of diffidence she began wearing these new clothes for their evening meal and was rewarded both by Nathan's compliments on her appearance, and by the way his eyes would sometimes follow her as she moved about the room.

They also shared a love of music, and again Kristin was

excited by Nathan's breadth of knowledge. He would not allow her to make slip-shod judgments, making her justify all her statements in a way that challenged her intellect as it had never been challenged before. She felt alive in his company, and if she occasionally contemplated his eventual departure from the island, she would push the thought aside. The prospect of life without him seemed unutterably flat and empty.

One evening stood out in particular in her mind, perhaps because it contained all the elements of this exciting new relationship that she knew was inexorably changing her life; she would never again be the same girl that she had been a week ago.

The study curtains were drawn against the lonely vista of open sea, and the flames leaped and danced in the hearth. Kristin was wearing the long red skirt with a white silk blouse, of a severe style, that emphasised the slender line of her throat and the delicate bones of her wrists. Delighting in her new femininity, she had swept her dark hair into a smooth loop on the crown of her head; a few stray tendrils brushed her neck and curled about her ears. She had lengthened her lashes with mascara and touched her eyelids with a silver eye-shadow.

She was quite unaware of the new assurance in her bearing as she crossed the room to put on some music. She knelt by the long shelf that held all the records, flipping through them abstractedly. Nathan was seated in one of the deep armchairs by the fireplace, an open book on his knees.

She finally found what she wanted. 'Baroque trumpet music—do you like that?' She glanced over at him, to find he had been steadily watching her, his blue eyes inscrutable, his mouth grim.

'What's wrong?' she said anxiously. In one graceful movement she got to her feet and hurried over to his chair, kneeling beside it. 'Are your ribs hurting?'

'No, they're fine.' As though compelled by some force greater than himself, he reached out one hand and stroked the hair back from her forehead. 'You look very beautiful tonight,' he said huskily.

Her expressive eyes glowed with pleasure, and a smile lifted the corners of her mouth. He had neither touched her nor kissed her since the night of his illness and now she waited tremulously for the next move. His hand slid down the side of her face and with one finger he traced the soft curve of her lips, almost as though he was memorising it. She closed her eyes, feeling herself begin to tremble. And then it was not his fingers but his mouth that caressed her and between them leaped the flame that had been smouldering since their first meeting. She swayed closer to its scorching heat.

But then his hands were rough on her shoulders and he was pushing her away so that her mouth was torn from his. Her eyes dark with bewildered pain, she whispered, 'Why did you do that?'

'I kissed you because you looked very desirable ... and I stopped because you're far too innocent.'

'That could be changed,' she heard herself say recklessly, the words seeming to come from a long way off.

'Of course it could. But not by me.'

'Why not?' It was a cry from the heart.

He looked down at her, picking his words with care. 'You've lived an exceptionally sheltered life, Kristin, for this day and age, and you're very young. I'm older and I can only assume'—he smiled crookedly, although the smile did not reach his eyes—'I'm more experienced. Because your father's away, we happen to be alone together all the time; inadvertently we've been put in a situation of considerable intimacy. I can't take advantage of that, Kristin, don't you understand? Apart from any other considerations, how would I ever face your father?'

She stared down at her hands, linked in her lap, like a child who has been reprimanded. Everything he had said was reasonable and logical, she thought miserably, and she supposed he was right. But when he kissed her, reason and logic fled. So was it wrong of her to long for his touch, and to ache for that ultimate fulfilment that he could give?

As though he had read her mind, he said softly, 'Don't look so upset, child.'

She looked up, his endearment bringing a flush to her cheeks. 'I'm not——'

'And don't for a moment think that there's anything wrong with you for wanting more than just a kiss or a caress.' His voice deepened. 'There's nothing I want more right now than to pick you up in my arms and carry you into the bedroom and make love to you. Promise you won't ever forget that.'

His words filled her with wonder. The firelight flickered over her face, tiny flames reflected in the smoky depths of her eyes. 'I promise.'

Deliberately he moved, making his voice prosaic as he said, 'I'll put another log on the fire. Why don't you put on that record?'

As the brilliant tones of the trumpet soared into the room, Kristin sank down on the bearskin rug by the hearth.

'I heard that played in concert once,' Nathan said casually. 'The baroque period is one of my favourites.'

Careful to sound just as casual, she asked, 'Where was the concert held?'

'Vancouver.' He tensed as he realised the implication of his words. 'Kristin, I remembered that concert! I can see the hall and the conductor and the soloist just as clearly as if I was there.'

'Who were you with?'

'I—don't know. I don't know if I was with someone or alone. And I don't know when it was——' He banged his fist on the armchair in utter frustration. 'How can I remember some things and not others?'

'It seems when you're relaxed and thinking of something else, you remember things from the past.'

'You're right. So the moral of that is, don't worry about losing your memory, and maybe it will come back.' He grimaced. 'It all sounds fine in theory, doesn't it?'

'I don't see what else we can do,' she said helplessly, longing to erase the strain from his face. She paused thoughtfully. 'Well, that's not strictly true. If the weather's okay, we could go to the Landing tomorrow. The supply plane flew in yesterday, and Luther always gets the Vancouver and Victoria papers. Perhaps you're from Vancouver, in which case surely there'd be some mention of your disappearance.'

'That's a great idea. Good girl!'

Pleased to have some kind of a tangible plan to help him, Kristin leaned back against her chair, feeling suddenly very tired. She gazed into the hypnotically dancing flames until they blurred into a shimmering orange mass. She closed her eyes . . .

'Kristin, wake up!'

She shifted her position, and muttered 'ouch' at the crick in her neck. Nathan was crouched beside her, too close for her peace of mind. Had he been watching her while she slept? 'What's the time?' she murmured.

'Past midnight.'

She stretched unselfconsciously, giving a wide yawn. 'Oh dear, I feel awful. You shouldn't have let me go to sleep.'

'So it's all my fault! Is my company that boring?'

She wrinkled her nose at him, and said, wide-eyed, 'Well, as you happen to mention it ...'

'I'll teach you to fall asleep,' he teased, beginning to tickle her ribs.

She tried to wriggle away from him. 'That's not fair! You know I can't tickle you back.'

They were both laughing, their faces only inches apart, and it seemed the most natural thing in the world that he should lean forward to kiss her. But then he stopped, his hand tightening on her shoulder. 'God, Kristin, I can't keep away from you.'

Her rueful smile matched his, as she traced the firm line of his chin with her fingertip. 'Neither can I,' she said ruefully.

He got to his feet, and held out his hand, helping her up.

'Off you go. I'll see you in the morning.'

'Goodnight.'

Despite his restraint, she felt a glow of happiness as she got ready for bed. For a moment she stood in front of the mirror in her nightgown, seeing with new eyes the proud lift of her breasts, the curve of her hips, and the slender line of her legs. He wants me. He finds me desirable, she thought, taking a new pride in her femininity. And when she fell asleep, it was of Nathan that she dreamed ...

The next day dawned clear and bright, with only a light off-shore wind. As the skiff threaded through the rocks into the open sea, the sun sparkled on the water like a shower of diamonds. Seagulls lazily drifted behind the boat, their wings a dazzling white against the blue sky. Ahead lay the rounded hills and silver waters of the fjord with the brightly painted houses of Sitka Landing scattered over the sloping hillside at its estuary; misted by distance the snow-capped mountains of the interior made a jagged line of the horizon.

Nathan nudged the boat into the wharf and nimbly Kristin scrambled up the ladder and knotted the hawser. As they walked along the creosoted timbers of the wharf, skirting the heaped nets and boxes of bait, she waved at the crew of a seiner, all friends of Luther's, very conscious of their curious looks at her escort.

From Alice's kitchen came the delicious smell of newly baked gingerbread. 'We picked the right day for a visit!' Kristin called gaily as she opened the screen door.

'Hello, dear, what a nice surprise! Come in. And Nathan—welcome to Sitka Landing.'

Alice was far from the tidiest of housekeepers, but to Kristin Alice's kitchen was the friendliest place she had ever known. The sunlight streaming in the windows lit on a tangle of brightly flowering geraniums and on golden-brown loaves of bread cooling on the counter. The coffee pot bubbled on the stove, and from its cage in the corner a yellow canary chirped a greeting. Kristin cleared a pile of magazines off a chair and sat down.

'Can you put an extra cup of water in the soup for lunch?' she said cheekily.

Primly Alice addressed Nathan. 'The manners of this younger generation are dreadful, aren't they? However, you're in luck. I have a fresh salmon casserole.'

'It'll be the first decent bite I've had all week,' Nathan remarked to the ceiling.

Kristin gave an indignant gasp. 'For that you can cook supper tonight!' She looked up to catch on Alice's face a fleeting expression of satisfaction.

'There's some mail for you on the hall table,' Alice said quickly.

'Oh, good—anything from Dad?' Kristin leafed through the letters quickly. Two official letters for her father, and a couple of advertising circulars. She walked back to the kitchen, a worried frown creasing her brow. 'It's funny I haven't heard from him, he's had lots of time to write to me. I hope he's all right ...'

'I'm sure he is, dear. He's probably walking around with a letter to you in his pocket.'

Since Dugald had been known to do this in the past, Kristin stifled her concern. 'I expect you're right. Do you mind if we look through Luther's newspapers while we're here?'

The back door banged and Alice said comfortably, 'Here he comes. You can ask him yourself.'

'Ask me what? Hi, Kristin, Nathan. Don't tell me you smelled Ma's gingerbread all the way from the Island?' Luther began peeling off his rubber boots and yellow oilskins, a guileless grin on his tanned young face.

'Can we look through your newspapers?' Kristin asked, pointedly ignoring his last comment.

'Sure—looking for anything in particular?'

She was about to make some disclaimer when Nathan spoke up. 'As a matter of fact, yes.' For a minute he let his eyes wander around the kitchen and intuitively Kristin knew he had been sensitive to its open and friendly welcome. With a little thrill of pleasure she knew also that he must like Alice and Luther. She waited with bated breath for him to go on.

'I'm afraid I was guilty of not telling you the whole truth the other day, and I apologise,' he said bluntly. 'The blow I got on the head before I was shipwrecked made me lose my memory. I don't know my last name or where I'm from or why I was sailing in these waters.'

Both Alice and Luther had their attention riveted on him.

'I wondered why Kristin told us so little about you,' said Alice. 'Now I understand.'

'We have reason to believe I might be from Vancouver, so we thought if we went through the papers, there might be mention of a missing person.'

The four of them spent the next half hour scanning the pile of newspapers that had been delivered the day before, but to no avail. Although he took pains not to show it, Kristin knew Nathan was bitterly disappointed.

'I must have a home and a job,' he said slowly. 'Surely I couldn't disappear without anyone realising. We'll wait another few days, Kristin, and if nothing new turns up, I guess I will go to the police.'

'In the meantime, let's have lunch,' Alice suggested, her panacea for all ills being a good square meal.

After they had eaten, Luther and Nathan went to look over

Luther's fishing equipment; an instant liking seemed to have sprung up between the two men. Kristin helped Alice with the washing up, and then left to go to the general store. For almost an hour she poked contentedly among the diverse array of goods; she bought a couple of paperbacks, a sweater to go with her new jumper, some new bras, and finally a tiny flacon of perfume. She piled her purchases on the counter, searching for the right change in her wallet.

'Kristin, I figured I'd find you here.'

It was Del. 'Hi,' she said casually, trying not to blush as she saw him eyeing the lacy underwear.

'I saw Luther with that guy Nathan on the wharf. Is he staying at the Landing now?'

She moved towards the door, not wanting everyone in the store to hear their conversation. 'No.'

'You mean he's going back with you?'

She nodded. He grabbed her by the sleeve, his eyes narrowed. 'What kind of a game are you playing?'

'I don't play games, Del.'

'Then why is he staying with you?'

'Nathan was shipwrecked on the Island and he's my guest. That's all there is to it.'

'I think he should stay at the Landing, Kristin, for his own good. If he goes back with you, I just may get in touch with the police—there's a patrol boat not thirty miles from here. They're always interested in tips about dope runners.'

'Are you trying to blackmail me?' she said coldly.

'It's just a friendly warning, Kristin.' But his pale blue eyes were watchful and there was unspoken menace in his broad-shouldered bulk.

'You're wasting your time! Nathan's going to stay on the Island. And he's already decided to go to the police.' She added childishly. 'So there!'

Her display of temper fanned his anger. 'I never was good enough for you, was I, Kristin? But some guy gets himself shipwrecked and makes you feel sorry for him and you fall all over him.'

'That's not true!'

'No? Don't tell me you haven't kissed him?'

She was silent, biting her lip in vexation.

Abruptly he changed tactics. 'You don't think a guy like that will be content to stay here for the rest of his life, do you? He's city, Kristin, you can tell that just by looking at him. Don't go falling in love with him, because sooner or later he'll up and leave you.'

She was shaken by his words. Del was right—there was the indefinable stamp of the city about Nathan; and if he came from the city, to the city he would return. Why should that thought fill her with a nameless apprehension? 'Don't go falling in love with him,' Del had said; she hadn't—had she?

Wordlessly she stared at Del and he was shrewd enough to know he had said enough. 'Just remember that when he's gone, I'll be around if you need me.' He turned on his heel and went back into the store.

Lost in thought, she stood still in the sunlight, the breeze playfully tugging at her hair. A hand touched her arm and she jumped.

'Are you all right?' Nathan asked. 'You look as though you've lost your best friend—what was he saying to upset you?'

She could hardly tell him. Trying to shake off the mood of foreboding that Del had instilled in her, she said dismissively, 'It was nothing.'

'You can't expect me to believe that.'

Goaded beyond endurance, she cried, 'Oh, please, just leave me alone!'

His mouth tightened. 'Are you in love with him?' As she swallowed a hysterical giggle, he went on, 'You deserve better than Del Clarke, Kristin.'

'I've just about had enough of everyone offering me free advice.'

'Then perhaps we'd better head back,' he said in an even tone that did not deceive her at all; she knew he was violently angry.

'I'll have to say goodbye to Alice first.'

'Fine. I'll meet you at the boat.'

He strode away and she watched him go, a lump in her throat. With all her heart she wished Del had not mentioned that little phrase 'falling in love'. She could not afford to fall in love with Nathan. Whoever he was, wherever he lived, he was a stranger from a very different world from hers, and that world would claim him sooner or later.

She managed a brief and cheerful goodbye to Alice, who in-

sisted on presenting her with a loaf of homemade bread and
a big chunk of gingerbread. Then Kristin made her way to the
wharf. The trip home was accomplished with a bare minimum
of conversation, and although she and Nathan ate supper together and spent the evening in the study, the old ease and
intimacy had gone; their silences were strained rather than
restful. Kristin went to bed early, for once glad to be alone.

She was the first one up in the morning. Dressed in jeans and
an old shirt, she pulled on her boots and went across the dew-
wet grass to the barn. From the woods came the irregular
hammering of a woodpecker and the thin chirping of warblers;
high overhead a dark-winged osprey soared. The early morning sun bathed the scene in a pale golden light, burning off the
wisps of mist. Kristin drew a deep breath of pure delight,
savouring the delicate scent of wildflowers and the mingled
tang of forest and ocean. How she loved this place!

'Want a hand with the chores?'

She smiled at Nathan, forgetting the constraint of the evening before. 'Isn't it a lovely day?' she said, a lilt in her voice.

'You know what we should do?'

'What?'

'Let's pack a picnic and you can show me the other side of
the island.'

'That's a super idea!' What could be better than to share
the beauty of her beloved island with him?

By the time they were ready to go, the sun had climbed in
the sky and was shedding a steady warmth. Although Kristin
was wearing jeans to protect her legs from the underbrush, she
had thrown a pair of shorts and a halter top into the picnic
basket at the last minute; it showed signs of being the first
really hot day of the year. Swinging the basket between them,
they set off along the trail that wound through the woods.

'It's like a different world in here, isn't it?' Kristin said in
hushed tones. The sunlight filtered through the tall trees,
dappling her upturned face in a pattern of light and shadow;
the breeze stirring the branches sighed like the distant sound of
the sea. They were enclosed in a green cocoon of hemlocks,
spruce and cedar. The air was resin-scented. Content to be
silent, they strolled along the trail, surprising a chittering
squirrel and startling two grouse into an explosion of wings.

The trail ended abruptly in a wide expanse of open meadow that sloped all the way to the sea. A wide turquoise-blue channel, sprinkled with smaller islands, separated them from the hills of the mainland.

'Every year Dad and I uproot any brush that starts to grow in the fields—and we cut hay here in the summer for the cow,' she told Nathan.

'A lot of the work you do on the island is more concerned with day-to-day living—milking the cow, collecting the eggs, your vegetable garden—than it is with the actual running of the lighthouse, isn't it?'

Nathan had hit upon one of her secret worries. 'You're quite right. All the equipment is fully automatic and takes very little maintenance. They're phasing out a lot of the lightkeepers along the shore just because of that. I hope they don't do it to Dad before he retires—this island is his whole life, and to be told he's redundant would kill him, I'm afraid. I just can't imagine him living anywhere else.'

'I see.'

And Kristin knew he did. 'Well, there's nothing I can do about it, so let's not worry about it today,' she said philosophically. 'Come on, I'll show you the old farmhouse.'

They wandered down the hill through the knee-high grass, which was sprinkled with daisies and scarlet poppies. An orchard flanked the hillside, the trees gnarled and contorted with age. Surrounded by lilac bushes and rambling wild roses, the farmhouse faced the quiet waters of the cove and the white crescent of sand.

'I can't imagine a more perfect location for a house,' Nathan said softly.

'It's my favourite place on the island.'

They put down the picnic basket in the grass and approached the house. Its shingles, long unpainted, were a weathered grey, and the door squealed on its hinges as they entered. Nathan seemed to have forgotten his companion. He went around tapping the window frames and testing the beams in the walls; he inspected the roof for leaks and even crawled down into the mud-floored root-cellar.

'You know, structurally it's sound,' he said thoughtfully. 'A hell of a lot better made than some of the modern houses.'

'You must have done some carpentry work,' she commented.

'I suppose I must have. I seem to know about these things, don't I?'

They stepped out on to the front step—a great slab of beach stone. Without warning Nathan rested his hand on the sun-warmed door frame, almost as though for support. Alarmed, Kristin saw him give a shudder, his face ashen pale.

'Nathan, what's wrong?' she demanded.

'I—I don't know,' he said uncertainly. 'I had the strangest feeling . . . I suddenly knew what I've been running away from all my life—and I'm sure I was running from something.' He paused. 'It was a kind of emptiness, a lack of meaning. And it's as though this place is what I've always been looking for.' He gave himself a shake. 'Crazy, eh? Talk about someone walking over my grave! Let's go down to the beach.'

He obviously did not want to talk about his experience any more. Wanting to distract him, Kristin said, 'We'll climb over these rocks first. Go very quietly, okay?'

Hand in hand they crossed the meadow to the rocks. Crouching down, and waving Nathan to do the same, Kristin crept to the edge of the cliff. Nathan knelt beside her, his arm about her waist.

The seals were out in full force. Some lay basking in the sun, their fur a mottled brown; others flopped their ungainly bodies into the sea, where they instantly became transformed into creatures of grace and speed.

'You knew they'd be here,' Nathan whispered.

'They often are—they're such fun to watch, aren't they?'

Very conscious of the weight of his arm on her back, she could have stayed for much longer, but as she pointed out the antics of two young seals cavorting in the waves, her foot slipped, and a tiny avalanche of stones clattered down the cliff. There was a concerted rush of movement, a dozen splashes into the sea, and the seals were gone.

Nathan got quickly to his feet—as if he was glad to move away from her, Kristin thought painfully. The brightness of the day dimmed a little as she followed him down the path to the shore. Once there, however, the beach worked its usual magic. She unlaced her sneakers and rolled up her jeans, feeling the sand hot on her bare feet. For an hour or more they meandered contently along the beach, poking among the tidal pools for starfish and crabs and brightly coloured snails. At peace with the world, Kristin said finally, 'I'm starving!'

'I thought you'd never mention it!'

She splashed him playfully, then ran ahead up the slope. The sheltered hollow behind the house had trapped the sun's heat; it could have been July, Kristin thought. Anyway, it was far too hot for jeans.

'Excuse me a minute,' she murmured, and going behind the old wood shed swiftly changed into her trim white shorts and halter top. Nathan had spread the rug on the ground and was unpacking the picnic when she came back into the clearing, but beyond one swift, searching glance, he made no comment on her appearance.

They ate cold chicken, crisp salad, and Alice's bread, thickly spread with butter, washing it all down with chilled white wine. Kristin finally licked her fingers in repletion. 'Mmm, that was good!'

'Aren't you glad I thought of this?' her companion said lazily, lying back on the rug.

'You wouldn't be fishing for a compliment, would you?'

'Never—— Lord, the wine's made me sleepy! Do you mind if I take a siesta?'

'I gather that's a rhetorical question,' she chuckled, packing away the remains of their lunch and putting the basket in the shade of the house. By the time she had done this, Nathan was asleep, and for a few minutes she sat quietly in the grass beside him, a deep contentment pervading her.

He looked younger, more vulnerable in sleep, his arrogance dimmed. With secret pleasure she allowed her eyes to explore the strong contours of his face, already so familiar to her. The tiny silver amulet gleamed in the sun ... Nathan. When, she wondered, would she find out more about him? Did she even want to? For once he remembered who he was, he would leave her—other people then she knew would have claims on him.

But what if he didn't leave? She remembered the strange little interlude by the farmhouse door ... dared she hope that the island had cast its spell on him? If only it had ... the possibility, however remote it might be, opened before her a vista of incredible happiness ...

Unable to sit still any longer, she got to her feet and walked up the hill to the orchard, the grass tickling her bare feet and brushing against her legs. She stooped to gather some of the long-stemmed wildflowers, plaiting them into a brightly coloured wreath that she playfully wound through her long hair. Leaning against a tree trunk, she idly gazed at the waves rolling into shore and breaking into pristine white foam. Near at hand the crickets chirped and bees hummed drowsily among the branches . . .

'You look like a wood nymph.'

She turned to face him, a slow, mysterious smile curving her lips, her face serenely beautiful under its crown of purple and white flowers. They were alone on an island paradise, she and this man . . . a delicious lassitude crept over her as he walked steadily towards her. He was naked to the waist, the muscles rippling under his bronzed skin. The deep blue of the sky was reflected in his eyes; they mesmerised her with their intensity. Slowly she went to meet him, until they stood only inches apart.

Dazzled by the sunlight, its golden rays bathing her in a pagan warmth, Kristin felt her blood quicken with primitive desire. Deliberately Nathan cupped her face in his long fingers. He bent to kiss her, his mouth hungry for hers, demanding a response she was only too ready to give. Her hands clasped his waist and suddenly she was strained against him. His lips moved to the scented softness of her hair. With a sensuality at once daring and shy, she laid her cheek on his shoulder and began kissing his smooth, sun-warmed skin, nibbling at his flesh. Her fingers fondled the rough hair on his chest.

He tilted her chin with a hand that was not quite steady. 'Do you know what you're doing to me?'

She shook her head wordlessly.

'You've bewitched me—you and your island.'

She felt a tremor of superstitious fear, so uncannily he had echoed her thoughts. 'Spells are made to be broken,' she heard herself say.

She did not think he even heard her. He went on exultantly, 'You've become my whole world, Kristin.'

Once again his lips plundered hers, his embrace crushing her to him, so that the heavy beating of his heart became the beating of her own. Then she felt him undo the clasp of her halter top and slowly slide it from her shoulders. Unheeded, it fell to the ground.

For a moment Nathan stood back from her, his eyes devouring the proud firmness of her breasts, the delicate arch of her ribcage. Her cheeks flamed with colour as she tried to cover herself with her hands.

'Don't—you're so beautiful.'

With an exquisite slowness that tormented her with longing, he stroked her breasts so that they swelled and throbbed with life, the nipples teased into hardness. And then somehow she and Nathan were on the ground, their limbs entwined, and he was kissing her, his hands moulding her hips and thighs to his masculine hardness. She cried out with pleasure. Her nails dug into his back as she felt his pulsing strength.

Dimly she was aware that he had pulled away from her and was fumbling with the waistband of his jeans. Her whole body was swept by the torrential passion he had aroused in her. Unable to bear the distance between them, she thrust her body against his, aching for fulfilment that only he could give. She whispered huskily, 'Take me, Nathan—oh please, take me.'

So suddenly that she felt the shock rip through her, his body shuddered to stillness. Her grey eyes huge in her face, she said uncertainly, 'Nathan——?'

He twisted away from her, burying his head between his knees. She could hear his laboured breathing, see his fists clenching and unclenching.

She shivered. Her heart fluttered against her ribcage like a trapped bird. She *was* trapped, she thought in a flash of incredulous insight. She loved Nathan, loved him with every fibre of her being. Body and soul she was his—and he did not want her.

Almost blinded by pain, she felt a cool breeze waft over her half-naked body. Flushing with mortification that she could have behaved so shamelessly, she fumbled in the grass for her top and fastened it with shaking fingers. She had practically thrown herself at him, she thought wretchedly.

'Get up, we're going back to the house,' he said coldly.

'Nathan, please——'

'Shut up!' he said savagely.

Feeling as though she had been slapped, she fought back the tears crowding her eyes. He took a half step towards her, then stopped, his face bleak and bitter. When he spoke, there was still an undercurrent of violence in his voice. 'God, Kristin, I can't talk now—don't you see that? Let's get our things and go.'

She trailed behind him to the farmhouse, where they gathered up their belongings. When they set off on the return trip across the island, she kept up with Nathan's long strides with difficulty; he walked like a man pursued by demons. Kristin's throat was tight with unshed tears, for their day of enchantment lay in ruins about her. Spells are made to be broken . . .

When they reached the house, Nathan carried the picnic basket into the kitchen, then turned to face her.

'Kristin, I'm going to the Landing.'

'Now?'

'That's what I said, isn't it?'

'But it'll be dark soon. How will you get back?'

'I'm not coming back.'

'Never?'

'Why don't you let me finish?' he said curtly. 'What I was saying was that I won't be back tonight. I'll drop over to-morrow just to make sure everything's okay.'

Deep within her, she felt the first stirrings of anger; it warmed her, bringing life back to her ice-cold limbs.

'Why, Nathan?' she said clearly. 'Just tell me why.'

'God, Kristin, do I have to spell it out for you?'

'Obviously you do.'

With heavy patience he said, 'If I stay here tonight, I won't be accountable for what happens. I want you, I want to make love to you. And next time I may not be able to stop.'

He was not saying that he loved her, she noted with a cold detached part of her brain. But her traitorous tongue said in a tiny voice, 'I want you, too.'

He seized her by the shoulders and shook her, his mouth a grim line. 'I mustn't make love to you, Kristin. You know that as well as I do.' His fingers tightened unconsciously. 'So I'm getting out of here before we do something we'll both regret.'

'You're hurting me!'

For a moment he looked blank and she was sure he had not

even realised how hard he was holding her.

'Sorry.' Automatically he released her.

She rubbed her arms, leaning back against the counter for support; the tension between them had gone on too long and was taking its toll. Too proud to cry in front of him, she said with assumed coldness, 'There's plenty of fuel in the skiff. You'd better go before the wind comes up.'

'Damn it, Kristin, you don't think I want to go, do you?'

'I'm not a mind-reader, Nathan, so I have no idea.'

He ran his fingers through his hair, his eyes brilliant with anger. 'You don't understand at all, do you! Is this all a game with you?'

His cruel words cut her to the quick. 'Just go, if you're going.'

'If that's the way you feel, I'll be glad to oblige.'

He pivoted and left the kitchen; she heard him in the bedroom gathering up his few belongings. When he came back, he said emotionlessly, 'I'm doing the only possible thing, Kristin. I'll stay at Alice and Luther's—so you know where I'll be if you need anything.'

'What will you tell them? They'll think it strange, you walking in like this.'

He brushed her objection aside. 'Luther and I had already talked about going out fishing together first thing one morning, so it'd be logical that I'd spend the night with them.'

He seemed to have it all worked out. Neat, tidy, no loose ends . . . She said flatly, 'Say hello to them for me. And if there's a letter from Dad, be sure and bring it back with you, please? If you come back, that is.'

'I've already said I would. I'll see you tomorrow afternoon.' He hesitated, keeping the space of the room between them. 'Goodbye, Kristin. Take care of yourself.'

'You too,' she said almost inaudibly, hardly able to believe he was really going. He shut the door quietly behind him. In a few minutes she followed him out of the door, running swiftly to stand by the lighthouse. From high on the bluff she saw him steer the skiff down the inlet, skilfully navigating the channel rocks. Then he was out into the open sea, headed for the Landing. He never once looked back. So he did not see the girl's lonely figure standing by the lighthouse, her hair whipped into a dark cloud by the wind.

When she could no longer distinguish the skiff among the waves, Kristin slowly went back to the house. She had spent many hours by herself on the Island, but never had she felt as alone as she did now. It was a convincing—and frightening —demonstration of how Nathan had changed her life. By showing her the delights of companionship and the turbulence of passion, he had taken away her self-sufficiency; no longer could she be content with her own company. For the first time in her life she saw how uncaring was the sweep of sky overhead ... how indifferent the dark mass of the forest ... how cruel the jagged cliffs. Even her surroundings were betraying her, mocking her loneliness.

Terrified by her new vulnerability, she ran to the house, bolting the door behind her. In the familiar haven of her room she sank down on the bed, too tired to think any more, nor could she hold back the tears that finally began to trickle down her cheeks. She threw herself face down on the pillows and sobbed out all her heartache and loneliness.

CHAPTER FIVE

KRISTIN struggled from the depths of sleep. She had been dreaming, and the nebulous horror of the nightmare still haunted her ... someone was banging on the door and shouting. She buried her head in the pillow, wondering fretfully why they couldn't go away and leave her in peace.

'Kristin, open the door!'

She pushed herself upright, rubbing her eyes; her dark hair tumbled over the cap sleeves of her short green nightgown. Someone *was* at the door. Still half asleep, she stumbled into the kitchen. There were voices outside. Dazed and uncomprehending, she heard Nathan say, 'I'll get the axe and break the lock. I hope to God she's all right——'

Then Alice's tones, attempting to be comforting, but nevertheless anxious, 'She's just sleeping in, I expect.'

'But she never locks the door——'

Slowly Kristin slid the bolt back in the latch and opened the door. She stood still, a slender figure in a cotton nightdress, her grey eyes confused in her pale face.

Nathan seized her in his arms. 'Thank God!' he said huskily.

For a moment she relaxed in his embrace, his solidity and warmth comforting her. Then she tensed and steeled herself to pull away. 'Alice?' she said questioningly. 'What are you doing here? And Luther—why aren't you fishing?'

'We'd better go in the house, dear,' Alice said quietly.

Kristin's nerves tightened. 'Something's wrong?'

'Come inside.'

The girl turned to Nathan, knowing instinctively he would tell her the truth. His blue eyes were deeply compassionate, and her heart constricted with fear. 'Please tell me,' she pleaded. 'It's Dad, isn't it?'

'Yes, Kristin. The coastguard vessel came to the Landing this morning. Last night they found wreckage from his boat on the reef by the Cape.'

'Did they find—him?'

'No. They made a thorough search of the area—but the currents are offshore and they didn't hold out much hope of ever finding the body.'

Alice interrupted in distress, 'Nathan, please, is all this necessary?'

'Yes, I think so,' Nathan said soberly, and indeed Kristin was grateful for his honesty, brutal though it might seem to Alice.

'When do they think it happened?' she whispered.

'In the same storm that brought me here.'

She closed her eyes momentarily, overwhelmed by the bitter irony of Nature: the storm that had given her Nathan had taken her father from her ... 'That's why he never wrote ...'

'Kristin dear, you'll get cold—let's go in, and I'll make you a cup of tea.'

Numbly Kristin looked from one to the other ... Alice, trying hard not to show how upset she was ... Luther, his young face solicitous, concerned ... Nathan, serious and watchful. The sensible thing to do was to go in the house and make a cup of tea and something to eat—just as though nothing had happened, she thought in desperate rebellion. But she didn't want to go in the house. The walls would close in on her, stifling her. She wanted to be by the sea, the sea that had claimed her father's life. But they were all crowding around her, trying to decently smother her sorrow.

Frantic with grief, she whirled and ducked past Alice's out-stretched hand, and began to run. The grass was damp under her bare feet and once she slipped and almost fell. Her heart pumping in her breast, she raced along the forest trail, heedless of the branches slapping at her, scratching her bare arms and legs. She was scarcely aware that she was crying, the tears streaking her cheeks.

Then she heard Nathan's voice shouting her name. 'Kristin, stop!'

Glancing over her shoulder without slackening speed, she saw he was chasing after her. She tried to go faster, but she was tiring, and her legs would not obey her. But she was nearly there, and she could hide among the rocks—she knew the cliffs like the back of her hand. Oh Dad, Dad ...

A root protruding from the forest floor caught her foot. Caught off balance, she was thrown to the ground, the breath driven from her body. And then Nathan was beside her, his big hands gentle as he turned her over.

Hysterical with pain, she beat at his chest with her fists. 'Let me go!' she sobbed, 'Let me go—he's dead, he's dead!' Like a wildcat she writhed in his arms, fighting to be free.

'Stop it, Kristin!'

But she struck at him again, inadvertently catching him in the ribs. He grunted with pain and lightning-swift she rolled out of his grasp, scrambling to her feet. She began to run again, her whole being concentrated on one mindless need: the sea—she had to get to the sea.

The field ... the orchard ... the old farmhouse ... the cliffs were just ahead of her. She put on a last desperate burst of speed, hearing the thud of Nathan's footsteps close behind. But then he seized her shoulder and she stumbled. She tried to twist free, sobbing with frustration. 'Let go!' she screamed, kicking out at him. Deliberately he raised his free hand and slapped her hard on the cheek.

She drew a shocked breath. Her cries died in her throat as she gazed at him from drenched grey eyes. Then suddenly she collapsed against him. 'Nathan—oh, Nathan!' As his arms folded her close, she began to weep.

He held her firmly while she sobbed out the first intolerable wrench of grief. Gradually she quietened, and only then did he speak. 'Let me look at you.'

She raised her head from his chest, and stood trustingly still as he wiped her tear-wet face with his handkerchief.

He was white about the mouth and she could still feel the laboured beating of his heart. In swift compunction she remembered how short a time it was since he had been injured in the wreck.

'I—I'm sorry I hit you in the ribs,' she faltered. 'I didn't mean to hurt you.'

His face softened and he gave the ghost of a chuckle. 'Remind me to duck if you ever intend to hurt!'

'I'm sorry I ran away, too. I just felt I had to be near the sea —can you understand that?'

'So that's what it was,' he said slowly. 'You scared the hell out of me. I thought you were going to throw yourself over the cliffs.'

'Oh, no!' she gasped, realising now why he had pursued her so desperately. 'It wasn't that at all.'

'Well, there wasn't really time for explanations, was there?'

'No ... I just knew I couldn't bear to be shut up in the house.'

He turned her in his arms, so that her back rested on his chest, and linked his arms in front of her. She could feel his chin resting on the crown of her head and knew he would patiently remain here with her as long as she wanted him to. In front of them stretched the ocean, its waters deceptively calm, glinting in the sun.

'I wish he wasn't dead,' Kristin said finally in a low voice, 'but if he had to die, I'm glad it was at sea. He loved the ocean —its freedom and its unpredictability. Even its ruthlessness ... I was so afraid he would be forced to retire, or else sent to a desk job. He would have hated that ...'

She leaned back against Nathan, feeling emptied of all emotion except an overwhelming weariness. 'I'd like to go home now.'

'If you're sure you're ready.'

'Yes—I am now.' And she knew it was true. She turned her back to the sea and looked up at her companion. Standing on tiptoes, she kissed him softly on the mouth.

'Thank you, Nathan.' Her eyes misted with tears, for she had never felt as close to him as she did now. 'All I can say is thank you.'

He hugged her briefly. 'You're welcome.' His face crinkled into a smile. 'And now, my dear, if I were the hero of a book, I'd sweep you into my arms and carry you home. Unfortunately, as my ribs are hellish sore, you'll have to walk.'

She gave a tiny chuckle of genuine amusement. 'In that case I shall refrain from swooning at your feet—it wouldn't do me any good, would it?'

'Not a bit.' Arms about each other, they walked up the hill together.

Back at the house the kitchen once again welcomed Kristin into its sunlit warmth. Alice had started breakfast and the aroma of coffee met them as they entered. Kristin missed the quick nod of reassurance Nathan gave Alice; she was only glad that all the older woman said was, 'I'll pour you a coffee, dear.'

It seemed natural to all of them that Nathan should take control. 'Have you any boiled water, Alice? I want to bathe the scratches on Kristin's arms. The first aid kit's in the bathroom, isn't it, Kristin?'

She nodded. After one swift discerning glance at her face, he said matter-of-factly, 'Why don't you go in your room and sit down—you look bushed. I'll bring the stuff in there.'

She did as she was told, sitting on the edge of the bed, her hands slack in her lap. Nathan wrung out the cloth and gently wiped the scratches on her arms and hands, patting her dry with a towel. Then, kneeling beside her, he did the same for her ankles and feet. There was no passion in his touch and when she reached out and stroked his thick black hair, it was a gesture of simple gratitude. He smiled at her. 'Where do you keep your nightdresses?'

'Second drawer down.'

He fumbled among them, his masculine hands oddly at variance with the froth of lace and ribbons. 'Will this do?' He dropped a long cream-coloured gown on her lap.

'Turn your back.' Standing up, she hastily shed the stained and torn green nightdress and put on the fresh one. Her eyes were heavy-lidded with weariness as he helped her into bed.

'Do you want anything to eat? Or do you need an aspirin?'

'No—I just want to sleep.' She laid her fingers on his wrist. 'Nathan, promise you won't go away.'

'I promise. Sleep well. We'll be in the kitchen if you need anything.' He went out, closing the door behind him.

She lay back on the pillows, her eyes already closed, and almost immediately was asleep.

Luther went to the fishing grounds the next morning, leaving Alice on the Island. 'He can manage without me for a couple of days, dear,' she said comfortably to Kristin.

'It's good of you to stay,' the girl answered seriously.

Although the first raw grief had passed, driven out of her by that wild flight across the island, she felt a deep sadness and an overwhelming tiredness. The thought of preparing a meal was beyond her, and even such a minor task as making the bed seemed to have taken on gargantuan proportions. But without any fuss Alice took over, preparing delicious meals to tempt Kristin's appetite, and unobtrusively making sure the house was running smoothly.

Nathan was working outside that first day, and after a while Kristin got dressed and went out to find him. He was painting the windward wall of the toolshed—a job Dugald had been planning to do. Easy tears filled Kristin's eyes, but she blinked them back.

'Hi,' she said, her voice almost normal, hoping he would not ask any of the usual trite questions like 'how are you feeling?'

She should have known him better. 'Pass me that rag, would you?'

She did as he asked. 'You've got more on you than on the wall,' she remarked, and indeed there were droplets of paint on his face and bare forearms and his fingers were liberally streaked with white.

He grinned at her, wiping his hands. For a moment her heart almost stopped in her breast for love of him. Without conscious thought, she rested her fingers on his wrist. 'I'm glad you're here,' she said huskily.

He patted her shoulder in an almost brotherly gesture that nevertheless melted the bones in her body. 'Alice got the coffee pot on?' he enquired casually.

At least it didn't show, Kristin thought ruefully, this love of hers, so bright and shining and new. It was her secret and so it had to remain. Especially now ... with a catch of disquiet she recognised that today at least Nathan seemed to be treating her as though she were a younger sister. Was it because of Alice's presence? She had no way of knowing ...

She preceded him into the kitchen, and after a while excused herself to go to her room, where she lay down to rest. She seemed to have an unending appetite for sleep ...

The next morning she felt a little better. It was a perfect summer day, bright and sparkling and clear, so Kristin wasn't surprised when Alice shooed her outdoors. 'I'm going to turn out the back bedroom,' the older woman said. Kristin winced, for that had been Dugald's bedroom. 'So off with you. Nathan is somewhere around.'

Glad to escape, Kristin went outside. The rhythmic bite of the axe echoed in the still air and for a moment she hugged to herself the comfort that Nathan's presence on the island brought her; she did not know how she would have got through the past two days without him. She found him behind the barn, splitting wood with an economy of movement that bespoke experience. He was stripped to the waist, and as she came into sight he hauled a handkerchief out of his pocket and wiped the sweat from his face; his keen blue eyes unobtrusively noted the pallor and the dark smudges under her eyes.

'Hi, Kristin.'

She would have liked him to kiss her. 'Good morning.' Indicating the pile of freshly cut wood, she added, 'I'm impressed! But are your ribs okay?'

'Fine so far. I'll stop in a few minutes and split some kindling.'

'I'll pile this in the barn, then.'

As she trudged back and forth to the barn with the armloads of sweet-smelling wood, a kind of peace came over her. Dugald might be gone, but surely the routine of life on the island would continue ... and he would want it to. And besides, to work side by side with Nathan was a pleasure in itself. She stacked another armload neatly against the barn wall, then gave a tiny exclamation of pain as a splinter was driven into her finger.

'What's happened?' asked Nathan.

'A splinter—ouch!'

'Let me see.' He dropped the logs he had been carrying and walked with her to the window, where the sun's rays streamed in, spangled with drifting dust motes.

'It's a big one—I'd better not touch it now. I'll get it out for you when we go back to the house.'

He stood still, continuing to hold her hand in his, a strange expression on his face. Slowly, he lifted her hand to his mouth and kissed her palm, his lips warm on her skin. A frisson of sheer delight rippled down her spine. She loved him so much ... unconsciously she swayed towards him. And then she was in his arms, her pliant body moulded to his. His mouth was almost brutal in its demand, but an answering fierceness leaped into life within her as her lips parted under his. Her slender fingers dug into the muscled hardness of his back and her blood sang with desire.

His urgent hands went under her shirt, rediscovering the swelling fullness of her breasts and the curve of her waist. She felt herself being consumed by the fire of passion he had so swiftly ignited and fanned to flames. But before she could give herself up to it completely, a tiny warning bell rang in her brain. Remember what happened last time you made love to him, it said; Nathan left you. He went away and left you alone . . . do you want that again?

She knew she could not bear it. With her hands flat on his bare chest she tried to push him away. 'No!' she gasped. 'No, don't!'

He fought for breath. 'Come here, Kristin,' he said thickly.

She backed away, pinned by the hypnotic brilliance of his eyes, until the heavy beams of the barn were against her back. With the last of her strength she flung the words at him. 'No! I don't want you to touch me!'

His body was frozen to stillness. 'Kristin, what are you saying?'

She gazed at him dumbly, one thought reiterating itself over and over again in her brain—she could not bear for him to leave the island. With the weight of despair she saw the cruel dilemma in which she was caught, helpless as an animal in a trap. If she allowed him to make love to her, he would go away . . . yet, because she loved him, her traitorous body could deny him nothing.

'I'm waiting for your answer.' His big body loomed over her. His eyes were bleak and hard, without mercy.

'I don't want——'

'You want me as much as I want you.'

'Oh, want, want!' she cried wildly, 'that's all you think about!'

Her fingers gripped the rough beams behind her. Spacing her words, desperately holding on to the last shreds of her control, she said clearly, 'Leave me alone, Nathan. That's all I'm asking.' He made an angry move towards her and she shrank back. 'Please——'

'Oh, for God's sake!'

Her body sagged as he pivoted and strode out of the barn; within moments she heard the vicious thud of the axe. She

had handled it all wrong, she thought despairingly—but what
else could she have done? He had left once before because of
his need to make love to her; if he left now, she would be
completely alone.

For the first time since her father's death she tried to look
into the future. Sooner or later she would be turned out of
the house, she supposed; they would not let her stay here for
ever. Then where would she go? If she was to earn her own
living, she would have to leave the coast and go to a city; she
would have to live in an apartment and work in an office.
Hundreds of girls did it—but could she? Almost sick with
fear, she walked across the barn to the side door, and let herself out. The green grass stretched to the cliff's edge; beyond
it the sea was a limpid, innocent blue. To live anywhere else
but here was too dreadful to contemplate——

'Kristin!'

It was Luther; he must have come to get Alice. She waved
and ran to meet him, and he hugged her briefly. Without
preamble he said, 'I was talking to the priest from the mission
downshore; if you'd like a memorial service at the Landing
tomorrow afternoon, he'd be glad to fly up and conduct it for
you.'

'Yes, I'd like that.' Her lips trembled.

'Okay, I'll get back to him on the radio. Oh, hi, Nathan.'
Nathan had approached them so soft-footedly that Kristin
had not even heard him; she hoped Luther would not notice
the constraint between them.

They all went to the kitchen together. 'Time to go back
home, Ma,' Luther announced cheerfully. 'I seem to have
emptied the refrigerator.'

'And cleaned out the cookie jar, I'll be bound,' his mother
replied.

'Come on, a guy's got to eat!'

'You don't look as though you've been wasting away,
Luther,' Kristin smiled. 'Anyway, thanks for lending Alice to
me. I couldn't have managed without her.'

'By the way, Father Duncan said the service would be
around three—a memorial service for Dugald,' Luther added
in explanation to Alice and Nathan. 'Are you ready to go,
Ma?'

'Yes—my case is in the hall.'

A half-formed plan sprang into Kristin's mind and she spoke without thinking. 'Can I come back with you?'

'You mean now?' Alice tried to cover her surprise, glancing sideways at Nathan.

'Yes.'

'Why, of course, dear, if you're sure that's what you want to do.'

'Yes,' Kristin replied firmly, 'I'd like that. I'll just go and pack a few things—I won't be a minute, Luther.'

She went past Nathan with her eyes downcast. In her room she folded the only dark dress she owned, and added shoes and a matching handbag. The door creaked and Nathan came in. He closed it behind him. Even though she had been half expecting him, she felt her nerves tighten with apprehension. She folded her night clothes and added her make-up kit. 'There,' she said lightly, 'I think that's all I need.'

With dangerous quiet he said, 'What's this all about?'

'I—I just need to get off the Island for a while.'

'I've never known you to want that before.'

'Well, the circumstances are a little different from what they've ever been before, aren't they?' she said tightly, aware of how unfair she was being, even as she spoke.

Almost invisibly she saw him retreat behind an impenetrable barrier; he was too proud a man to beg. 'Very well,' he said quietly. 'I'll see you at the service tomorrow.'

She opened her mouth, scarcely knowing what she would say, but he forestalled her.

'No, Kristin—there's nothing more to discuss.' And with that she had to be satisfied.

There was a fine drizzle falling the next day, so that ocean and sky were a uniform blur of grey. The bell in the tower of the little log church tolled solemnly as the mourners came out of the church to stand in groups in the roadway. Kristin had been comforted by the age-old rituals of the service and by the gathering of all her friends at the Landing. She was grateful that so many of them wanted to share their memories of Dugald with her: he had saved more than one fisherman's life in the wild storms that lashed the western coast, and the people of the Landing would not forget that. Also she was much aware of Nathan in deep conversation with Luther; he had arrived only minutes before the service began, and Kristin had not yet spoken to him.

Someone touched her on the sleeve. It was Del, looking unaccustomedly formal in a dark suit. 'I'm sorry about your Dad, Kristin,' he said gruffly. 'I won't pretend we were the best of friends, but he was a damned good man to have around if your boat was in trouble.'

His rough honesty touched her. 'Thank you, Del.'

Then he had to spoil it. He glanced over at Nathan, who was now talking to the priest. 'The story's going around that your friend Nathan's lost his memory.'

Warily she replied, 'That's right.'

'And you fell for that!'

'It happens to be true.'

'What's he waiting around here for then?'

'What else can he do?'

'I can think of several things. Kristin, you're heading for trouble.'

'Why, Del?' she asked, barely bothering to disguise her hostility.

'It's obvious, I would have thought. He's probably got a wife and kids back home—wherever that is—and he's having himself a vacation from them.'

'That's a despicable thing to say!' she cried.

'Not half as bad to say it as to do it.'

Unbidden there came to Kristin's mind the name 'Carla' ... Carla who must have shared Nathan's bed ... unaware of the look of anguished enquiry on her face, she saw Nathan approaching.

'Del, I have to go,' she said flatly.

'I'll be over to see you one of these days.' After Del had exchanged a barely civil nod with Nathan, he went to join his friends.

'What was he saying?' Nathan demanded. 'Nothing pleasant, by the look of you.'

For one crazy moment she thought of bursting out with the truth, but then her courage failed her. Coldly she said, 'I'd rather not discuss it.'

'What's between you two anyway?'

'Between us?' she said blankly. 'Del and me, you mean?'

'Exactly.'

His sarcasm brought a flush to her cheeks. 'Exactly nothing, that's what's between us!'

'It doesn't look that way to me.'

'Well, for once you're wrong,' she said sweetly.

His eyes narrowed, he glared at her. 'Just thank your lucky stars there are lots of people around—or I'd pick you up and shake the truth out of you.'

'I told you the truth!'

'Sure——' He controlled himself with an effort, and when he spoke his voice was remote. 'We'd better start back soon—the fog could come in. That is, if you are coming back?'

His very remoteness gave her no clue to his feelings. She stared at him in futility. Although she suddenly longed for the comforting familiarity of her own surroundings, she was too proud to force her presence on him—her unwanted presence, it seemed.

'You don't have to worry,' Nathan added, 'I won't bother you. Luther and I plan to go fishing together the next couple of days, so I won't be around that much.'

Kristin flushed at the barely disguised boredom in his tone. But in the end the desire to be home—and, she thought wretchedly, the desire to be with Nathan—overcame the rags of her pride. 'Yes, I'll come,' she whispered. 'I'll get my case from Alice's and meet you at the wharf.'

More than once in the next few days Kristin found herself wishing she was a hundred miles from the Island, or at least, a hundred miles from her self-imposed exile with Nathan. He had turned into a stranger, and she was helpless to break through his reserve. He was polite—bafflingly, infuriatingly polite—until she felt she could scream. The delightful companionship they had once shared had vanished in a sea of inanities. 'Good morning ... goodnight ... how are you? ...'

True to his word he went fishing every fine day, often not returning until late afternoon. During his absences she seemed to accomplish very little. All the contentment that had so blessed her placid life up to now had vanished, ephemeral as fog. She knew now that she was living on borrowed time on

Sitka Island: an official letter of condolence had come from the head office in Victoria, and with it the ominous announcement that a junior official would call on her within the next two months. It did not take much intuition for Kristin to realise that she would then be given her notice. She would never be allowed to stay here ... not, she supposed miserably, that she would want to live here alone, after Nathan had gone. For he would be bound to leave sooner or later, even though right now he never raised the subject of any future plans. So the weeks ahead looked bleak and uncertain, frighteningly empty of purpose.

As the slow days passed, Kristin could feel the tension mounting within her. The isolation she shared with Nathan should have brought them closer together. Instead, it was driving them apart, for it was a false intimacy. The bungalow seemed too small to hold the two of them. When she went to bed at night she was achingly conscious of the sound of him moving around his room, of the creak of his bedsprings, the click as he switched off the light. She would lie tense on the bed, her eyes straining upwards into the darkness ... each morning she insisted on getting up early and cooking his breakfast before he left to meet Luther at the fishing grounds; they stepped around each other in the all-too-small kitchen, making stilted conversation, and she would both long for him to leave and dread his departure.

In the hall one afternoon she almost bumped into him on his way from the shower; his hips swathed in a towel, his chest bare, his wet hair curling around his ears. Another evening she found him asleep in the study, his body loose-limbed and relaxed in the armchair. His presence pervaded her life, yet for all the real communication between them, he might just as well not have been there.

As was inevitable sooner or later, matters came to a head. One morning about a week after Dugald's memorial service, Kristin got out of bed to the shrill of the alarm, feeling as though she had not slept at all. She looked at herself in the mirror without any enthusiasm: pale face, smudges under clouded grey eyes. Viciously she dragged a brush through her hair and splashed cold water on her face before struggling into her oldest housecoat. What did it matter what she looked like? Nathan never looked at her anyway.

She stalked out into the kitchen, filled the kettle and set it on the stove with unnecessary vigour. Hacking up some bacon, she threw it into the frying pan.

Soft-footed as a cat, Nathan came into the kitchen. Quiet as he was, she was instantly aware of his approach, even as she cursed her overly sensitive nervous system.

'Good morning,' she said coldly, not turning round.

'Morning. It looks like it's going to be a nice one too.'

She burned her finger on one side of the frying pan and swore crossly. She hadn't even looked out of the window to see what it was like out—normally the first thing she did—but she was damned if she was going to be drawn into one of their oh-so-polite discussions of the weather.

'Do you want beef or egg sandwiches?'

'Beef, please. I'll carve it if you like.'

She sliced some bread and recklessly slathered on the butter, then turned the bacon, its fragrance temporarily allaying her admittedly foul mood. Toast in, make the tea ... automatically her nimble fingers went about their usual tasks. She could cook the eggs now ... But as she straightened up from the bottom shelf of the refrigerator, the eggs in her hand, Nathan turned to put the meat back, and bumped into her. The eggs were jerked from her fingers and fell to the floor, smashing into a mess of yolk and shell.

'Oh, damn!' she cried. 'Now look what you made me do!'

He checked the retort he had been about to make. His forbearance only made her angrier. 'I'll clean it up,' he offered.

'No, I will.'

'You're determined to make a martyr of yourself, aren't you?'

In one glorious surge of emotion, she lost her temper. 'What the hell do you mean by that?'

'I would have thought it was obvious. Even to someone in as bad a mood as you——'

'I am not!'

'You're spoiling for a fight, Kristin, and you have been ever since you got up. Be careful that you don't start one you can't win.'

His hard-eyed stare made him a formidable adversary, but

she was past caring. 'Tell me one thing, Nathan. You make it very obvious you can't stand the sight of me—so why do you stay here?'

'Any time you want me to leave, say the word.'

'You haven't answered my question!'

'No, I haven't, have I?' He gave an unpleasant laugh, that inadvertently sent a shiver down her spine.

He stepped carefully over the puddle of egg on the floor, his blue eyes blazing with an emotion that set her heart banging painfully against her ribs. Unable to stop herself, she backed away from him towards the stove.

'Scared, Kristin?'

'Of you? Of course not,' she lied valiantly.

'Then come here.'

She held tightly to her anger. 'No!'

Behind her the frying pan sizzled and spat, and she glanced over her shoulder to find the bacon had burned to a crisp. It was the final straw. Ridiculously she felt tears prickle in her eyes, as her anger evaporated into self-pity. 'Can you give me one good reason why I ever got up this morning?'

To her consternation, Nathan began to chuckle, quietly at first, then throwing back his head and laughing so infectiously that she could not help the small smile that pulled at the corners of her mouth.

'What's so funny?' she said uncertainly.

He finally collected himself and grinned at her, his teeth white and even against his tanned skin, his blue eyes dancing. Her heart caught in her breast, for with his laughter he had restored all their old camaraderie and she was totally unable to resist his charm. He glanced at her dark blue robe.

'You looked like a bad-tempered peacock a minute ago—all ruffled feathers.'

'I was certainly screeching like one!'

He seized her by the shoulders, his eyes still glinting with merriment. 'Why do I stay here? Because you're bad-tempered in the mornings. Because you never bore me. Because you're honest and kind and distractingly beautiful, and'—he paused for a moment, becoming more serious as he searched for the right word—'and somehow very real. There's nothing fake about you, Kristin.'

Strangely breathless she looked up at him, not knowing how to respond. All the misery and anxiety of the past few days slid from her shoulders like snow from a tree, and soft colour suffused her cheeks.

'You've never told me anything like that before,' she said shyly.

Abruptly he sobered. 'How could I? I didn't even know who I was—I still don't, but at least I'm beginning to be sure that whoever I am, I'm a loner—no wife, no children, no family out searching for me.'

'I don't understand.'

'I hadn't told you about this earlier—I've been in touch with the police and the coastguard people through Luther, and so far they haven't found me on any of the missing lists. No one's enquiring after me—at least in British Columbia. If the police don't turn up anything in B.C., they'll start enquiries across the rest of the country. Luther took a couple of photos of me, too, and put them in the mail last week. He said yesterday I should hear in a couple of days. And then I'll be in the clear.'

Kristin gazed at him, dumbstruck. It seemed incredible—and somehow sad—that a man like Nathan could vanish without anyone caring enough to look for him. Yet if no one cared —then he must be unmarried, without a family ... free ...

'Ever since I first saw you, Kristin, I've been torn in two.' His voice deepened and unconsciously his fingers tightened, pulling her a little closer. 'I wanted you—oh God, how I've wanted you! But how could I kiss you, make love to you, when for all I knew I might be married to someone else?'

'I thought you didn't want me any more,' she said in a small voice.

'Oh, sweetheart, you couldn't be more wrong. It's been torture for me—being with you so much, and yet unable to touch you and tell you how much I love you——'

'You love me?'

'Yes, I love you. It's pretty obvious, isn't it?'

Her knees felt weak. She clutched at his waist, scared to believe the evidence of her own ears.

'No, Nathan,' she murmured, 'it hasn't been obvious at all. The last little while I thought you hated me.'

'Hated you? God, no! I think I've loved you from the very

moment I saw you ... when you came through the storm to me.'

Suddenly overcome with emotion, she leaned her forehead on his chest, her heavy hair falling about her face. He went on anxiously, with a humility that touched and disarmed her, 'It's all right, Kristin, I don't expect you to love me too. I know it's too soon. You don't even know who I am. But maybe in time——'

She raised her head, her delicate features transformed with joy. 'I love you, Nathan. I know you—I know you're trustworthy and strong and generous and good, and that's all that matters.'

'Kristin. Oh, Kristin, my dear love ...' He gathered her into his arms and she buried her face in his shirt front, feeling the heavy beat of his heart against her cheek. A singing happiness filled her and when he raised her face to his, her eyes glowed with all the love she had never dared to reveal. He bent and kissed her, his lips firm and sure, claiming her for his own. When he spoke, his voice was exultant. 'You really do love me, don't you?'

It seemed strange to her that Nathan, so strong and sure of himself, needed such reassurance. 'Yes, I love you more than I can say.'

This time his kiss was more demanding, and the passion that had so long been denied between them leaped into flame. Fiercely Kristin clung to him, aware with every fibre of her being that his hands were pushing aside the heavy folds of her gown so that he could caress the satin softness of her skin. Her breasts grew taut with desire. Longing to feel his flesh against her own, she undid the buttons of his shirt.

'Sweetheart, I want you so much.' His hands moved to her elbows and for a moment he held her away from him, devouring her brilliant eyes and flushed cheeks, the tumble of disordered hair across her breast. He drew a deep steadying breath.

She came back to earth with a thud. 'I suppose you've got to go?'

'Yeah—Luther'll be here any minute. I guess he'd better not find us like this.'

She made a face. 'I don't want you to go.'

'I know. But I'll be back, Kristin. And when I do get back, we won't have to worry about Luther coming.'

She blushed, her lashes fluttering to hide her shining grey eyes. 'Hurry home, won't you?'

'Yes, my darling.'

'And Nathan'—she laid her fingers on his sleeve—'be careful.' Anxiety sharpened her tone. 'I couldn't bear it if anything happened to you.' For the first time in her life she fully understood the lonely fears of the women who stayed behind on shore, watching their men set out to sea, and not knowing whether they would return.

Yet had she but known it, it was not the peril of the sea that would soon threaten her happiness. Ignorant of the true danger, she spoke urgently. 'There are the currents off Bird Island, and the barometer's dropping a bit——'

'Don't worry, love, I'll be all right.' With deliberate sensuality Nathan ran his finger from her cheek down her throat to one pink-tipped breast. 'Nothing can keep me from coming home to you, Kristin—I swear that.'

His deep sincerity allayed the worst of her fears. She brushed his cheek with her lips, and then said with determined lightness, 'Heavens, you haven't had any breakfast!'

'That's okay—Luther always brings something to eat.'

She laughed, for Luther's appetite was notorious. 'I'll have supper ready for you, then.'

'Okay.' He kissed her, biting gently at her lips. 'Mmm—that tastes better than breakfast any day.'

She shoved him playfully. 'You'll be late.'

He raised his eyes heavenwards in mock horror. 'Nagging me already!'

'Oh, Nathan, I'm not!'

He kissed the tip of her nose and grabbed his jacket from the back of the chair. 'Must go—'bye, love. See you later.'

The door shut briskly behind him. She hugged herself, savouring her happiness, then on impulse she left the house as well. Lifting her long robe clear of the dew-wet grass, she ran to the fence and looked down into the inlet. Luther had just nudged his boat close to the wharf and Nathan was climbing on board. As the gill netter backed into the open sea, Kristin waved goodbye. As though Nathan sensed her presence, he looked up, and even from that distance she could see his smile as he raised his hand in farewell.

Only when the boat was too far away for her to distinguish its occupants did she turn away and wander back to the house. The sun gilded the drooping tips of the hemlocks, while the dew sparkled underfoot like jewels. The sea's endless rhythm murmured in her ears. From a clump of spruce a flock of tiny kinglets burst into the air, wildly wheeling after each other yet never colliding, their cries piercing the golden air.

Sun, sea and forest ... all merged into one rapturous moment of pure joy. He loves me, Kristin thought incredulously ... Nathan loves me. For the rest of her life she would remember that perfect moment ... and in the days that were to follow she would wonder how her happiness could have been untinged by any foreboding of what was to happen.

CHAPTER SIX

AFTER breakfast she decided to give the study a good cleaning. Beethoven's Fifth Symphony, played fortissimo, seemed well suited to her mood, so she turned the record player on and got to work, dusting off all the books to start with and humming along with the music. It was little wonder that she did not hear the knocking at the back door, or the fall of footsteps through the kitchen.

It was some instinctive recognition that she was being watched, rather than any actual sound, that made her look up. A man was standing in the doorway, watching her.

Her nerves jumped. The ornament she had been dusting slipped from her fingers and fell to the floor, smashing into tiny pieces. 'Del! Did you have to creep up on me like that?' she cried, too startled to be particularly logical.

'I knocked. There could be a dozen people at the door and you wouldn't hear them with that racket on.'

'That racket happens to be a Beethoven symphony!' She knelt to pick up the shattered china. 'You seem to make a habit of appearing out of the blue and frightening the wits out of me.'

'I told you I was coming the last time I saw you.'

She sighed with exasperation. 'I suppose you're right. What did you do, wait until you knew Nathan had gone?'

'Yeah—that's just what I did.'

She had expected him to deny it. An aggressive tilt to her chin, she said, 'Why did you do that, Del?'

He leaned against the doorpost, his stocky body relaxed, his pale eyes calculating, and she had the feeling that he had taken control of the conversation. A tiny feather of fear brushed her, but she pushed it away. Nathan loved her, so nothing Del could say or do could harm her. Armoured with this new security, and swept anew by the joy that the mere thought of Nathan could arouse in her, she said calmly, 'Would you like a cup of tea?'

As she filled the kettle, she found herself wishing Del had chosen any day but today to visit. His presence was an intrusion. If she couldn't be with Nathan, she wanted to be alone, to savour her new happiness and to rejoice in the prospect of Nathan's return this evening. As she automatically searched for the teabags, she found herself wondering if Nathan would kiss her this evening as he had this morning ... would he hold her and caress her? Her body tingled with anticipation, and it was an effort to bring her thoughts back to the present.

More and more she resented Del's unexpected visit; he seemed to have a genius for turning up at the wrong time. Reluctantly she sat down at the table with him to wait for the water to boil. Picking up a pocket book that was lying on the table—one she had been reading—she idly riffled through its pages. 'Have you seen Alice lately? I'm rather surprised she hasn't been over to see me.'

'I met her at the store yesterday.' His movements unhurried, Del lit a cigarette, tossing the match into the ashtray.

'Well—how is she?'

'Fine, I guess.'

'I suppose she's busy with her garden, and the sewing and cooking she always seems to be doing. It's funny she hasn't been over for a visit, though.'

Del grinned slyly. 'Oh, I'm sure she has her reasons.'

Again Kristin felt a flutter of disquiet. 'Stop hinting, Del, and come out with it. You're obviously working up to something.'

'I suspect Alice is leaving you and Nathan alone together as much as she can ... she's kind of hoping something will develop, isn't she?'

A painful blush coloured Kristin's cheeks and her silence was more expressive than any words could have been. Finally she sputtered, 'That's nonsense!'

He pounced, like a cat on its prey. 'I sure hope so.'

A blanket of fear enveloped her. Fiercely she fought free of its folds, calling up Nathan's beloved image like a talisman. 'I wish you'd go home,' she burst out, too upset to be polite.

'I'll go when I've had my say, Kristin, and not before.'

'Then quit being so long-winded!'

The kettle chose that moment to boil over and she leaped up from the table, taking it off the heat and wiping up the water. Inevitably this reminded her of the burned bacon earlier in the morning, and in sudden desperation she wished Nathan would walk in the door. She needed his strength, the support of his love, for she was becoming more and more convinced that Del was out to do mischief. 'Why don't you just tell me why you've come, Del?'

'Alice is making a bad mistake trying to throw you and Nathan together.'

'Maybe it isn't such a bad mistake. Did you ever think of that? Not that it's really any of your business. Nathan and I do happen to be adults and can surely look after ourselves.'

'Oh, he's certainly looking after himself,' Del sneered.

'Stop it, Del! You've never liked him, right from the beginning.'

'Maybe I was the only one to see through him. And now I've come across something that proves my point.'

With a kind of fascinated horror she watched him pull his wallet out of his hip pocket and extract a folded piece of newspaper. Almost suffocated by a fear as vivid as it was irrational, she said faintly, 'What's that?'

The tone of her voice must have alerted him. There was something very like compassion in his expression when he spoke. 'You've fallen for the guy, haven't you?'

She stared at him dumbly, unable to deny it.

He pulled out another cigarette. For the first time since he had arrived, she saw he was at a loss. 'Damn it, Kristin, what did you do that for?'

'Why can't I be in love with Nathan, Del?'

'He's no good, that's why.'

'That's not true. And that's not your reason. You can't hide what you've come to tell me, Del. You've gone too far for that.'

Still he hesitated, twisting the piece of newspaper round and round in his calloused hands. An insane urge to scream rose in Kristin's throat. 'Tell me! Del, you've got to tell me.'

He stared at her. 'Sit down.'

Limply she sank into the chair, her eyes great pools in her white face. He held out the scrap of paper. 'I'm sorry, Kristin,' he said roughly. 'I wish I hadn't come—although you'd have to find out sooner or later.'

For a moment she closed her eyes; she would have given anything to be able to set a match to the paper and forget it had ever existed. With fingers that shook, she unfolded it.

Afterwards, she supposed she had been more or less prepared for what she saw. It was a photograph with a caption beneath it. The picture blurred momentarily, but then resolved itself into five figures: Nathan, tall and handsome, unfamiliar in a tailored business suit, yet unquestionably Nathan; an equally handsome boy of ten or eleven, whose features were almost a mirror image of the man at his side; a woman—a beautiful woman—chic and elegant in a long gown, one hand resting in a proprietorial way on the boy's sleeve; a shorter, stockier man, whose face nevertheless bore a resemblance to Nathan's; and finally a petite curly-haired woman who was smiling at the camera with infectious gaiety.

The words beneath the picture dragged Kristin's eyes downwards. 'Mr Nathan Raines is seen relaxing with members of his family in their palatial home in Victoria. Mr Raines is a well known businessman and world traveller.'

All the colour drained from Kristin's face. The paper fluttered to the table. Vaguely she heard Del's chair scrape back and then his hands roughly forced her head between her knees.

The dizziness faded. She pushed him away; as though drawn by a magnet her eyes flew back to the photograph. Nathan . . . Nathan's son . . . Nathan's wife. The other two, she supposed, must be his brother and sister-in-law. It didn't seem to matter much. Nathan was married . . . the three damning little words pounded a maddening echo in her head. She had fallen in love with a married man . . .

She did not notice Del folding the newscutting and shoving it between the pages of her book, his only motive being to remove it from her sight. When he spoke it was as much as she could do to focus on his words. 'I'm sorry, Kristin,' he repeated. 'I never knew it would hit you like this.'

She looked at him dully, knowing he was speaking the truth. Del had neither the imagination or the sensitivity to have anticipated the effect of his disclosure. All of a sudden his sympathy was more than she could bear. She had to be alone, to decide how . . . if . . . she would tell Nathan.

'I need to be alone for a while, Del, before Nathan gets back from fishing.'

'You'll be all right, though, will you?'

She would never be all right again, but there was not much point in telling him that. 'Yes, I'll be fine.'

'I guess I'll be going, then,' he said awkwardly.

Go, please go, she screamed inwardly. But the face she turned to him was a frozen mask, only her stricken eyes revealing her true feelings. 'Goodbye, Del.'

'Look me up next time you're at the Landing.'

She nodded, unable to speak, and finally, blessedly, he was gone. She slumped down in one of the kitchen chairs ... a motionless figure staring sightlessly at her hands flaccid on the table.

However, this merciful numbness soon wore off, and as it did pain awoke in her. She had felt grief at the death of her father, but that had been a normal grief; her father had had a long and useful life. She and Nathan, in contrast, had had so little time together. Their love was too new, too fresh and sweet to be cruelly destroyed. The pure, undistilled happiness she had felt that very morning now seemed aeons away, almost as though it had happened to another person.

It would have been better, she thought miserably, if she had never found out that Nathan loved her, if she had never reached that pinnacle of joy. How brief her happiness had been! A matter of hours ... was that to be her measure for a lifetime? For the love she felt for Nathan was a lifelong love ...

She pushed her hair back from her face. Her hands were ice-cold and she was shivering. She should get up and do something ... the dishes needed washing, and the frying pan was still on the stove, complete with the burned bacon. She and Nathan had laughed about that bacon and then he had kissed her ... it was too much to bear. She put her head down on the table and wept.

Eventually the deep, shuddering sobs ceased. Drained and exhausted, Kristin bathed her face in cold water in the bathroom, then went back into the kitchen. It was two o'clock. In less than three hours Nathan would be home.

She cudgelled her tired brain into action and began to think. Somehow she would have to tell him that he had a wife and son. She pictured him as she had last seen him, happy and confident, his blue eyes ablaze with his love for her. What would happen when she told him?

There was no question in her mind. He would leave, she knew him well enough for that. He would go back to his family in Victoria and she would never see him again. Pain struck her like a knife, pain so intense that she doubled over the sink, fighting back a wave of sickness that left her shaking. She couldn't tell him, she couldn't—yet she had to. She had no choice.

Or did she? She straightened slowly, as another possibility slid into her mind. She could at least put off telling him until tomorrow; they could have one last evening together before their world collapsed about them. The temptation to do this was so strong that she felt almost faint.

But could she deceive him? She looked at herself in the mirror. A wan face, lacklustre eyes . . . he would know immediately that something was wrong and he would not rest until he had discovered what it was. And even if her outward appearance did not betray her, he knew her too well, was too sensitive to her every mood, for her inward misery to escape him for long. It was impossible. She'd have to tell him the minute he walked in the door.

Back and forth she vacillated, one minute convinced she could hide her secret from him, the next moment equally convinced she could not. And then the clock in the living-room chimed the hour: three o'clock. It jolted her into action. Whatever she decided, Nathan must not come home and find her like this.

She finished cleaning the study, shoving the Beethoven record to the back of the cupboard, certain she would never listen to it again. Then she showered and washed her hair, carefully made up her face to hide the last marks of her tears, and dressed in her flowered jumper and flared skirt, narrow-strapped sandals on her feet. This whole procedure both calmed and strengthened her; she would show a brave face to the world, no matter what. She went into the kitchen and began to prepare supper.

It was shortly before five when she looked up and saw Nathan striding towards the house, his yellow oilskin jacket slung across his shoulder, the wind ruffling his black hair.

Emotion welled within her, a mingling of love and sorrow and fear that almost overcame her with its intensity. As he walked into the kitchen she could not stop herself; she ran to him, flinging her arms around him and hiding her face against his chest. 'Oh, Nathan! Hold on to me, please.'

His arms came around her, tight and hard. 'Sweetheart, what a welcome! I've been waiting for this all day long.' But then, as she continued to cling to him, he demanded, 'Kristin? Is something wrong?'

She shook her head wordlessly, not wanting to leave the comfort and security of his embrace—false security though it might be.

'Look at me,' he said.

Obediently she raised her head.

'What's wrong?'

She gazed at him, her heart aching with love for him. She couldn't tell him the truth, she simply couldn't. 'I—I missed you, that's all. It seemed a long day.' And that *was* the truth, she thought grimly.

'Mmm, I know what you mean. But there's no need to get so upset, Kristin.'

'It's frightening when you love someone—I never realised before today how vulnerable it makes you.' She gave herself a shake, feeling a little better now that she had shared at least that with him. 'Roast chicken and all the trimmings for supper. How does that sound?'

'Great—I'm ready for it. Do I have time for a shower first, to wash the worst of the fish off?'

By some miracle she was even able to laugh. Wrinkling her nose, she said cordially, 'Go right ahead.'

'Which is a polite way of saying I smell,' Nathan rejoined, slapping her on the bottom as he headed for the bathroom.

Encouraged that he had not divined the true extent of her unhappiness, Kristin was able to maintain the sense of ease between them throughout the meal. At times she almost forgot Del's nightmare visit, and when they adjourned to the study she sank gracefully on to the rug by the fire, feeling that Nathan's very presence had granted her haven from the storm. She sipped her coffee as he put on a record of guitar music, then smiled at him as he joined her by the hearth.

VISIT 4 MAGIC PLACES
FREE!

AFRICA

...me of the Temptress by Violet Winspear
...apped in the jungles of Africa, Eve's only
...hance for survival was total dependence
...h the mercenary Major Wade O'Mara. He
...ad the power to decide her fate. But only
...e could make him give in to desire.

GREECE

Say Hello to Yesterday by Sally Wentworth
Seeing Nick after seven years made Holly
realize it was her parents who ruined their
marriage. Now that she had found him, she
knew that their love had never died. And
she was determined to make him
love her again.

CARIBBEAN

...orn Out of Love by Anne Mather
...harlotte had paid for one night's pleasure
...ith years of pain and loneliness. Ten years
...ter Logan had deserted her and the baby,
...ey met unexpectedly on San Cristobal...
...here their love affair seemed destined to
...egin again.

ENGLAND

Man's World by Charlotte Lamb
She had everything going for her. Brains.
Beauty. And a sterling wit. Her only problem
was men. She hated them. That is, until Eliot
decided to make her see otherwise.

Love surrounds you in the pages of Harlequin Romances

Harlequin Presents romance novels are the ultimate in romantic fiction . . . the kind of stories that you can't put down . . . that take you to romantic places in search of adventure and intrigue. They are stories full of the emotions of love . . . full of the hidden turmoil beneath even the most innocent-seeming relationships. Desperate clinging love, emotional conflict, bold lovers, destructive jealousies and romantic imprisonment—you'll find it all in the passionate pages of **Harlequin Presents** romance novels.

Let your imagination roam to the far ends of the earth. Meet true-to-life people. Become intimate with those who live larger than life.

Harlequin Presents romance novels are the kind of books you just can't put down . . . the kind of experiences that remain in your dreams long after you've read about them.

Let your imagination roam to romantic places when you...

BUSINESS REPLY CARD

First Class   Permit No. 70   Tempe, AZ

POSTAGE WILL BE PAID BY ADDRESSEE

Harlequin Reader Service
1440 South Priest Drive
Tempe, Arizona 85266

'Do you know what's wrong?' he demanded.

Her eyelids flickered momentarily. 'N-no.'

'I haven't kissed you since I came home.'

Relieved, and lulled into a false sense of security, she murmured, 'That's easily remedied.'

She should have remembered the cataclysmic effect of Nathan's lovemaking. Because, of course, he did not stop with a kiss. Before she knew it she was lying back on the rug, Nathan's big body lying across her, his mouth raining kisses on her mouth, her hair, her throat. Like a finely tuned instrument her body began to sing to his touch. Her truant hands caressed his neck, running through his thick hair.

She heard his breathing quicken. His hard thigh forced her legs apart as with strong demanding hands he pulled her jumper to her waist, hungry for the softness of her breasts. 'Kristin, my beautiful Kristin.'

She went still in his arms. One night not long ago he had said another woman's name ... 'Carla, Carla.' And today Kristin had seen the image of that woman in all her perfectly sculpted beauty. Jealousy and pain ripped through her and with the strength of desperation she fought free of Nathan's hold.

'Kristin! Did I hurt you?' He reached out for her, anxious and concerned.

Her heart smote her. She was hurting him already and she would have to hurt him more. It was the ultimate in cruelty to have to destroy the very one you loved more than life itself. She choked back a sob. 'We can't make love, Nathan,' she blurted.

'What are you scared of, sweetheart?' he said gently. He made no further attempt to touch her, as if he knew she would flinch away like a frightened deer. 'I'll try not to hurt you— it's bound to be a bit frightening the first time.'

He was trying so hard to understand and sympathise and she loved him so much ... 'This morning——' she murmured finally. 'I've never been that happy before in my life. It scares me. I'm afraid it won't last ...'

'It will last, Kristin,' he said with deep conviction. 'I love you. You love me. Together we're invincible!'

'But we still don't know who you are. What if you do have a

wife, Nathan?' He made an impatient movement, but she ignored him. 'Somebody, somewhere, must have a claim on you.' Weakly she attempted to joke about it. 'You're far too gorgeous to be unattached!'

'That's very flattering! But listen to me a minute, Kristin—Luther was in touch with the police again last night and they still haven't come up with anything.' He stared sombrely into the flames. 'I don't have to tell you how much this whole loss of identity has bothered me. There've been times I've thought I'd go crazy if I didn't soon find out who I am ... and times I've thought perhaps I already was crazy, because I couldn't remember.'

He shifted his gaze to meet hers, his eyes intense with the need to make her understand. 'I have no past. It's gone. All I have is the present and the future—and you are part of both of those, Kristin.'

Her lips trembled. 'But——'

'I've given a lot of thought to the future. I've decided to go to Victoria myself very soon, and from there, if necessary, to the mainland. It seems pretty definite that I haven't got a family'—his mouth twisted—'unless I'm such a bastard that no one wants me to turn up.'

'Don't be ridiculous!'

'Thanks,' he grimaced. 'But just the same I have to find out who I am. Apart from anything else, how can I marry you when I don't even know my last name?'

For a moment the wonder of these last words overcame all other considerations. 'You mean you want to marry me?' she said with childish simplicity.

'Kristin, for someone with your intelligence, you can be terribly obtuse. Of course I want to marry you—and as soon as possible. Hence the trip to Victoria. The sooner I go, the sooner we can get this mess cleaned up and start on our new life ... together.'

In Victoria you'll find you have a wife and son, she thought, with such clarity that for a minute she was scared she had spoken the words out loud.

With uncanny perception he said, 'Kristin, you've really convinced yourself that some woman's going to appear out of the woodwork, haven't you?'

She nodded, avoiding his eyes. She ought to tell him—but, oh God, how could she?

'For what it's worth, I'm sure I'm not married. I can't explain it rationally and I certainly have no proof one way or the other. I just don't feel as though I've ever been married.'

She made no response, her slim shoulders bowed, her hair hiding her face from view.

'Come here, Kristin.'

She looked up in surprise, for his voice was harsh as he peremptorily beckoned her to his side. Sensing that his patience was wearing thin, she moved closer to him, her nerves tightening.

'I love you, sweetheart. But you've got to trust me; the two go hand in hand. I'll never knowingly deceive you—I promise that. And I expect the same from you.'

This was getting worse and worse. She could feel an inward trembling spread to her limbs. Then he pulled her towards him, fastening his mouth on hers.

Her entire body recoiled, shrinking away from him. She felt him freeze to stillness. Opening her eyes, she saw for an instant how bleak his features were, how pain-filled his eyes, before a mask of cold anger closed over his face, obliterating any other emotion, so that she wondered if she had imagined that fleeting agony. In one lithe movement he stood up.

'There's not much point in continuing this, is there? Go to bed, Kristin. I'll see you in the morning.'

She scrambled to her feet. 'I'm sorry,' she whispered, holding out one hand in unconscious appeal.

He struck it down with barely controlled violence. 'Spare me the histrionics. It's too late for that.'

Frightened, she retreated towards the door. The muscles of his throat were taut as he fought for self-control; he looked dangerous and unpredictable. She, Kristin, had done this to him. Her attempt to shield him from the truth had been an exercise in futility; in deceiving him, she had driven him away anyway. With the calmness of despair she said, 'Nathan, I have something to tell you——'

'No, Kristin, I've had all I can take for one night.'

'You must listen!'

'Get out! Before I do something I'll regret.'

His eyes raked her slender form with unmistakable intention and with a sob of fear she whirled and fled to her room. Slamming the door shut behind her, she undressed with feverish haste and got into bed, huddling under the covers. The house was quiet and still, as though she was the only person in it; there was no sound from the room next door. For a long time she lay awake, too tired to think, and beyond the point of obtaining relief in tears . . .

A sudden noise dragged her from the black depths of sleep. She found herself sitting bolt upright in bed, her heart pounding as though she had been running. Her ears strained the silence.

There it was again . . . a hoarse, straining cry. In a flash she was out of bed and running along the hall to Nathan's room. He had not drawn the curtains and a shaft of moonlight silvered the carpet, casting a pale luminous light over the bed. He was dreaming. He muttered something under his breath, his restless body tangled in the covers. Again that wordless sound of pain burst from his lips.

She could not bear to hear it again. Half kneeling on the bed, she shook him by the arm. 'Nathan! Wake up!'

He wrenched away from her so that she fell across him. 'Nathan, please——' she begged. 'Wake up.'

In the semi-darkness she saw his eyes open. 'Kristin?' he said uncertainly.

She sagged against him. 'You were dreaming, Nathan.'

With one arm he encircled her shoulders, pressing her to his naked chest in an unspoken need for human warmth and closeness. 'I was in a desert,' he said slowly, 'an empty desert that stretched for miles around, with the moonlight throwing black shadows on the dunes. I knew I was alone, the only human being for miles. And I was lost. I had no idea which way to go, and I didn't know who I was or why I was there. And yet for some reason it was desperately important that I should find out. God!' He wiped the back of his hand across his forehead. 'I've never known such loneliness . . .'

She was swept by a wave of compassion that left her trembling from its force. 'I'm here—you're not alone now. It was only a dream.' Acting without thought, only wanting to comfort him, she kissed him, her hands clinging convulsively to his shoulders.

He must have felt the tremors that rippled through her frame. 'You're cold,' he murmured, pulling the blankets around her.

She cuddled against him, craving the warmth of his body, feeling the familiar ache of desire stir within her. And suddenly she abandoned herself to it, as everything—past, present, and future—dissolved into a passionate need for his love-making. It was the only reassurance she could give him, a primitive and instinctive assuagement for the pain he had suffered.

Sensuously she moved her thighs against his and with a quickening of her breath realised he was sleeping naked. 'Make love to me, Nathan.'

'Kristin, do you know what you're saying?'

'Yes!' she whispered fiercely. 'I'm sorry about this evening But that's over now, and I want to be yours. I love you so much.'

'I love you too. I won't rest until I can make you my wife.' He kissed her, his lips parting hers, and she moaned with pleasure. Pushing her nightdress from her shoulders, he fondled her breasts, then slid his hands over the swell of her hips.

Kristin gave herself up to the sheer magic of his mastery over her body. She revelled in the torrential passion he evoked within her, no longer fighting it or trying to subdue her natural impulses. Every touch of their lips, every caress, was an expression of love, of generosity and caring.

His weight crushed her into the mattress. Pinned by his masculine hardness, she cried out his name; then she gave herself up to a crescendo of desire that carried her beyond herself to a place where she had never been before—a place of mingled pain and pleasure that exploded into a throbbing white heat.

Slowly reality returned. Her body's hunger was appeased, and in the aftermath of their lovemaking Kristin was filled with lassitude and contentment. She smiled drowsily into Nathan's face, so close to her own. 'I love you,' she said softly.

He kissed her. 'And I love you ... they're such small words to mean so much, aren't they?'

She nodded, her eyes heavy. For several minutes they lay quietly, their limbs entwined. Then Nathan kissed her again, a thread of laughter in his voice as he said, 'Do you realise the alarm will go off in exactly four hours?'

'Oh no!'

'Oh yes.'

'*I* don't have to get up.'

'You most certainly do! You don't expect me to get my own breakfast?'

'I don't see why not.' She tickled him in the ribs and he twisted away, chuckling in the darkness, 'Leave me alone! Or you know what'll happen——' Gathering her in his arms, he pulled her head down on his shoulder, where her hair lay in a scented tangle. Warm and safe, she drifted off to sleep ...

The jangle of the alarm woke them both. Nathan reached over and turned it off, swearing under his breath.

'Don't tell me you're cross in the mornings,' Kristin teased, stretching lazily.

'Only when I have to leave you.' He smiled at her, watching the delicate colour tinge her cheeks and noticing the purple shadows that smudged her eyes. 'You look as though you didn't get much sleep,' he remarked.

She blushed fiercely, as he pushed back the sheet, letting his eyes wander possessively over the slender curves of her body. His big frame loomed over her, and with secret delight she admired the dark mat of hair on his chest, the smooth play of his muscles. 'You'd better get up,' she said regretfully.

'Yeah.' He stretched, sinuous as a mountain cat, and left the room.

Filled with a nameless content, Kristin got out of bed; a reminiscent smile tugged at her lips as she found her night-dress on the floor. She went to her own room for her house-coat and then to the kitchen to start Nathan's breakfast.

It was only as she placed the cutlery on the table that she recalled Del's visit and his shattering revelations. She was living in a fool's paradise, she supposed, remembering the heart-ache of yesterday. But it all seemed very far away ... the present, with its memories of Nathan's tempestuous lovemak-

ing, was far more important. There was a new pride in her
bearing as she moved around the kitchen, for she felt confirmed as a woman—a woman loved and desired by the man
she loved.

Nathan ate his meal quickly, while she finished packing his
sandwiches and preparing a thermos of tea. He shoved them
into his jacket pocket. 'Oh, that reminds me,' he said casually.
'I'm going to take a book—there was an hour or so yesterday
with nothing much to do. I'll get one from the study.'

Kristin waited quietly, thinking that when he'd gone she'd
probably go back to bed and catch up on her sleep—he was
right, she hadn't had much sleep! He was taking a long
time ... 'Nathan?' she called.

There was no answer. Suddenly worried, she padded down
the hall to the study. He looked up as she walked in, and she
gasped with shock. He had turned into a stranger, white-faced,
hard-eyed.

'What's the matter?' Her eyes fell to his hands. 'That's my
book, not yours,' she said, puzzled. 'Yours was underneath it,
wasn't it?'

'I guess it was,' he said evenly. 'I dropped yours when I
picked it up.' He paused meaningfully.

Completely lost, she said in perplexity, 'So what? I don't
understand.'

'You really are quite the actress, aren't you?'

'Nathan, what are you talking about?'

'Cut it out, Kristin! And take that innocent look off your
face—it makes me sick!'

'For the last time, I don't know what you're talking about!'

'No? What about this?' And from the pages of her book
he held up the newspaper photograph.

The colour drained from her face, and she looked the picture of guilt. Her book had been lying on the kitchen table
while Del was there; she had assumed Del had taken the photo
away with him ... but she had been wrong. He had left it in
the book. Her grey eyes appalled, she blurted. 'I only——'

Ruthlessly he interrupted her. 'You hid it where you
thought it would be safe, didn't you? It's a pity you didn't find
a better hiding place, and then your little masquerade could
have gone on indefinitely.'

'It wasn't like that!'

'Oh, you were planning to tell me about it, were you?' he said silkily. 'What were you going to say? Something like this—oh, by the way, Nathan, last week I discovered you have a wife and son. Is that what you planned to do?' Savagely he demanded, 'Answer me!'

She fumbled for words that would somehow stem the vicious flood of his rage, but her mind had gone blank. Her wan-faced silence seemed to infuriate him further.

'How could you do it, Kristin? You of all people knew how much I hated not knowing who I was or where I was from'— he held out the clipping—'and here it all is. "Nathan Raines of Victoria". Why didn't you tell me—out of ordinary human decency? I told you about the enquiries I'd made, and that I'd be going to Victoria. I told you, God help me, that I didn't feel married. I told you I loved you. And you sat and listened, and all the time you knew who I was.' He banged his clenched fist on the top of the bookshelves so hard that the ornaments rattled. 'How could you do it?' he repeated, his voice anguished.

She took a step towards him. 'Nathan, you've got to believe me—I only found out yesterday.'

'Believe you?' he said bitterly. 'I'll never believe you again, Kristin.' Grabbing her by the elbows, he shook her like a puppy. 'My God! Don't you even know what you've done? You've destroyed all the trust between us. You've deceived me, lied to me.'

His words beat at her like flails so that she flinched away from him, her eyes twin pools of agony. He loosed his hold and turned away, his shoulders sagging. 'What's the use? It's over—finished.'

She leaned against the wall, for she would have fallen without its support. 'No! It can't be over—I can't live without you!'

For a moment she thought he would strike her, so wild and frenzied did he look. 'You should have thought of that sooner, my dear,' he said with bitter sarcasm.

She had reached the end of her endurance. Her one desire became to hurt him as he had hurt her. 'Well, of course it's over,' she spat. 'But my shortcomings are scarcely the point any longer, are they, Nathan? Because while you've been busily condemning me without even trying to listen to my side of the story, you've forgotten one thing——'

'What the hell are you talking about?'

'Your wife, Nathan. That's why it's over. Because you're married, remember? I even know her name—I didn't tell you that, did I? Her name's Carla—Carla Raines.'

He said hoarsely, 'How did you know? It didn't give her name on the paper.'

'When you were ill after the shipwreck, you started kissing me one night—and then you called me Carla. That would seem to clinch it, wouldn't it?'

'You little bitch! So you've known all along.'

'Oh no—I've only known since yesterday. And I don't give a damn if you believe me or not!'

He didn't seem to have even heard her. Ashen-pale, he sat down abruptly on the arm of the nearest chair, rubbing his forehead with his fingers. 'Carla,' he muttered. 'Carla ... and my son. How could I have a son and not even remember his name?'

Paralysed by the pain and defeat in his attitude, Kristin watched him speechlessly. Slowly he straightened, with the air of a man picking up an intolerable burden. His blue eyes rinsed clear of any expression, he said tonelessly, 'I'll get Luther to take me to Tofino and I'll catch the first plane out.'

He got up and walked past her, moving like an automaton. She followed him into the kitchen. He shrugged into his jacket and turned to face her. 'I won't be coming here again,' he said evenly. 'Goodbye, Kristin.'

'Goodbye,' she whispered.

He walked out of the door, closing it behind him with an air of finality. Through the window she watched him walk to the steps and then disappear from sight. He had not once looked back.

CHAPTER SEVEN

AUGUST, hot, drier than usual, was upon them. There had been less rain this month than Kristin could ever remember. She had been frantic, bereft when Nathan had left. For weeks she had refused to go to the Landing—not for anything—for the face she yearned to see was missing. Luther and Alice came often to the Island, pleading with her to come to the mainland with them for a few days, but always she refused.

She was losing weight and was feeling tired most of the time. Alice and Luther kept insisting that Nathan would return, but Kristin worked desperately hard reconciling herself to his absence. At first she wanted to believe he would come back to her. Then she struggled to accept the fact that he could not—he was married and had a young son. He couldn't leave them.

She loved Nathan and would love no other as she had loved him. But now she would have to work to forget him. Her father had not only left her a little money—enough to enable her to stay on the Island, but also his will had revealed that she now owned the old farmhouse and most of the land on the Island. Yes, she would stay on Sitka Island, for now most of it was hers.

Eventually she began to make the journey to the Landing again, sitting quietly on the beach helping Luther mend nets, or just visiting Alice in the afternoons, often chatting, staying for supper and returning to the Island at dusk. Alice never pushed her to talk about Nathan but left her to decide the direction of their conversation.

Late one afternoon Kristin and Alice stood in the living room. It was time to go—time to go back to the Island. They had had a pleasant afternoon together, with Kristin helping Alice around the house, then preparing supper for them all. They had waited for Luther to come, but strangely enough he had missed supper. Now it was dusk—and time to return to the emptiness of the Island. It suddenly struck Kristin—this emptiness, this aloneness. Before Nathan had come to her she had never felt loneliness. Now, she realised that it was a feeling she fought to control nearly every waking moment. Suddenly she didn't want to go back to Sitka. There was no place —no place on earth to go and be at peace. Tears welled in her eyes and she turned back to Alice, wanting only to be held and comforted.

'Oh, Alice——' she threw herself against her friend, burying her face in her shoulder, tears running down her pale cheeks. 'This is crazy,' she sobbed brokenly, 'I'm acting so stupidly lately. I do so well some days—then this terrible emptiness just washes over me and I don't know how I'll ever live without him. I feel such a fool!'

The older woman patted her on the back, hugged her, then held her from her, looking into the depths of her grey eyes. 'Love has a habit of making us act that way, child. It just does, that's all—not just you, but all of us.'

'I hurt him so, Alice. It was wrong, terribly wrong of me not to show him that picture right away.'

'But understandable, when you consider your feelings for him.'

'He didn't understand. He's gone.'

'He'll be back, Kristin. Luther says so and so do I.' Alice smiled gravely and patted Kristin's hand. 'He's a good man and he loves you, I know he does.'

'But he can't come back. He's married,' Kristin replied despairingly. 'He can't forgive me for what I did.'

'You saved his life, Kristin, and you loved him—honestly and openly. How could he not forgive?'

Kristin started and pulled back from Alice, searching her face for some clue to the meaning of her words. Did Alice know she had slept with Nathan the night before he'd left? How could she possibly know? No, they were words, just words.

'Are you all right, Kristin?' asked Alice anxiously.

'Yes—yes, of course.' She went quickly to the door, pushed open the screen and walked out into the cool evening air. No, I'm not all right, she thought desperately, not since he left. A wave of dizziness washed over her and she felt nauseated. Her thin fingers gripped the railing. Oh God, don't let me faint, she thought, not here. She bent down over the railing feigning interest in something in the grass below them. In a moment the dizziness passed and she felt stronger.

'Kristin?' It was Alice, a concerned question in her eyes.

'Truly, Alice, I'm all right. These past weeks have been a strain, that's all. I'm just tired. I'm going to bed early tonight and get a good rest. I promise.'

Alice nodded her agreement, then looked down towards the beach. 'Here's Luther coming. Wonder what kept him so long tonight? Not like that boy to be late for a meal!'

Luther waved to them from the path and ran across the grass towards them, taking the steps two at a time.

'Darn you, Kris—— How long have you been here?' he demanded.

'Why? What's wrong?'

'Nothing, you goose, except I've just been to the Island. We—I—didn't know you were here.' He picked her up and swung her round, hugging her with brotherly affection. 'Kept me late for my supper, kid, and that's an unforgivable sin in my book.' He put her down, kissed her on the forehead, then turned and flung open the screen door.

'Well, what did you want, Luther? Anything special?' Kristin called after him.

He looked at her and laughed, a devilish glint lighting his eyes. 'No, nothing special. Just checking up on you, that's all. But next time,' his fingers jabbed the air in a mock command, 'be there!' He bowed, continuing his charade, 'and now, my dear, you must excuse me, but my grub awaits in yonder kitchen—I hope.'

'Oh, Luther, you're crazy!' She laughed, for a moment forgetting the terrible pain which held her in its icy grip.

'Ah, and so I do keep the right company, don't I, Kris?'

She waved him off and turned to Alice, kissing her lightly on the cheek. 'Got to run, I guess. Thanks for supper and the comfort. I'll see you in a few days. Maybe you can get Luther to bring you over to the Island and we can have a picnic lunch together soon.'

'Sounds good, child, we'll see what the week brings us. Take care, and,' Alice paused, her voice dropping to a whisper, 'trust him, Kristin. He'll be back. Believe that.'

Kristin didn't respond but ran down the steps, across the

lawn, and on to the path that led down to the beach.

As she approached the wharf she saw Del Clarke walking towards her, and a wave of fear swept over her. Always now, something in the very sight of that man frightened her, threatened her. She nodded without speaking, lowering her eyes to the ground as she started to walk by him.

But he caught her roughly by the arm and swung her round to face him. Startled, Kristin cried out and twisted her arm quickly out of his grip. 'Don't you touch me, Del Clarke—don't you ever lay a hand on me!' Her eyes flashed angrily as she turned abruptly and walked towards the wharf where *Seawind* was tied up.

Del caught up with her. 'Don't be so damn touchy, Kristin. I only wanted to speak to you—I didn't mean any harm.' He was puffing hard, seeming to find it difficult to keep up with her pace. 'I called out to you, but you didn't hear, I guess.'

'No—I didn't.' She didn't slow down but marched determinedly on, not wanting to have to stop and converse with him.

His large hand once again closed over her slim arm, and this time she did not try to pull away, for his grip was strong and demanding. 'I want to talk to you.'

She looked at him closely and was surprised to see he was smiling and seemingly trying to act in a friendly way. She relaxed under his hold and he dropped his hand to his side, fidgeting a little, scouring a small trench in the sand beneath his foot.

'I just wanted—to say—well, he's gone for good, isn't he, Kristin?' He saw her tense and withdraw and put up a hand to explain. 'No, I don't mean to hurt your feelings—I was just saying that I know it must be hard for you out there, all alone on the island with no one to help you—your dad being dead and all, and ... Well, I just wanted to tell you that I'm more than willing to lighten your load and lend a hand.' He looked down at her small figure, slim and straight before him. His voice softened. 'We're the same kind of people, Kristin. We belong here. This place is what we are—we wouldn't do badly together you and me—I know it. I'd treat you good, I promise——'

She could scarcely believe it was Del speaking. This was a

man who seemed drastically different from the man she had known, and who, she now admitted to herself, she had feared from childhood. 'Please, Del—I've got to get back. It's getting late.'

'Just give me a fair hearing, Kristin.' He started walking slowly. 'Come on, I'll walk you down to the wharf.' They moved along the beach together and now Kristin was more uncomfortable than afraid. He continued, 'I know your dad and me, we didn't always see things eye to eye. We had our differences, for sure, but I always respected him, Kristin, I always did. He was a good man, Dugald MacKenzie was. And we were both from the Landing—we had that in common.' For a split second Kristin wondered if her father and Del really had even the remotest thing in common. But she didn't interrupt him. 'Your dad would want to be sure you were taken care of properly, and not by an outsider who doesn't know or care about our ways, but by someone from the Landing.'

He cleared his throat and hurried on with his words. 'And this is what I want to say—I want to marry you, Kristin.' He saw the startled look in her face and quickly added, 'No, don't say anything yet. We could do fine together—we could make it, I know we could. And some day I'll have a lot of money and you can have anything you want—anything at all.'

'Del, listen to me, please'—her voice was quiet and almost lost in the sound of the waves against the shore—'I don't—we don't . . .'

'No, don't say anything right now. Just tell me you'll promise to think about it. That's all—just promise me that.' He took her hand in his and looked pleadingly into her eyes. 'Just give it a chance, that's all I ask. Please.'

As if suddenly aware of what he was doing, he dropped her hand. 'If it's all right with you, Kristin, I'll come on out to the island soon and check on you—see if you need anything done—and to see what you've decided.'

Before she had a chance to answer, he turned away and strode across the beach to the path that led to his storage shed.

She watched him as he flung open the door, saw the yellow light hanging from the ceiling, and saw too the figures of the men, his crew, leaning over a barrel and playing cards. She heard the sound of their gruff laughter break the early evening silence. What she did not hear, as she turned and walked slowly towards the wharf, was Del's gruff comments about catching more flies with honey and 'meaning to have that girl, one way or the other'.

Despite everything it was good to be home, she told herself. The Island was the only home she'd ever really had, she realised. The only home she'd ever know—or ever want now that Nathan was gone. Never would she leave the island—never. Over and over in her head she told herself that this was all she needed. Nothing and no one was necessary to her life. But she knew that wasn't so—she needed Nathan. She loved him as she had loved no one ever before in her life—as she would love no one ever again.

She secured the boat, climbed out on to the wharf and ran up the steps which were wet with the spray of the crashing waves, the sound of the sea drowning the rhythm of her own pulse. In was dusk and night shadows changed the look of everything. The lighthouse stood alone and straight before her. She stopped and looked around her, for a moment sensing a presence that had not shown itself, sensing watchful eyes. Silly woman, she told herself as she hurried on—you're imagining things. But once again she realised how unutterably alone she was here on the island, and once again she knew that her aloneness had become loneliness. This was the legacy Nathan had left her. Slowly she approached the house, fighting the feeling of desperation rising within her.

Pushing open the side door, she went in, hung her jacket on a hook in the hallway, and walked into the kitchen. Suddenly she stopped. A lamp flickered in the darkness in the living-room.

'Who's there?' she called out. There was no answer. She moved slowly to the doorway, her hand gripping the wall.

'Who is it?' she asked again, her voice small and frightened.

There had been no other boat but hers tied at the wharf, so how had anyone got here? She forced all thoughts from her mind. It didn't matter now. Someone was here—who she didn't know—but someone. She backed slowly towards the door, escape the uppermost thought in her mind—to get back to the wharf and away from here——

A voice, deep and resonant, sounded from the hall. It stayed her panic and flight. 'Don't run away, Kristin—I've come back.'

Nathan. It was Nathan's voice. Nathan had come back. He stood, tall and straight, his body blocking the hallway.

Kristin stood absolutely still, only her mind and emotions now in frantic flight, and watched as he walked towards her, stopping finally only a few feet in front of her. For a moment all she could do was stare. 'How did you get here?' she finally asked in a small tight voice.

'Luther brought me over a few hours ago—I've been waiting for you.' As he spoke he reached out to touch her, but she moved back abruptly, cutting his words in mid-sentence.

'No, don't touch me—don't you dare come near me!'

'Kristin—please——'

'No! There's nothing here for you. You don't belong here any more.' She raised her hands, emphasising her words, and trying to camouflage the racing beat of her heart. She couldn't let him know the truth of her feeling for him, or the depth of her yearnings. She had to learn to live without him, for he could never stay with her—and if he touched her again she would be lost to him.

She looked up into his eyes, so devastatingly blue, as deep as the sea. Something stirred in them momentarily—a look of pain mingled with regret.

'I had to go, Kristin—I know I've hurt you, but . . .'

She turned her back to him, holding herself in check. 'Don't bother to take the time to explain, Nathan. I want you to leave. I want you out of my home now. You aren't welcome here any more,' she said coldly and succinctly. 'You can take the boat and ask Luther to bring it back in the morning—as you did the last time.'

Silence filled the air, the space between them. She held her breath waiting for some movement—some sound. But he did not move, neither did he speak. Finally she turned to look at him, standing tall and straight and motionless before her, staring at her—as if searching for the answer to some question he dared not give form in words.

'Won't you please go, Nathan,' she said wearily, pushing past him into the living-room. He followed her and she saw that his jacket lay on the couch, flung carelessly over the back of it. A duffle bag lay on the floor. Quickly, without thinking, she grabbed his jacket and threw it across the room at him. 'I told you to get out—now go, damn you!' The jacket struck him in the chest and fell to the floor at his feet as he made no move to catch it. Then he bent and picked it up and threw it back on to the couch.

'What's the matter with you?' she blazed at him. 'Why don't you go? Or have you lost your hearing as well as your memory?' He flinched at the cruelty of her words. As soon as she had spoken them she regretted them. She sighed, fighting back the tears that threatened. 'I'm sorry, that was a cruel thing to say.' She pushed her hair away from her eyes. 'Please, Nathan. Please just go away from me—just leave me alone. Until you came a couple of months ago, I was happy here.'

'I don't believe you,' he said quietly and firmly. 'You were content, perhaps—but not happy, and I was far from being either—until I found you.' The sound of his voice, so deep and so warm, shivered through her and she wanted nothing more than to lean against him, to lie in his arms and be held. But he would leave again. He could never stay with her. He had a life of his own and a wife and son—a life entirely foreign to her—one he could never give up and one she could never be a part of. She could not bear him leaving her again, like the last time—and so as much as she loved him, she had decided that she must send him from her, for one final time.

'I don't want you here, Nathan. I want you off my island,' she said tonelessly.

'You can't mean that, Kristin. We have things to say to each other, things to explain—plans to make.'

'You're a fool, Nathan Raines! You're a fool who can't see that when you left you decided for us both that we have nothing else to share with each other——'

'Damn you, Kristin,' he flared angrily, 'listen to me! I hurt you when I left like that. Do you think I don't know that? I've lived with it day and night since I left. And I came back as soon as I could.' He paused, running his hands through his hair in a gesture whose familiarity tore at her heart. 'I'm only human, Kristin. For that you'll have to forgive me, but I went through hell while I was on the island—not knowing who I was, having no idea at all what I might have been or done, wanting you and afraid to touch you—afraid of being with you and then maybe finding out something that would make it—make us impossible. You have no idea——'

'Don't I? I know the despair you speak of,' she cried desperately. 'Well, you did have me—and you *are* married. You even have a son ...' her words rushed and mingled with her tears '... and there can be no us, as you say. There can never be us—together—never.'

'Dear Kristin,' he said softly, touching her face with his strong fingers, seeking to wipe away the tears, to ease the pain. 'I have something——'

'No more, Nathan—I can't stand any more! I meant to show you the picture. I never intended to keep it from you. Yes, I was afraid—I knew you would have to leave the island and me when you found out, but I'd already faced that fact and I never intended to keep that picture from you. I could never have done that to you—I loved you too much. You left without knowing that. You left thinking that I——'

'I left hurt and angry—thinking that after everything we shared you were no different from all the others—believing in my mind that you'd cheated me. I admit it,' he said huskily. 'That's why I left—I wanted to hurt you as I believed you had intentionally hurt me.'

He drew her gently into his arms and this time she could not protest—could not hold him off—too crushing was her pain and too strong was her desire for his soothing touch. He buried his face in her silken hair. 'But God knows, Kristin, I knew in my heart that you could never have done that to me. I wasn't a day away from you before I came to my senses and knew with a certainty that I should have given you a chance to explain.'

'But you didn't come back.'

'Didn't I?' He laughed and held her from him. 'Take another look, my girl.'

'I mean—it's been weeks—three weeks——'

'I wrote to you, Kristin—I explained everything: that my memory had returned, how I felt about you, my plans with Luther, and why I'd be delayed. I prayed you would understand till I could come to you, but then you didn't answer my letter. I came as soon as I could get away.'

She shook her head. 'I got no letter, Nathan—nothing. You left that morning and I've heard nothing of you or from you since you'd gone back to Victoria.'

'Oh, God! Believe me, Kristin, I did write. I don't know why you didn't get the letter, but I did write to you.'

'It doesn't matter what I believe,' she replied sadly. 'It makes little difference in any case.'

Frustration glared from his eyes. 'It makes a great deal of difference. We have plans to discuss—I wrote to you about what I intended to do—but since you didn't get my letter——'

'Plans—how can we have plans?' Her control snapped and she pulled free of him. 'I don't want your explanations, Nathan. You can't stay here—you just can't. You have to leave —now.'

He reached out and swung her round to face him. 'Stop it, Kristin! Just give me a chance, for God's sake.'

'And will you stop it! It would have been better for both of us if you hadn't come back here. I wish'—she faltered—'I wish you'd never come here in the first place.'

Anything Nathan was about to say was stilled by a loud pounding on the door. Startled by the sharp sound, Kristin moved cautiously to the door and opened it. Del stood facing her, his face red with anger. He pushed her roughly out of his way so that she nearly stumbled, and came into the kitchen.

'Heard he was back. Came to see for myself.'

'You have no right to come here like this—none at all. I want you to leave,' she ordered. She could smell the reek of liquor on his breath. 'You've been drinking. Get out, Del—I don't want any trouble.'

'Don't you tell me what to do, Kristin—don't even pretend to. I do what I want around here.' His eyes narrowed and a leering smile etched itself on his face. 'Have you told Mr Raines of our arrangement yet?'

Nathan had held himself in check, his jaw tightly clenched, hands balled into fists at his sides, although Kristin was keenly aware of the tension that gripped him. He spoke calmly but with obvious effort. 'Get out, Del, or by God, I'll throw you out! Don't you ever lay a hand on her again—do you hear me?'

'Listen to the threats from the fine city boy here—you think you can make me leave, do you?' Del was swaying on his feet now. 'She doesn't mind me touching her. And you—why, I'll squash you like a bug, Raines—just like a bug.' He lunged for Nathan, who agilely stepped aside. Del went crashing into the kitchen table, upsetting chairs as he sprawled over it. Nathan was on him in an instant, pulling his right arm behind him and propelling him swiftly across the room and out the door. With a shove he sent him sprawling in the grass, wet with the early evening dew.

'I meant what I said, Del—never touch her—never!' The fury in his face threatened a violence so devastating and powerful that Del was silenced. He awkwardly got to his feet and stood for a moment without saying anything, his eyes narrowed with hate. Then he started along the path by the lighthouse that led down to the wharf. He hesitated and then stopped.

'You'd better tell him about us, Kristin. No outsider's going to come in here and take what belongs to me—what was mine before he came. He's been gone three weeks. He had his fun with you before he left, but he's a fool if he thinks he can come back here for more. You're mine now—like before he came. And I'll kill him—I'll kill him if——'

Kristin's hands went to her mouth in horror. 'What are you saying, Del? Don't talk like ...'

'Shut up, you bitch—just shut up! Ask him if second-hand goods will satisfy him for long. Ask him that—after you tell him about us. And make sure you tell him how things are handled round here, Kristin. I'm not finished with him—not by a long shot. I'll settle with him in my own way and in my own time, and you'd better believe it.' He turned and plodded down the path, slipping and falling twice before he disappeared from their view.

Kristin stood transfixed, her face pale and stricken. 'Oh God, he means it——'

'What does he mean?' Nathan's voice was as hard and cold as ice. She did not answer. 'Tell me, Kristin'—his voice rose in the darkness—'tell me why he's here at this time of night— tell me what he meant by all that?'

'Nothing ... nothing ...' She felt ill and dizzy. All of a sudden she knew she had to get inside—to sit down—to lie down. A sound, a whirring, filled her head and darkness cloaked her vision. 'I need ... I must go——' her words drowned in the depths of their desperation and she turned and groped at the air for support. It was Nathan's strong arms that caught her before she fell. As he carried her easily into the house, she could feel the power and the strength in him, could smell the sweet odour of his clean skin, could feel the gentleness of his touch as he placed her on her bed. 'Oh, Nathan——' she whispered weakly.

'Be quiet for a moment.' She couldn't tell if there was still anger in his voice. He undid the top button on her shirt and laid a warm hand on her forehead. It was cold and clammy with sweat. She heard him go into the kitchen, then moments later felt him sit down on the side of the bed. A cool cloth touched her forehead.

'I feel so sick,' she muttered. 'Just go away—I'm going to be sick—please leave me ...'

'I told you to be quiet. Do what you're told for a change, Kristin MacKenzie!'

She wanted to open her eyes—wanted to look into his face. What was he thinking? He must leave or Del would try and kill him. Del was crazy enough to try and do that, she was certain. He wouldn't give Nathan a chance, for he wouldn't fight fairly.

'Del meant it, Nathan—he'll kill you, if he can. You must leave ... please!'

She opened her eyes slowly, wanting the world to stop spinning. Nathan—strong, beautiful Nathan—sat, shoulders tense and sloped, beside her.

'Go easy, Kristin. Just go easy.' He took the cloth from her forehead. 'I'm not leaving until we settle things, until some important things get said. Then, if you still want me to go alone, I'll go—and I'll never bother you again, I promise.' He cleared his throat, looked at her for a long moment, then got up and walked to the window.

'What do you have to tell me about you and Del, Kristin?' Still his back was to her. He stood as if braced for a mortal wound.

'I have nothing to tell you about Del and me—nothing. What do you think I have to tell you?'

'No more games,' he replied harshly. 'Tell me the truth!'

'I have *nothing* to tell you about Del and me. How many times must I say that?'

'He implied—he . . . I want to know if you've been with him since I left?'

She lay perfectly still on the bed and did not answer him.

'Have you slept with him, Kristin?' He turned and faced her, anguish filling his eyes. 'Tell me, for God's sake, tell me if you've slept with him.'

'Would you believe me, Nathan, after the newspaper—the picture, after everything that's happened, would you believe anything I told you?'

'Yes. Yes, I would, because I believe the truth is all you know.' He came close to her, looking down at her slim body which lay perfectly still on the bed below him. She closed her eyes tightly, tears rolling down her cheeks.

'No, I haven't slept with him. I've only been with you, Nathan—only you.'

Relief spread across his face, although the hardness in his voice bespoke of the marked anger inside. 'If he had—if he'd touched you—I think, God forgive me, I think I would kill him.'

The look in his eyes told her that he spoke the truth and its violent power filled her with terror. 'Don't talk like that—it's insane!'

'There's nothing insane about it. After what we've shared—knowing what we are to each other——'

'We aren't anything to each other any more, Nathan, and there's nothing to keep you here. There's nothing more to say—can't you see that?' she replied desperately, fighting to keep her voice even and controlled. 'That's why you must leave Sitka—why you must leave me alone so I can try to find some peace. You must never come back here again—not ever. You have your wife and son to think about—you can't do this to them.'

He looked at her with vacant, wounded eyes. 'I have no wife. I have no son.'

Time stood still. Kristin closed her eyes, wondering if she had indeed heard him say those quiet words, 'I have no wife . . .' Had she dreamed them? Somehow she found her voice. 'But the picture—the picture?' she faltered.

'The woman with me in the picture is a family friend, Carla Monteroy. And the boy is my brother's son. It was taken before I left in the spring.' He stared down at the floor and repeated almost mindlessly, 'I have no wife and I have no son.' She could not move; she could do nothing but stare.

'Oh, God! Oh, dear God——' She turned and wept, her face buried in the pillow. Nathan sat next to her again, his hands touching her hair, stroking it, soothing her.

'Don't send me away, Kristin. I can't leave you, I can't. I love you too much.'

He pulled her into his arms, holding her tightly. 'You love me, I know you do. I couldn't have been wrong about the way we were together. Tell me, Kristin—tell me.'

'Yes, I do love you—I do. There's never been anything with Del—never. I love only you, Nathan.'

'I want you, Kristin, as my wife. The past will be past.'

It was all that she ever wanted—to be with Nathan, to be his wife. Now there would be time and the chance to heal the hurt they had inflicted on each other.

'Will you come back with me? Tomorrow? And marry me as soon as possible?'

'Yes, oh yes,' she breathed. 'I'll marry you, Nathan.'

He drew her fiercely to him. 'I love you more than the breath I draw. Remember that—no matter what.'

'And I love you,' she whispered.

CHAPTER EIGHT

EARLY the next morning they sat at Alice's table. Nathan had radioed the mainland and an amphibian plane had arrived, bobbing placidly at Sitka Landing waiting for his two passengers. Alice was ecstatic as they ate breakfast together.

'I told you, Kristin MacKenzie. I told you he'd be back for you!' She came round the table and hugged the girl. 'You both deserve the best, and the best is what you've finally got—each other.'

Kristin blushed fiercely. 'Please, Alice——'

'Don't try to shut me up, my girl. Why, I feel almost like having champagne—not this coffee that Luther threw together which is obviously mixed with the sand from the beach.' She turned to Nathan. 'When will you be back?'

'In a few weeks—three weeks at the latest, I'm hoping. My brother Charles is taking over the running of our business interests. We've run into a few snags, but nothing that has proven to be more than time-consuming. As I said to Kristin, that's why I wasn't back here sooner.' He reached out and gently touched her cheek with his strong hand. 'But soon—very soon—we'll be back to stay,' he said softly. He finished his coffee and quickly stood up. 'It's getting light—time to go.'

'Look, Kristin,' Alice clucked, 'you'd best be taking more than you've got packed in that uselessly small bag—why, there's nothing in that to hold you for more than a day or so——'

'She'll be shopping in Victoria, Alice, having the spree of her life—just wait!'

Luther put a hand on Nathan's arm and drew him outside on to the veranda. 'Just wait a minute, Kristin,' said Alice. 'I'll get my sweater and we'll walk you down to the wharf.' She disappeared into her bedroom and Kristin turned to join Nathan and Luther on the front veranda, but stopped abruptly when she heard Luther's hushed and concerned voice.

'I tell you, Nathan, he's trouble, and he'll be real trouble

124

later, if you come back here. I thought last night he was really going to blow the lid off—he and those drunken friends of his were out for blood. I thought they were going to head out to the island.'

'What stopped them?'

'Too much drink and finally inertia.'

Nathan sneered, 'Inertia gets his kind in the end.'

Luther shook his head. 'You don't understand. They're dirty dealers, Nathan, and they've got it in for you. If you come back here like you plan, I don't know what'll happen. I just don't think it'll be safe for you and Kristin with them here.'

'What are you suggesting I do, Luther?' Nathan asked harshly.

'Look, don't get mad at me. I'm telling you straight what I think—and I'm telling you because I care about you both. I'm thinking maybe you should find some other place—or maybe you should stay in Victoria, working with your brother Charles.' Luther shrugged his shoulders. 'I'd miss you both— you're family to Mom and me—but I'd still feel safer. I've just got this awful feeling inside.'

Kristin shivered at the sound of his ominous words, but Nathan's voice halted her response.

'Look, Luther, we're coming back. For a lot of reasons—we have plans, you and I, and we can make more than a comfortable living here, doing something we both like. Do you have any idea what it's like to be chained to a job in a place that drains the very soul from you—day after day, year after year? I dread going back, even for a few weeks. I've found a place for myself finally,' his voice told of the depth of his feeling, 'and the person I want most in the world to be with. Kristin and I have a chance to be happy here and I'm not going to throw it away. This is her home and she loves it here. She couldn't live her life in a city—she just couldn't. And anyway, you and Alice are her family—she needs you both.'

'She needs you, Nathan—no one else.'

'That's not true, Luther, she loves you both a great deal. Tell me why I should take her away from the people she loves when we both want to be here.'

'Damn it,' Luther grated, 'I've just told you. You have no idea of the things Del Clarke is capable of, Nathan. And right now I'd say you're at the top of his vengeance list.'

'And you, Luther,' Nathan said quietly, 'obviously have no idea of the things of which I am capable. I am no man's doormat—and I protect what's mine. Neither Del Clarke nor anyone else will force me to live where I don't wish to be, or to live in fear.'

They continued to speak for a few minutes so quietly that Kristin could not hear their words. She stood transfixed, her heart pounding in her breast. Luther knew, he was no fool. He knew what Del was like—maybe they shouldn't come back. But this was her home—she loved it here—and she knew too that Nathan had come to love it as she did. She heard Alice come up behind her.

'You heard what Luther said?' Kristin questioned softly.

Alice nodded.

'I ... I don't know what to do ... I ...'

'Trust Nathan, honey. Trust him, and stay with him, no matter what happens.'

'What do you mean—no matter what happens?'

For a moment Alice hesitated, about to speak, then decided not to. 'Nothing. Nothing at all—just go with him and we'll be waiting for you to come right back to where you belong—right here with us.' She kissed the girl on the forehead. 'We're your family, Kristin, and we want you with us. Now get going—you've got an exciting time ahead of you.' She moved past Kristin and out on to the veranda, the sound of the screen door echoing in the early morning stillness. 'What are you two gabbing about? Come on, Nathan, you've waited long enough for this wedding—why put it off any longer by talking to my mouthy son here?'

The four of them walked down the steps, across the wet grass, and along the beach to the wharf, as the tip of the sun filled the morning greyness with the glow of gold.

The flight to Victoria was a memorable one for Kristin. She had never flown before and was at first more than a bit dubious and slightly frightened. After a while she relaxed and marvelled at the sight of the coastline over which they flew. Nathan sat back and enjoyed her comments and sharp cries of surprise and joy. 'Oh, Nathan, look down there! Just look at it! Have you ever seen anything as lovely in all your life?'

'Indeed, yes.'

'What? What could possibly be as beautiful?'

'A certain young woman who in a few short hours will be Mrs Nathan Raines.'

'Oh, Nathan!' She blushed, unable to find words for her happiness.

'Happy, Kristin?'

'Yes—oh yes. Tell me about the city, Nathan, tell me what it's like.'

'Why don't you wait and see—I don't want to spoil it for you.'

'But——'

'No buts—wait and find out for yourself. Besides, I love to watch that look on your face—that look that lights your eyes when you're seeing something for the first time.'

'Nathan Raines, you're as much a romantic as I am!'

He nodded, obviously enjoying their light banter. 'Maybe so, madam—maybe so.'

'Don't tease me.'

He reached out, his hands cupping her face. 'I'm not teasing you—I'm loving you to distraction, sweetheart.' His mouth sought hers in a kiss of utter tenderness.

'If you won't tell me about the city, at least fill me in on your formidable family,' she invited.

He laughed. 'Listen to the size of the words rolling off that slight tongue of yours! I told you about my family last night.'

'You did not. You listed them, that's what you did. And,' she rushed on, 'don't just tell me to wait and see for myself. It's not fair—I need to be a little prepared for them.'

He looked at her, considering what she had said. 'Yes, perhaps you're right, but there really isn't a lot to say. They're a normal family, I guess, with perhaps one exception—my mother. My brother Charles and his wife Annabel and their son Jon live with my mother.'

'Heavens! Don't they find that cramped and small? I should think they'd like to live on their own where they would have more room.'

Nathan chuckled. 'Wait till you see the place, then decide if you think they're living in close quarters.'

'Why? What do you mean?'

'I mean, dear naïve Kristin, that my family home is a regular museum—small is not a word I would use to describe it. I think you could wander for days in it and not meet a soul.'

'Now you *are* exaggerating!'

'Yes, I am. But truly, it's large enough to house four families, I'd say.'

'Do you live there as well?'

'No! Decidedly not. I moved out long ago—I have an apartment. But Charles and Annabel do, and I'd say they're very comfortable there. Annabel seems to be able to deal quite handily with Marion, so there's really no problem.'

'Marion?'

'Yes—my mother.'

'Is she difficult? To deal with, I mean?'

He smiled. 'Well, you could say that.'

'What has she said about me?' asked Kristin.

'Nothing.'

'Nothing? She must have said something—she . . .'

'She doesn't know about you yet, Kristin.'

Startled, Kristin looked into his eyes, searching for some message hidden in their depths.

'Why not?' she murmured.

'Because I haven't told her about you—that's why.'

'Why ever not?' she persisted.

He shifted in his seat and raised his hands in mock supplication. 'Oh, please, don't go looking for some deep dark reason. I haven't told her because—very simply—you are mine, Kristin MacKenzie, all mine. And for the next few hours you are still my secret.'

'But I don't understand. They won't be expecting me or anything—how can we marry when nothing has been planned and——' Tears threatened in her eyes.

'Kristin, I've told Charles and Annabel, so you're not a complete secret. They're anxious to meet you—to welcome you. But my mother . . . she . . . damn it——' he muttered. 'How do I make you understand? My mother likes to own people and run things according to her own design, and for a long, long time I've let her do just that with my life. Nothing mattered at all that much to me—until you. I want you and I want us to live our lives together from the very beginning according to our own design, not my mother's. And I guess that's why I haven't told her and,' he added firmly, 'I won't tell her until after the wedding.'

'After the wedding? I don't understand. I thought you'd want your family to be there.'

'No, I don't want them there.'

'Not even Charles and Annabel?'

'I thought—for a while I considered perhaps having them stand for us—then I realised that it would put them in a bit of a spot, knowing about my plans and not telling Marion. So I decided against it.'

Kristin sat perfectly still, the moments of silence expanding and filling the air around them.

'Have I upset you?' he asked pointedly, in a voice that for a moment, she almost couldn't recognise.

'No. Yes. I don't know, I'm confused, that's all. It seems such a strange way to deal with your family. It doesn't seem honest, in a way.'

A look of impatience crossed his face, then faded. He tried again, taking her small hand gently in his.

'Please try to understand, Kristin. I want this to be ours, all ours, from the wedding on. I want no one to change it for us— to ruin what we share. I want to protect us, that's all.'

'But your mother—she loves you, and we'll hurt her if . . .'

He drew in a deep breath. 'Dearest, my mother loves no one but herself and her social position. Anything or anyone else is purely to be utilised to enhance either herself or her status. Until a few months ago I was a part of it all, then I took the summer for myself and found you. I can't and I won't go back to the way if was before, so please stay with me and do it the way I ask.'

He spoke, not with bitterness, but with a trace of sadness— as if he had been hurt and hurt badly in some way. Kristin wanted to ask more, but knew that he had told her all he was going to—for now. She squeezed his hand lovingly.

'It's you I'm marrying, Nathan Raines, not your mother. We'll do it your way, as you ask.'

A chauffeur-driven car met them at the dockside and whisked them away to Nathan's apartment. Kristin had not time to grasp her surroundings before Nathan presented her with a soft white silk dress—her wedding dress, that he had chosen for her himself.

A few hours later she stood proudly beside Nathan in the small chapel of a church in downtown Victoria, listening to the solemn voice of the minister pronounce them husband and wife. As Nathan gathered her into his arms, she felt the sheer power and wilful strength of this man, now her husband. And also—a sudden, almost terrifying moment of strangeness. He seemed different somehow, so different, since they had left the island. But as quickly as it had come she drove the thought from her mind, admonishing herself for having let it lodge in her consciousness for even one foolish moment. This was Nathan—her Nathan. He had not changed. He loved her and she loved him and they would share a joyous lifetime together, for no one else, she believed, had ever before loved as they did.

They dined in a secluded corner of a very expensive restaurant, where the subdued lighting and hushed excellence heightened the excitement that filled her to near bursting. Kristin leaned across the table and whispered furtively, 'Are you sure we can afford to eat here, Nathan? It looks awfully expensive to me.'

He smiled and joined in her whispering conspiracy. 'It is awfully expensive. And yes, we can definitely afford it.'

She realised that he was well known here when the maître d'hotel came to speak to him, smiling graciously. 'Good evening, Mr Raines. We're glad to see you again. It's been a while, sir.'

'Good to see you, Emerson.'

'May I suggest a bottle of our finest wine?'

'I think we prefer champagne tonight, please, Emerson— your finest champagne. For we, this lady and I, are celebrating something very special.'

'Yes, sir.' He turned and walked away, the sound of his footsteps buried in the deep pile carpet.

'He knows you,' Kristin whispered again.

'Yes, he does, doesn't he?'

'You've been here before then?'

'Yes—many times.' His soft tone mimicked her own.

Suddenly she laughed, her voice light and dancing with life. 'This is just too much!'

'What is too much?'

'Is . . .' she giggled, 'is his name really Emerson?'

He looked at her in amazement. 'You, dear child . . . But it's you who are too much!'

She'd never in her life tasted champagne and she loved it. 'Oh,' she murmured ruefully, 'what shall we do, Nathan? How shall we live on Sitka without champagne?'

'You, dear Kristin, have had enough, I think . . .' Nevertheless he poured her another glass.

They had a wonderful meal—champagne, poached salmon, and a flaming flambert for dessert. The light from the candles danced in the glow of her eyes.

'You're happy, aren't you, Kristin?' he asked solemnly, his fingers tracing the contours of her wrist.

'I have never in my whole life been happier,' she beamed back at him.

'I want you always to have that look about you, child—that look of pure joy and fresh life——'

'May I remind you that I'm not a child, Nathan,' she responded.

'I'm only too aware of that at this moment.' His voice was husky with a desire that burned in his eyes, a desire that she felt reflected in her own.

'Come——' he stood up, 'I think it's time to go home.' They walked towards the door, his arm resting possessively around her small waist.

Outside the warm moist air of an August evening drifted around them. Nathan led her to the waiting car, but she pulled back. 'Would you mind awfully if maybe we walked for a while—just a short distance? It's such a warm night—and the lights—I've never seen anything like this in my life, Nathan, never.'

He spoke to the chauffeur and seconds later the long black car moved silently away and they walked, hand in hand, down the street, with Kristin excitedly looking in store windows filled with the glitter and glamour of clothing, of daring styles—all so very new to her. They passed hundreds of people, saw cars moving quickly up and down the street. Someone bumped into her, and absently apologised while continuing to stride down the sidewalk. She held Nathan's hand more tightly.

'It's another world here—so amazing! It's exciting. But—but it's frightening too. I shall never be able to find my own way around here. I shall be lost in no time.'

'Don't worry, you won't have to find your own way around this city—I'm not going to let you out of my sight, not for an instant. We're going back to Sitka soon, don't forget.'

'Yes—yes, that's right,' she said seriously. 'I like it here—what I see of it. But I couldn't live here for ever. It would wear a person out, having to live here all the time, wouldn't it, Nathan?'

He stopped in the stream of human traffic flowing all around them, bent, and fiercely kissed her, all his passion and desire for her flaming in his touch. No one seemed to take any notice of them. 'I think,' he whispered thickly, 'I think we need to go home now.'

'I didn't realise that your apartment was on the top floor,' Kristin observed in awe, 'and that you needed a key for the elevator!'

'My apartment is the top floor, Kristin.'

'Oh,' she said, feeling a little stupid at not having noticed earlier when they had come to the apartment to change.

It was night now, and she was moving in an environment entirely strange to her. A mixture of light and dark, gold light and blackness, and a myriad city night colours.

The elevator door slowly opened. Nathan crossed the foyer, unlocked and opened the door to his apartment. It was as if she was seeing it for the first time. 'It's like the restaurant,' she whispered breathlessly. He took her wrap and set it on a nearby chair.

'How's that?' he asked.

'It's expensive here too, isn't it?'

'Yes, I guess so.' He was watching her closely,   ching her reactions. She looked directly into his eyes.

'Do you have a lot of money, Nathan?'

'Would it matter to you if I did? Would it make a difference between us?'

'No, I don't think so.' She walked slowly across the room to the huge glass window that formed one wall and tentatively drew back a shimmering light drape, feeling its sheerness with her fingertips.

'What do you mean, you don't think so?' she heard his voice ask calmly behind her.

She stared out over the harbour, for his apartment faced the water. The lights of the city and of the ships and smaller boats in the harbour gleamed in the darkness. The sight which lay before her took her breath away.

'I asked you a question, Kristin——'

She looked back at him. 'What?'

'Never mind,' he laughed, 'go out on the balcony and look at it all from there.' He slid the balcony door open and held back the curtains as she walked hesitantly in front of him and out into the warm night air. She stood gazing out over the city, her hands gripping the railing of the balcony. 'I—I ...' she stammered, but didn't continue.

She felt his fingers under her chin, pushing her face gently up until her eyes met his.

'What were you going to say?'

'I think it's beautiful, Nathan,' she breathed. 'You live in a beautiful, wonderful place. I'd heard about cities before and I've seen pictures in Dugald's books, but never did I think they were like this.'

He sighed heavily. 'And they aren't really like this, either, Kristin. Only once in a while does someone see it as you are. But it's only a sparkling, glittering show on the surface of it all. If you remember that that's as far or as deep as it goes, then yes, it's beautiful. But if you expect more, you'll be very disappointed.'

She frowned at him, not understanding the sadness in his voice, but he looked away and silently stared out over the city. She felt his change of mood but could not understand it and could not, for some reason, question it. An amazing new world lay before her and she turned back to it, forgetting his words whose meaning she had not even begun to understand.

They stood on the balcony for what seemed to her a very

long time, breathing in the fragrant night air. Nathan put his arm about her and held her close to him, then finally took her hand and led her back into the apartment. It was in darkness except for the dim glow of light that reflected up from the city.

'Nathan?' She stood looking up at him.

'Yes?'

'I love you so very much,' she said quietly.

His mouth gently covered hers and sought the sweetness of her. 'And I,' he whispered, 'love you, so very much.' He lifted her easily into his arms and walked down the darkened hallway to the bedroom.

He put her down and stood looking down at her, not saying anything. He touched her face and her hair and ran his fingers along the fine contours of her collarbone. She shivered with the delight at his touch.

'Are you frightened?' he asked huskily.

'No,' she replied evenly, and waited.

'It's been so long—so long since Sitka.'

He reached out and undid the tiny buttons that held the front of her dress, and slipped it off her shoulders. It fell quietly to the floor and lay there in a silken heap. Still she stood facing him. He watched her face and the play of emotions on it, her love for him written in her eyes. His hands not quite steady, he removed her underclothes so that she stood before him, naked in her love. He picked her up and placed her gently on the bed. She lay there, her eyes now closed, listening to the thud of her heart, and the sound of his movement in the darkness. Then the feel of his skin on hers, the touch of his body, strong and smooth and powerful. 'Oh God, Kristin, how I've missed you—how I've longed for the touch of you these past weeks!' His hands roamed her body, proclaiming his possession of her. He buried his face in the warm valley between her breasts. 'You're mine,' he groaned, 'you're mine.'

And Kristin responded to the desire that consumed him. She did belong to him, and to no other. Her body cried out for the completeness that only he could give her, and they came together in the darkness of the night with a desire for each other so strong that neither felt it could ever be satisfied. Afterwards, Nathan lay beside her holding her small body against his. Her hand rested on his bare chest, fingers moving lightly among the curling dark hair.

'You'll never know how much I love you, child. You'll just never know,' he whispered to the darkness as much as to her.

'I do, Nathan. I do know.'

CHAPTER NINE

DAWN lightened the sky above the city, gradually staining the early morning greyness a gentle pink. Kristin had awakened often during the night, pleasuring in the feel of Nathan's body next to hers; and now she lay there gently stroking his thick, silky hair, which was black like soot against the white satin pillow. He lay on his stomach, one arm flung out across the bed, the other holding her possessively close. She loved the touch of him, the smell of him, everything about him. And she loved being his, truly and completely his. He stirred and rolled over on his back, not opening his eyes, and asked drowsily, 'What time is it?'

'I don't know, but the sun'll be up any minute,' she replied.

'Lord! It's early—what a nerve you have wakening me at this hour, woman!' She could hear the sleepy teasing tone of his voice. 'I'll have to train you better than this, and punish you properly.' He pulled her easily on top of him and held her close. 'Now try and get away—you're to spend the rest of the day in my arms, Kristin Raines.'

She sighed and rested her head against his chest. 'Such a sweet punishment, my love—I shall be begging for more.'

'All right—the rest of your life in my arms—will that suit you?'

'Quite nicely,' she murmured.

His mouth sought hers, at first gently, then more demandingly as she felt his desire for her rise in him again. He groaned and pulled her down beside him. 'Kristin, my Kristin,' he moaned, 'never shall I have enough of you.' His hands sought every inch of her and aroused her to meet his demanding passion. Later, they lay quietly entangled in each other's arms, sharing a silence that spoke of the completeness they had granted each other.

And so it was for the next few days—they spent every waking and every sleeping moment together, glorying in the love they shared. They roamed the city, lunching at quaint little out-of-

the-way restaurants, wandering through magnificent gardens
in the hot summer afternoons, watching the yachts move in
and out of the harbour. They walked hand in hand along the
rocky shoreline, and along the teeming city streets at night.
But always together. On the fourth day they were sharing
breakfast on the terrace when the intercom buzzer sounded.
Kristin jumped. 'What's that noise?'

Nathan smiled wryly, and got up from the table. 'The Outside World, sweet Kristin, come to fetch us, I'm afraid.' She
watched him as he moved easily across the room. He was a
large man, but his movements were smooth and gracefully
controlled. This morning he was dressed in white jeans and a
navy cotton shirt, sleeves rolled up to his elbows. She never
tired of looking at him. She loved absolutely everything about
him. She smiled, content in the knowledge of their love for
one another. These past few days had been good for both of
them. They had relaxed and lived only for themselves and
until now the outside world had left them alone.

He returned to the balcony. 'Well, my beauty, you're about
to meet my family, or at least part of it. That's Charles and
Annabel—they're on their way up.'

They heard the bell of the elevator, the apartment door
open and close, and then the muffled sound of footsteps on the
carpet. Nathan held out his hand to her, she rose, and came to
stand beside him. He squeezed her hand gently. 'Don't worry.
They're very nice—they don't even eat little people like you
for breakfast.' Kristin smiled nervously, and then checked herself impatiently. They're Nathan's family, she thought, of
course they'll be good people. Just like him.

'We're out here on the terrace,' Nathan called out.

'Right,' a voice, even deeper in tone, replied. The man who
appeared was clearly Nathan's brother. He had the same thick
black hair, a little coarser than Nathan's, and he too was
tanned and fit. He was younger and shorter but very good-
looking. The young woman who stood beside him was slim
and pretty, with curly red hair and a friendly smile that lit
her face. They were unmistakably the couple whose photo
Kristin had seen so long ago in the newspaper clipping.

Charles grasped Nathan's hand, after which the woman
reached out and hugged him. 'You devil!' she scolded, 'we'd

thought you'd decided not to come back after all—but now I
see why you didn't bother with any of us.' She looked at Kristin, a friendly smile still on her face. 'Hi! I'm Annabel and
this is my husband Charles, sister-in-law and brother, respec-
tively, to the notorious and elusive Nathan Raines.' She
hugged Kristin affectionately. 'Welcome to the Raines clan—
and may you survive them all!' she added laughingly.

'Stop it, Annabel—you're going to scare the girl away!'
Charles grinned. 'Don't listen to a word she says, Kristin.
She's a scattered lady, let me tell you.'

Nathan squeezed Kristin's hand gently. 'Don't listen to
either of them—they're both scattered. And don't worry, my
dear brother, she won't be scared away.'

'Well, she obviously hasn't met mother Marion yet,' Annabel
added mischievously.

'Not even Marion, Annabel, not even Marion. Come and
sit down and have some breakfast.'

Charles waved a hand. 'We've had breakfast, thanks. We've
been up since the crack of dawn. Jon's spending the day with
John and Marilyn'—he looked over to Kristin and explained—
'Jon's our son and John and Marilyn are Annabel's parents.
They've taken him sailing—which he loves beyond reason,
thanks to my brother, who's thoroughly infected him with the
disease. But we will have a coffee if it's made.' Kristin nodded
and went to get two mugs from the kitchen.

Annabel followed her. 'Truly, Kristin, we welcome you.
You've done wonders for Nathan, believe me. He's not the
same man since he found you. You've made him very happy.'
She spoke earnestly and with an obvious depth of caring.
Kristin knew she was going to like her. 'Do you play tennis,
Kristin?'

'No, I never have. I don't know the first thing about it.'

'What about squash?'

Kristin shook her head. 'Perhaps Nathan's told you—I
come from an island quite a distance north of here. There's no
opportunity there for ...'

'Doesn't matter. You look more than fit to me—I'll bet you'll
be whipping Champion Nathan in no time. I'll teach you if
you like.'

'Yes, thank you, I would like it very much.' Kristin picked

up the two mugs and moved towards the terrace. 'I can sail quite well if you'd like to——'

'Oh no!' Annabel threw up her hands in mock horror. 'Not another sailor in the family—I can't bear it!'

Charles' voice echoed from the terrace. 'Annabel, the poor girl will think you're crazy—leave her alone.' Annabel pulled a face at him and just laughed. They obviously enjoyed each other and had fun together. Yes, she liked these people a lot.

Nathan and Charles seemed to be discussing business, Nathan suddenly looking very serious and none too pleased. 'They'll just have to accept it, Charles—I have no intentions of altering my plans. You've done well these past months—they have that to consider.'

Charles shook his head. 'Look, it doesn't upset me one way or another. I can do it, if that's what you want, or I can work just as easily for you, if you decide to stay. My self-image or ego isn't being tramped on by having to work for you.'

'I thought you understood me when I explained to you that I was through with the business,' said Nathan with marked frustration.

'I did understand and I do understand. But Marion says——'

'Damn Marion!' Nathan's eyes flashed anger. 'I'll bet she's behind the fact that MacIntyre and Collins are balking at your takeover.'

'I don't doubt it. She hasn't accepted your decision—not at all. She thinks that perhaps a rest will do you good, then you'll see things straight again.' Charles smiled wryly. 'Her way, that is, and get back to work as the Director and Chairman of the Board of Raines and Sons and all of their subsidiaries.'

Nathan slid the mug of coffee round and round in his fingers, staring sightlessly out over the terrace. 'I've given enough to her, Charles—and I've given enough to Raines Shipbuilding and Lumber Company. I've had all I can take. It's not the life I would have chosen or did choose for myself. Marion made the choices and I let her play me for the pawn. I'm thirty-six years old and I've worked hard for all of you, for fifteen of those years. Now I want, I need, a life of my own—a simple, straightforward, honest life of my own. And by God, I'm going to have it. Marion isn't going to stop me—not this time!'

The strained silence that followed lasted several moments but seemed to stretch into hours. Finally, made uncomfortable by the driven anger in her husband's voice, Kristin began to speak. 'Nathan, I don't understand all that you're saying, but if you spoke to Marion and told her how you feel, then surely she'd understand.'

Charles smothered a groan. 'If only,' he said sarcastically.

Nathan stood up and walked to the railing, looking out over the harbour at the ships anchored there. 'Kristin and I couldn't survive here, Charles. We have everything we want and everything we need back on Sitka and we're going back there as soon as we can. That's what we decided together and that's what we're going to do. And Marion and all of her cohorts will have to accept that as an accomplished fact.' He added calmly but forcibly, 'And I hope I have your support, for a great deal depends on you now, as you know.'

Charles got up and walked over to his brother, putting a hand on his shoulder. 'You know you can trust me. As far as I'm concerned, you'll have what you want. But,' he continued, 'don't underestimate Marion, that's all I ask. She's a powerful woman and has never been thwarted in anything she's ever wanted in her entire life. She won't sit calmly back and watch you walk away from the life she's designed for you, Nathan. She just won't.'

'She has no choice, Charles. None at all.'

Charles shrugged. 'I pray you're right—for your sake and Kristin's.'

'Oh, you guys——' Annabel interjected, 'this is unreal! Come on, let's get on to lighter things. Business—business— business—that's all you've talked since we've arrived. How about lunch together down at the Yacht Club?'

Nathan smiled and looked over at Kristin. 'What do you say, love? Shall we come out of seclusion and fraternise with these two?'

'I think that would be fun. I'd like to,' she replied.

Nathan drew a deep breath, 'After lunch then, if you'll pardon the cliché, we'll take the bull by the horns and I'll take you over to the house to meet Marion.' No one smiled at that pronouncement.

They had a very relaxed and enjoyable lunch together, sitting out on a terrace that edged the harbour, a light wind blowing off the water. They laughed and chatted as though none of them recalled any of the serious moments earlier in the day—but once in a while Kristin thought she saw in Nathan a tension, a concern clouding his blue eyes that had not been present in the past few days. She longed to speak about this, but when he realised she was watching him closely, he immediately joined in Annabel's joking banter. She must have been imagining things, she thought, telling herself that she was behaving stupidly. She was looking for trouble when none existed. Finally, lunch over, they parted, having agreed to meet back at the house later that afternoon. Nathan took her shopping, and if possible seemed even more attentive than before—almost, Kristin thought, as if he were trying to postpone the dreaded chore that faced him. They arranged to have her parcels delivered to the apartment and then began the drive to Nathan's family home.

For a while they drove in silence, then Nathan began tonelessly, 'It's called Maplewood.'

'What is?'

'Marion's place—my happy childhood home.' His voice was bitter and this new note added to her dread of the meeting with Marion.

'You don't make it sound so happy,' she commented.

'It wasn't, believe me.'

'Why not?'

'God knows.' He gestured futilely. 'When you were a child, Kristin, you were left alone too much, had no one to grow with and be with—while I never, not from the moment I can first remember, was ever left to myself. I had to be what my mother wanted. I never fully realised what it meant until—until you and Sitka. After I left the island and came back here, I knew just how empty and horrifying my life had been up to then.' Kristin reached out and touched his hand which tightly gripped the steering wheel. 'She did it to my father, too, you know. The same thing—drove him until he couldn't stand it any more,' he said thickly. 'And God help me, I can't forgive her for what she did to him. He killed himself in the end.' His words, despairing and sad, echoed in the silence between them.

He expelled a harsh breath through gritted teeth. 'And won't let her do it to us—I won't!' Suddenly he pulled the ca over to the curb, braked and turned off the ignition. H turned and looked lovingly at her. 'I'm sorry, Kristin. I'm do ing exactly what I told myself I wouldn't do—making thi meeting even more difficult for you.' He touched her face 'Have I told you today how much I love you, Mrs Raines?'

She held his hand to her lips, and kissed his fingers. 'Yes, do believe you have, Nathan.'

'Well then,' he drew a deep breath, 'that's all anybody needs isn't it?' He started the car and pulled away from the curb Kristin found herself praying fervently that their love woul indeed be enough.

'This is it?' she asked in wonderment.

'This is it,' he replied, watching her reaction closely, an with amused interest. 'As you can see,' he added calmly, 'it is in fact, a museum, as I already told you.' Before them lay massive grey stone mansion, huge and sprawling, surrounde by lawns and trees, all carefully cultivated and tended. An around all of that a high stone wall guarded the privacy of th inhabitants. A gateman swung back a wide wrought iron gate waving a friendly hello to Nathan as he manoeuvred the re sports car up the drive. Once inside, Nathan slowed to a sto and waited for the man to come to the car window.

'How are you, Mr Raines? Good to have you back.' H leaned down and greeted Kristin in the same friendly way 'And you'd be the new Mrs Raines Miss Annabel's told us al about. A welcome to you, madam.' He tipped his hat. A Kristin smiled a greeting, Nathan spoke to him.

'Thank you, Edward. How's your wife?'

'Much better, thanks, Mr Raines, a whole lot better. She' be home in a few days—not much can keep her down.'

'Good, I'm glad to hear it. If there's anything you need, le us know.'

'We'll be doing fine, thanks, sir.'

Nathan nodded and continued up the long drive. Kristi turned in her seat and looked back to see Edward swing th high gate shut.

'Edward and Nellie, his wife, have been here for years. The

worked for my father's family years before he married my
mother. They're fine people.'

'Do they live here at the house as well?' she asked.

'No, they live in the Gatehouse.' He flicked a hand behind
him and she saw a grey stone house, a small replica of the huge
mansion which lay before them.

The long gravelled drive approached the house, then moved
off through the tall maples that lined their way, to the side of
the house; Kristin realised then that what she had been looking at from the road and long driveway was the back of the
house. Nathan slowed for the turn before coming to a gradual
stop. Kristin didn't move but stared in amazement at the place.
In front of the house a massive lawn and a carefully designed
garden sloped gradually down to the water's edge. A number
of boats were tied up at the wharf and a boathouse was parti-
ally hidden by some trees. A marble fountain stood in the
midst of one section of the garden. She turned slowly to look
at Nathan who sat quietly beside her, waiting for her, but she
did not speak.

'Are you ready?' he asked.

'As ready as I'll ever be, believe me,' she replied.

He got out, and opened the door for her, helping her out,
not letting go of her hand as they walked slowly up the grey
flagstone steps together. Suddenly she felt as if she were going
to an execution. Horrified by the feeling and the thought, she
hesitated momentarily, but Nathan urged her on. 'It'll be all
right, Kristin.'

Nathan did not knock but pushed open the massive oak
door and moved inside, closing it carefully behind him. A tall
man dressed in black appeared mysteriously from one of the
many doors that lined the hall foyer, and walked stiffly towards them. 'Good afternoon, sir.' He bowed. 'Mrs Raines is
at present in the drawing room. Miss Annabel said you were
coming, so she's been waiting for you. She says you're to go right
in.'

Kristin could barely believe the formality with which
Nathan was greeted in his own home and shivered physically
with the coldness of it.

As if reading her thoughts, he commented wryly under his
breath, 'We Raines are very impressive with our household

entourage, as well as in our manners, aren't we, my dear?'

He led her across the hall and into a large room decorated entirely with shades of green and gold. Pale moss green carpets covered the floor and gold brocaded furniture filled the room. Heavy gold velvet drapes covered the tall floor-to-ceiling windows. Kristin gazed wide-eyed around the room, then her eyes came to rest on a woman who sat in a chair by the fireplace. This then was Marion, Nathan's mother. She looked up, coolly and casually—no flicker of surprise or gladness visible in her eyes or her face at the sight of her son and the slim young girl who stood nervously beside him.

Nathan did not move but waited—waited for some movement, some word from his mother. They stared at each other across the room. Finally she stood up and walked with precision and intention towards them.

In an instant Kristin comprehended the power and sureness of this woman. She was tall, with grey hair, hair that looked almost mauve in the light, and although Kristin guessed she was probably in her sixties, she was still very attractive. Her features were sharp and held no softness, no gentleness; her eyes were icy blue, very different from the deep penetrating blue of Nathan's. She wore a tailored tweed suit, and a double strand of white pearls. Everything about her spoke to Kristin of coldness and control. She stopped in front of them, her eyes flicking for a moment over Kristin, then dismissing her and moving to Nathan. A smile that was not really a smile formed on her thin lips. 'Why, Nathan—what a pleasant surprise. I hadn't expected you today.'

Still Nathan did not move but he said, his voice abnormally quiet, 'Annabel told you I was coming.'

Marion waved a careless hand, her smile still painted on her face, 'Until Annabel told me you were coming, I hadn't expected you.'

This was some game, Kristin thought frantically. A game she did not understand, played by rules she was sure she could never comprehend or learn. She looked up at Nathan for some clue or hint. His face was a mask; she couldn't see what he was thinking or feeling. Even his voice was different—as if frozen in his throat.

'Come and sit down, Nathan.' His mother turned and

walked back to her chair. 'And introduce me to your little friend.'

'Didn't Annabel tell you who she is?'

'Tell me what, darling?' She sat stiffly in the chair looking up at him.

'No, of course she wouldn't,' he muttered to himself.

'What? I didn't hear you, Nathan.'

They stood in front of her now, figures pasted on a page—in a book neither of them had written. A feeling of unreality filled Kristin, frightening her. She held on to Nathan's hand even more tightly than before.

'This is Kristin, Marion. My wife. Kristin—Marion, my mother.' Still his voice frozen and toneless.

The smile on Marion's face faded, the lips drawn tightly over it. 'I'm sorry, I don't understand,' she stammered; for the first time since they entered the room, she seemed thrown off balance.

'I said Kristin is my wife, Marion. We were married nearly a week ago.'

Kristin held out a tentative hand to the woman and smiled a greeting. 'Hello, Mrs Raines, I'm very glad to meet you.'

The woman moved not a muscle, but stared in astonishment at her son, then rose carefully from her chair. 'If this is some kind of a joke, Nathan, it's in very poor taste.'

Nathan's responding laugh was harsh. 'I'm not joking, Marion. Kristin and I are married.'

Now the older woman's composure was completely shaken, as she raised a thin hand to her forehead. 'How could you do such a thing, Nathan? How could you possibly ignore your position in this family? Who is she? Does she have family?'

'I'm Dugald MacKenzie's daughter, Mrs Raines,' Kristin replied innocently. Of course she had a family—what a strange thing for Nathan's mother to say.

'Dugald MacKenzie?' Marion's voice trailed off in horror. Her voice rose to a frantic pitch. 'Who is she? Who is this girl?' she demanded.

'Nathan told you, Mrs Raines. I'm his wife.'

'Be quiet, girl! Don't say one more word.' She turned to Nathan. 'I want to speak to you alone.'

'About what, Marion?' he asked with dangerous quietness.

'We will discuss it alone, Nathan.'

'No, we will not,' he said evenly. 'Kristin is my wife, Marion —and you have that, plus the other changes that are taking place around here, to accept. And that's all we have to say to one another.' He spoke calmly, but the muscle that moved in his jaw told of the tension and the controlled anger that burned in him. Despite his words of warning before they had come here, Kristin had not really believed it would be this way. How could they make Marion see what they meant to one another?

'We love each other very much, Mrs Raines, we really do. I'll be a good wife to him, you have no worry——'

Marion's muffled expletive cut Kristin's words off in mid-sentence. 'Love! What tripe is that?'

'Marion, I warn you!'

'You warn me? I'll warn you—get rid of her. Your marriage has already been arranged. You and Carla——'

'Damn it, Mother, will you listen to us? We're married and we're going to stay married. Charles is going to direct the family business and Kristin and I are going to make a life for ourselves—elsewhere, on our own, with interference from no one—least of all you.' He towered over her. 'Do you understand me?'

'Oh yes——' Marion replied coldly, her icy balance returned as she glared at him through narrowed eyes. As if she hated her own son, Kristin thought in fearful amazement. 'Oh yes, I understand perfectly. Now,' she turned her hate-filled look on Kristin, 'get her out of my house!' With that she turned and walked from the room.

CHAPTER TEN

THEY didn't speak during the interminably long drive home, nor was a single word uttered between them all the way up on the elevator. For the first time since Nathan had come back to her, Kristin felt isolated and deserted. He flung his sweater on the couch, then walked out on to the terrace and stood staring out into space, seemingly forgetting her presence. She joined him on the balcony and placed a tentative hand on his back, only to feel his muscles tighten beneath her touch.

'I'm sorry, Nathan. I didn't really realise——'

'Don't—just leave it alone, Kristin. I don't want to discuss it,' he said harshly.

'If you can't talk to me about it, then who can——'

He roughly pushed her hand from his arm. 'When I say I don't want to talk about it, I mean it—so forget it.'

Tears filled her eyes, and a sob broke her voice. 'You're ashamed of me, aren't you?' He turned suddenly to see the tears streaming down her face.

'Sweetheart,' he moaned, pulling her against him so that she felt his heart racing, pounding under her cheek. 'Don't you ever say that—don't you ever think that!'

All the tension and hurt finally found release and she sobbed bitterly in his arms. 'I don't understand. I just don't understand—— She doesn't even know me, she's never met me before in her life——'

'She didn't have to, love. You're not the one she chose for me, and that's the entire explanation of her reaction to you. She's my mother, Kristin, and she'll never know me, either—so don't feel too badly about it.'

He held her from him and gently wiped her tears. 'Come on, let's get a smile on that lovely face. We're still on our honeymoon, so let's not let anyone spoil that.'

That night they held each other and made love with an abandon and fierceness that was new to both of them, filled with a kind of fear and desperation. Finally, exhausted, they slept, holding tightly to one another. Then next day Kristin awoke to the sound of Nathan's movements in the room. She opened sleepy, contented eyes. 'What are you doing?'

'Getting dressed,' he replied softly. 'Why don't you go back to sleep?'

'But why are you getting up?' She turned to look at the clock beside their bed. 'It's only seven-thirty.'

He sat down beside her on the bed and smoothed back her dark hair. 'I've got work to do, Kristin. There's a Board Meeting at eight and I have to be there.'

She sat up. 'But you didn't say anything about it last night, you never mentioned it.'

'I didn't know then that I'd be going.' He shook his head and muttered, 'Marion works fast. I didn't want to do it this way. I wanted to stay in the background and just let Charles handle it, but he called late last night after you were asleep and he needs my help if he's to have the support of some of the most powerful of the Board members. Marion has seen to that, I'm afraid.' He got up, kissed her quickly and grabbed his suit jacket. He looked like a completely different man to her.

'Will you be gone long?' she asked.

'I don't know. I'll call you. Why don't you phone Annabel and go shopping with her this afternoon?'

'Won't you even be home by then?' she pursued unhappily.

'Stop pushing me, Kristin,' he snapped impatiently. 'I'll be back when I can get here. Leave it at that.'

It was late that night when he returned, and for the next few weeks each day followed the same pattern. Kristin tried to talk to him about it, but he refused to discuss it; he seemed to grow farther and farther away from her.

Annabel spent a great deal of time with her, teaching her the rudiments of tennis, lunching with her at the Yacht Club, and generally helping to alleviate her loneliness, but she could not replace Nathan nor heal the wound caused by his unexplained absences.

One morning after Nathan had left, Annabel called. Kristin had been sitting in the living-room reading a book. She ran to the phone, hoping against hope that she would hear Nathan's voice on the other end.

'Hi! What's doing this afternoon?' Annabel's voice sounded cheerfully over the wire.

'Oh, hi, Annabel.'

' "Oh, hi, Annabel," ' she mimicked. 'Is that all the welcome I get?'

'No—I just thought it might be Nathan.'

Annabel drew in a long breath. 'Look, Kristin, I don't know all the ins and outs of what's going on, but be patient and stick with him. From what Charles is saying, he's fighting for his life out there.'

'What do you mean?' asked Kristin, alarmed, thinking suddenly that Nathan was in some serious trouble of which he had not told her.

'Raines and Sons, that's what. I don't know the details, but I do know that Charles isn't happy about what's going on. He's as grouchy as a bear these days.' Annabel paused, then quickly changed the subject. 'Anyway, what I called about was this afternoon—are you busy?'

'No, I guess not.'

'Good—I'm having a bit of a cocktail party out in the garden later this afternoon. I meant to ask you last week, but it completely skipped my mind. But I'd like you to come. It would give you a chance to meet some people and it's such a lovely day—too beautiful to stay indoors.'

'I don't know, Annabel—I've never been to a cocktail party or whatever you call it. I don't think I'd feel comfortable.'

'Don't be silly—just be yourself.'

'Well, I don't know.'

'Nathan will probably be late, as usual, so no excuses from you, Kristin Raines.'

'Okay,' Kristin sighed. 'I'd be back by the time he gets home, I guess.'

'Of course you will,' Annabel said absently, 'just call a cab and come on over about four. I'll see you then.'

'Wait! Don't hang up. What'll I wear and how do I get there?'

Annabel laughed. 'Call a cab—a taxi—and tell him to take you to the Maplewood Estate in Uplands. And wear something pretty—to match you, my sweet innocent. Got to run now, I've got a million things to do today.'

Kristin arrived at Maplewood just after four. She paid the taxi driver and stood alone in the driveway as he drove off. Before her, the lawn was decorated as if for a child's magical dream, and at least a hundred people, men and women, wandered slowly about, chatting idly, sipping drinks. Panic rose in her throat as she looked at the simple cotton print dress and plain sandals she wore. She couldn't stay—there was no possible way that she belonged here with these people. She quickly counted the change the taxi man had given her, but it wasn't enough to get back to the apartment. She felt stupid—why hadn't she brought more money? Nathan had left her plenty; and too, she only vaguely knew the route they had taken. But she could find her way—she was sure of that. It was a fair distance to walk, but she was used to walking. All she wanted to do was to escape this terrifying place.

But as she started to walk along the drive, she heard her name being called. She turned to see Annabel beckoning to her. She hesitated—then knew she was caught. She couldn't possibly turn and walk away now. Drawing a deep breath, she moved shyly down into the crowd of people.

'Hello, Kristin,' Annabel greeted her happily. 'So glad you could come. I love parties, don't you?'

Kristin nodded, and Annabel continued, 'Come on, I'll introduce you to some people and then you can join the fun.'

They made the rounds, Annabel laughing and talking animatedly with everyone they greeted. She was introduced as the 'newest' Raines, Nathan's new wife, and she thought how strange that sounded, as if she were only the latest. She wasn't used to the way these people behaved and talked to one another. It all seemed too unreal. Shortly, one of the servants came up to Annabel and whispered something, to which Annabel nodded. 'Excuse me, will you, Kristin. Charles is on the phone.' She giggled. 'I'll try to persuade him to come to my party and drag that husband of yours along with him. Get yourself another drink, why don't you—and just mingle—I'll see you later.'

Abandoned so suddenly, Kristin felt the touch of terror once again. She seemed in the way, unable to think of anything to say to these sophisticated strangers. One man suddenly clutched her by the elbow. 'Watch where you're going, little girl!' His voice was slurred and his eyes stared glassily down at her. 'I'm heading in this direction, why don't you join me?' The pressure of his hand on her elbow prevented her from pulling away, but still she tried.

'Let go of me—I don't even know you,' she stammered.

'That could very easily be remedied.' He smiled crookedly at her.

'Now, Roger,' a cold, precise voice interrupted. 'None of your old tricks here, my boy. At least not with our young friend here—she's what you would definitely classify as "untouchable" —Nathan's new lady—his wife, to be exact.' Roger dropped his hand and quickly disappeared into the crowd and Kristin turned to look into the face of the woman in the newspaper clipping. Carla . . .

'Come,' she said, 'let's find a quieter spot and get acquainted.' She turned, leaving Kristin no choice but to follow. She indicated a table and chair at the edge of the crowd. 'Let's sit here, where we can see everything and still have a bit of a private talk.' She emphasised the 'private' and Kristin quickly tried to think of what they would have to say to one another that could be classified as such.

The woman who sat across from her was indeed beautiful, even more beautiful than the picture Kristin had seen of her. She was a tall, statuesque blonde, obviously very sure of herself.

'Don't let Roger bother you. Most of us have learned to ignore his games—when it suits us.' She laughed, but there was no mirth in her voice. 'I'm Carla—Carla Monteroy.' She waited for Kristin to respond.

'Yes . . . I know. At least——' she stammered nervously, 'I knew your first name and your face—from a picture I've seen of you.'

Carla raised her eyebrows, 'Interesting, very interesting,' and sipped casually from her drink.

'I'm Kristin Raines—Nathan's wife.'

'Oh, I know,' Carla replied, in a tone Kristin did not understand. Kristin did not know what else to say to this woman who sat in an almost exaggerated relaxed pose opposite her, staring at her as if trying to measure something. Her hands sweated and she fidgeted with the money she held tightly in her hand.

'What's that?' Carla asked sharply.

Kristin started. 'Oh—the change from the taxi ride. I—I didn't bring enough,' she laughed nervously, 'for the trip back home.'

Carla stared at her, then expelled a breath. 'You really are an innocent, aren't you?'

'I don't understand what you mean?' Kristin questioned, unsure of why Carla was looking at her in such a way.

'Oh, stop it! Your wide-eyed innocence doesn't fool me, not for a moment. Anyone who trapped Nathan into marriage can't be all that naïve, I'm sure.'

Kristin rose from her chair, the sting of the words whipping across at her, but Carla said sharply. 'Sit down—there are a few things I have to say to you that you might as well hear from me—and face—and accept.'

Kristin sank down into the chair. She wanted to run from this woman who so obviously hated her for no reason that she could see, but she couldn't move. She sat transfixed, staring into Carla's eyes, fascinated and hypnotised by the hate she saw there.

Again Carla drank from her glass—a longer, deeper sip. 'You know about Nathan and me, I presume.' It was a statement, not a question.

'No, I . . . I don't understand.'

'Is that all you know how to say—"I don't understand"?' Carla demanded cuttingly. She no longer looked beautiful to Kristin for her features were distorted with venom.

'What do you mean—you and Nathan?' Kristin asked in a small voice.

'Nathan and I were to be married. Nathan and I were lovers.' Carla paused and placed her glass firmly on the table. 'Nathan and I *are* lovers.'

Kristin felt as if someone had wounded her mortally—she couldn't breathe, the faces of people all around her fused and lost focus—a strange buzzing filled her head and all she could see was Carla's eyes, glittering with spite.

'No!' Her voice was a strangled whisper.

'Yes,' Carla said with finality, then added, 'I'm surprised Nathan hasn't told you—he's usually quite brutally honest about such things with his new women.'

'He's never been married before—never!' Kristin cried.

'No, that's true,' Carla said nonchalantly. 'But don't think marriage will be sacred to Nathan Raines. You won't stand in our way—as you've already probably discovered.'

'What do you mean?'

'He's been very very late getting home these past few weeks, hasn't he?' Kristin did not answer, but neither did Carla give her a chance to. 'He hasn't been alone, I can tell you. I've quite enjoyed his company—and his lovemaking—these past weeks. He has a new energy, that's for sure.'

'You lie—you lie——' Kristin cried, this time getting up and moving away from the table, frantic to escape. Carla was on her feet in an instant, her long fingernails digging into the soft flesh of Kristin's upper arm.

'Face it, Kristin—you're out of your depth here. You can't possibly hope to hold a man like Nathan—as it is, you have to share him, but it's only a matter of time before he throws you away, before he's no longer interested in you. Why don't you go back to your isolated little island, before you really get hurt?'

'How do you know where ...?'

'Nathan. He tells me everything—everything.' Carla smiled, then said in a pleasant voice, that belied the entire conversation that had just taken place, 'This is an adult game, Kristin, my dear. Have some fun, perhaps with our friend Roger, even, but don't expect to win the game with Nathan. You just can't keep him. He's mine. Enjoy the party, child.' And she turned and walked into the crowd, leaving Kristin shaken and bruised, her heart breaking.

'No—no—no——' she repeated, over and over again, as she moved blindly through the people. Faces, leering down at her, became twisted and tangled images. She couldn't breathe. They were crushing her, killing her, denying her existence. She pushed them aside and ran, driven by the demons Carla had unleashed, pursued by a nightmarish fiend who wanted only to destroy her, who had stolen Nathan from her.

'No!' her screaming voice and then silence, and Annabel standing there, holding her hand.

'Kristin, for God's sake—what's the matter?' Kristin suddenly realised that all faces were turned and staring at her. Silence. Silence all around. No movement. And a flood of em-

barrassment filled her—she'd disgraced Nathan. They knew
she was Nathan's wife and she had disgraced him by behaving
this way—by calling everyone's attention to her hysteria and
panic. They were all calm and sophisticated and able to deal
so easily with one another.

She would be that way too, she would. Then Nathan would
love her again, would be proud of her. 'Nothing's wrong,
Annabel,' she said in a tight voice. 'I'm sorry. I'm all right
now, thank you.' But away—she had to get away from them—
from the faces—the faces that threatened. She waited for the
silence to melt once again into chatter, then turned to leave.

But Annabel was beside her. 'Where are you going?'

'Home. I'm going home,' she replied decisively.

'Charles and Nathan will be here in a moment. Nathan'll
take you home. Why don't you go inside and lie down for a
while?' The look on her face told Kristin of her genuine concern, but nothing could allay Kristin's desperate need to flee
this place. Nathan would probably be late and she couldn't
stay here another moment, not a single moment more.

'I'll be all right, really I will,' she said tonelessly, walking up
the hill away from the guests—leaving Annabel to stare after
her.

But the nightmare wasn't over, for when she reached the
drive she looked up to see Marion standing there, her ice blue
eyes assessing her. 'I see you met Nathan's good friend Carla,
my dear. It's a pity you couldn't have met her before you
married my son—it might have saved you a great deal of
heartache.' She made a brief gesture of farewell. 'Do feel free
to come again, Kristin.'

Marion's words were an empty mockery; she would not care
if she never saw Kristin again. Kristin's hands flew to her
mouth, muffling a broken sob of horror as she turned and ran
wildly from the house and down the long driveway to the
road.

She ran until she thought her lungs would burst—running
and not really seeing the houses, the faces that moved past her
in a fluid blur. It was dark now—and colder. She shivered,
realising that it had started to rain. She stepped off a curb,
stumbled and fell, skinning her knees. But still she hurried on
—running from Carla and the words that tortured her by

repeating themselves over and over again in her mind. She was crying and her tears mingled with the rain that fell more heavily now. Her breath came in broken sobs.

Somehow she had made it downtown—she thought she recognised the street on which she and Nathan had walked their first night together. She slowed her pace, looking frantically for some familiar place—for some clue to where she was and where Nathan's apartment was from here. She wandered this way for a long time—finally realising that she was well and truly lost, as well as drenched and cold. She had worn no sweater this afternoon—just the thin cotton dress. Her brown hair was a slick helmet against her face. She had no way home and worse, she didn't know where it was. Then she remembered the money still clutched tightly in her hand. She opened her fingers and carefully counted—three dollars and fifty cents. She had change for a phone call. She would call Annabel and ask her for directions. Annabel would help her. She ran another couple of blocks until she came to a phone booth. She leafed through the book—searching for Annabel's name, then Charles'. But nothing. No Annabel or Charles Raines were listed. Frantically she trailed her finger down the list, searching for Nathan's name and finally for Marion's. But still nothing. Tears sprung to her eyes. 'What do I do? Oh God, what do I do?'

She searched the list of names again, but the list had become a meaningless blurr.

'Look, lady, if you can't find the number, call information or give up. I want to use the phone.' A large woman stood behind her, waiting impatiently to use the phone booth.

'Information?'

'Yah—information.'

'What number—I don't understand.'

'Oh God, a real dummy!' and the woman walked angrily away.

Trying to keep calm, Kristin looked at the list of directions printed on the phone, found the number marked information, put in a quarter and dialled cautiously. The phone rang a number of times before a woman's monotone responded, 'Information.'

'Yes—oh yes——' Kristin breathed with relief.

'Information. What number do you need?'

'Yes—ah—the number for Annabel Raines——' In the background she heard the rustling of pages.

'I'm sorry, we have no listing for that name.'

'Well, Charles Raines, then—of Maplewood——'

'I'm sorry—that number is an unlisted number.'

'What do you mean?'

'It means that I am not authorised to release that number.'

'But I'm his sister-in-law. Please——'

'I'm sorry, regulations will not permit me to release that number. Will that be all?'

'Yes—— No! No, please—don't hang up—give me the number for Nathan Raines, then.'

Seconds, then the same monotone—'I'm sorry, that number is also unlisted.'

'Oh, please—please—he's my husband—I need to know——'

'I'm sorry, I am not authorised to release——' then a click and a droning sound filling the silence. Kristin leaned her face against the side of the booth. What could she do now but walk and search? There was no other way.

Hours later she was too cold, wet and exhausted to recognise anyone or anything. She walked mindlessly along the street, passing the store fronts that she had the vague feeling of having seen before. No longer did she try to avoid them. She was just too tired ...

A hand heached out and pulled her roughly to a halt. 'Got a smoke, lady?' a rough voice demanded.

'No—no——' she tried to push past him. He reeked of alcohol.

'Want a smoke, lady?'

'No——' she pulled herself away from him but he caught her again by the sleeve.

'Don't be so unfriendly, no need to be unfriendly. I'm a very friendly guy——'

She pulled away from him abruptly and heard, as she turned and ran, the sleeve of her dress rip.

Out of the corner of her eye she saw a shiny red car pull up beside her and someone chasing her—coming after her; she ran—ran as fast as she could.

A strong hand stopped her frantic flight, but still she

struggled wildly with all the strength she could muster.

'Don't touch me—leave me alone—I don't want you to touch me!'

Then the voice that spoke her name, over and over again, penetrated and she saw the hand that refused to release her. She looked up into the man's face.

'Nathan—oh, Nathan——' she breathed as she leaned wearily against him. 'I want—I want to go home. Please take me home.'

The apartment was a warm and welcome haven. Kristin breathed a sigh of relief when the elevator door closed behind them. 'Oh, Nathan,' her voice quivered.

'Don't talk,' he ordered brusquely. 'Get out of those wet clothes, have a hot shower and dry your hair. We'll talk later.' His voice was hard and she could tell by the steel glint in his eyes that he was angry.

'Please, don't be angry with me—let me explain——'

He turned sharply. 'Oh, you'll explain all right—but after you do exactly what you're told.'

She stood rooted to the spot, shaken and hurt by the anger that he directed at her.

'Did you hear what I said—or do I have to undress you and bathe you myself, as if you really are the child you've been be-having like?'

She stared with large shocked eyes at him, but his eyes did not soften. White lines showed around his mouth.

'Go, Kristin!' he ordered again, then walked across the room and poured himself a drink.

She joined him half an hour later in the living-room, just as he was finishing a conversation on the phone. 'Fine, I'll see you in the morning, then. Goodbye. Yes,' he laughed mirthlessly, 'I'll tell her.' She stood before him waiting for him to speak, but all he did was glance at her then pour himself another drink.

In the interval she had calmed herself, and decided she must speak to him of Carla's accusations, but he was still clearly angry with her. 'How long am I to stand here and be punished by your attitude?' she asked evenly. He threw back his glass, drained his drink, and refilled it.

'Don't you think you've had enough, Nathan?'

'How long,' he asked in a voice that was slightly slurred, 'do I have to contend with your behaviour, Kristin—your childish unthinking behaviour?'

'What are you talking about?' she faltered.

'I'm talking about what you did at the party this afternoon and the manner in which you left it.' He raised a hand to emphasise his words. 'And that insane escapade of yours in the city.'

'You know nothing of what happened. You weren't . . .'

'It know exactly what went on—Annabel's been frantic about you—and Carla told me——'

'Carla!'

'Yes, Carla.'

'And just what did she tell you, Nathan?'

He stood towering over her, not hearing or not bothering to answer her question. 'Do you,' he asked succinctly, 'do you have any idea what could have happened to you out there? You're a fool if you think this city is all glittering, beautiful lights that are there to charm that stupid little romantic heart of yours.' He ran frustrated fingers through his hair. 'You seem to have no idea what hell you've put me through tonight.'

He was a stranger to her. His words, his anger had removed him from her. She turned to walk away, but he reached out and held her with a bruisingly tight grip.

'Don't you ever walk away from me like that,' he grated. 'No ever.'

She fought back, tears streaming down her face. 'Don' touch me! Don't touch me like that—as if being your wife makes me your property.'

'What are you saying?'

'I'm saying that all you seem to care about is if I embarrassed your family, or if I belittled you. You don't care about me and what I feel or what I went through tonight. You just care about the Raines' property, and I hate it. I hate everything here!' She was beside herself now—all the terror and panic of her experience flooding her senses. She pulled herself out of his grip. 'Don't touch me—don't come near me. I want to go home—I hate it here—I can't stand——'

She was crying uncontrollably now. 'You said we'd go back

to Sitka—you said that weeks ago. You lied to me, you just told me that. You're going to make me stay here, until——'

He cut her off. 'Is staying here with me such a painful experience, Kristin?'

'Yes! Yes, it is. And I'm going home. Alone, if I have to ...'

He straightened. 'You're my wife, Kristin—your place is with me,' he told her coldly.

'You promised,' she sobbed.

'Be quiet! All this is getting us nowhere—except that it's upsetting you.' He finished his drink and put the empty glass on the bar. 'I think we should get some sleep. Charles and I leave for Calgary early in the morning for a few days.'

She looked at him, not understanding his words at first.

'I'm taking you over to Maplewood—you're to stay there with Annabel and Marion while I'm gone.'

'No!' Her eyes widened with abject fear. 'I can't go there—I won't stay there!'

His eyes flashed with impatience again. 'I'm not arguing with you, Kristin—you're going to stay at Maplewood until I return. I'll be back by the weekend.'

'That's four days! I won't go there. I'll come with you, or I'll stay here—but I'm not going to Maplewood.'

'I'm not leaving you alone—not after today. You can't be trusted alone. I can't spend the next four days a thousand miles away worrying about you.'

'She hates me—she doesn't want me there,' Kristin replied brokenly.

'Don't be ridiculous—Annabel's your friend.'

'Not Annabel—your mother—Marion.'

'No,' he replied wearily, 'that isn't true. She's accepted you. It was Marion who suggested that you stay at Maplewood—after what happened today, knowing that I'd be away.'

CHAPTER ELEVEN

'WHERE's Annabel, Marion?' Nathan enquired.

'Now stop worrying, Nathan. Everything will be fine. We'll take good care of Kristin while you're gone. You'd better get going or you'll miss your flight.' Kristin stood in silence, watching Marion kiss her son goodbye and pretending to be glad to have her staying with her. Kristin did not speak but stood staring out of vacant eyes. At least Annabel would be here.

'Tell Charles I'm ready, then.'

Marion looked surprised, then laughed. 'That silly girl Annabel was supposed to tell you last night that Charles would meet you at the airport. He went to the office early and then drove straight out to the airport. I'm sorry, dear, I shall scold her for being so careless.'

'No matter,' he mumbled.

There were dark, tired lines under his eyes—he had not slept well last night. Perhaps her own tossing and turning had kept him awake. He bent and kissed her gently on the mouth, but she stood passively and did not return his kiss.

'Aren't you going to say goodbye?' he murmured.

'Goodbye,' she said blankly, not moving a muscle.

'All right, Kristin——' he sighed heavily, 'I'll see you in a few days.' Then he turned and was gone.

'Well, well my dear—now we have the perfect opportunity to really get to know each other. But first, excuse me—I'll have to give the servants their orders for the day. Annabel usually takes care of that,' Marion smiled graciously, 'but she and Jon are staying with her parents for a few days while Charles is away.' Still smiling, she swept from the room.

Kristin closed her eyes in despair. How was she to survive four days with this woman? Suddenly the shrill ring of the phone startled her. Marion called from the hallway. 'Get that, will you, dear? And take a message if it's necessary. There's paper on the desk.'

The phone persisted and slowly she lifted the receiver. 'Hello?'

'Hello? Marion?' It was Carla. 'Hello? Can you hear me, Marion?'

'It's Kristin.'

'Hello? I can't hear you,' Carla's thin voice repeated.

Kristin cleared her throat and spoke again. 'It's Kristin speaking. Marion is busy right now. Can I give her a message?'

Carla laughed. 'Oh yes—yes, indeed you can. Will you tell her, please, that I'll be unable to come to dinner this evening as we arranged. I'll be out of town for a few days. Can you hear me, Kristin?'

'Yes—yes, I can hear you,' she whispered.

'Good—it's rather noisy here. I'm at the airport. We're flying to Calgary shortly.'

Kristin's heart rose in her throat. Oh no—please, God—no!

Carla's voice persisted. 'Are you still there, my dear?' She could not answer. 'Kristin?'

'Yes,' she replied, her voice quaking.

'Don't take it too hard, Kristin dear, I told you that Nathan and I will be together—no matter what. You knew what to expect.' Carla hesitated for a fraction of a moment, then quickly added, 'Give my love to Marion—tell her I'll see her when I get back. Enjoy your stay at Maplewood, dear.' She hung up.

Kristin slowly replaced the phone in its cradle, her hands suddenly cold and stiff, her eyes pressed tight fighting back the tears that threatened and the lump in her throat that was choking her. So it was true. Carla and Nathan were lovers and now he was taking her with him to Calgary. All her instincts fought against this knowledge that was now a certainty.

Marion came back into the room. 'There, that's that. I'll be glad when Annabel returns—I have no head for household details myself. Who was that on the phone, dear?' Her voice was sweet and friendly and false when she looked up into Kristin's eyes.

'It was Carla,' she replied lifelessly.

'Yes? What did she say?'

'She said ...' Her voice broke, but she continued, 'she said that she can't come to dinner tonight. She's going to Calgary for a few days.'

Marion sucked in a deep breath. 'You know, of course, Kristin, that she's with Nathan,' she said almost reluctantly.

'Yes——' Kristin's voice was small and defeated. 'Yes, I know. She said that.'

'You must realise that they've been together for years, Kristin—long before he met you.' Marion motioned to her. 'Come sit over on the chesterfield and we'll talk.' She helped Kristin to the couch, her movements rigid as if she could barely stand to touch her daughter-in-law. 'What will you do now that you know for certain?'

'I don't know——' Kristin put her hands to her hot, flushed face. Suddenly she was feverish and freezing cold at the same time.

'Don't you think you should go back to your home, back to that island, before Nathan returns?'

'I don't know.' She shook her head—she just couldn't think straight.

'You know now that you don't belong here, Kristin. You could never accept the fact that Nathan will not give up Carla. Your life here would be miserable. I'm only trying to help you see that ...' Marion patted Kristin's thin shoulder. 'Look, why don't you go upstairs to your room? I've put you in Nathan's old room. You should rest for a while—I know this has been a shock to you. I'm having a few friends in this evening for supper. You can join us and afterwards we can talk again.'

She helped Kristin to her feet and led her across the room and upstairs to her room.

Kristin moved with sightless eyes—dulled by the pain of what she had finally come to realise about Nathan, her beloved Nathan, who, she knew now, had not, had never loved her as he had so fervently claimed. Soon she fell into a deep sleep that for a time deadened her pain.

'Kristin.' Her name over and over again, from a great distance. 'Kristin!' She opened her eyes, at first not realising where she was, then with a rush of memory, groaned and rolled over again. She felt so tired—and wanted only to be left alone.

'Come on, Kristin. You've slept all day. I can't believe that

anyone needs that much sleep—not a young thing like you.'
Marion pulled back the bedclothes. 'My guests are arriving and
I especially want you to dine with us. I'll expect you down
within the hour.'

They sat, twenty-eight people, around the long mahogany
dining table, lights dimmed through crystal chandeliers, the
clink of wine glasses and forks on precious china, voices low
and murmuring. Kristin tried to listen to the talk around her,
tried to focus on the faces, the mouths that spoke to her, but
it was impossible. All she could think about was the terrible
ache in her chest. She put a tired hand to her forehead—she
felt so warm. It was stuffy in this room, even though the terrace doors were opened.

She suddenly realised that Marion, sitting to the left of her
at the head of the table, was speaking to her.

'I'm sorry, I didn't hear you——'

'I'm not surprised, Kristin. You weren't listening,' Marion
scolded, then continued, 'I was just telling Doctor Anderson
here how difficult a time you've had adjusting to our way of
life. But then again you don't come from a very, shall we say,
sophisticated background and I guess one must make allow-
ances when one's training and upbringing has been found
wanting.'

'Really, Marion!' the older man interjected.

Anger and hurt stirred in Kristin, and she rose from the
table, glaring down at the rigid woman dressed in black silk
and pearls. She had taken all she could. 'You know, Mrs
Raines, my upbringing may lack a lot by your standards,' she
paused and swallowed with difficulty, 'but where I come from
I was taught not to intentionally and cruelly set out to hurt another person. My father didn't have a lot in the way of material
goods, but he taught me kindness, Mrs Raines. He gave me
manners and a basic respect for other human beings—all of
which you have worked very hard and very successfully to
prove you do not have.' She pushed her chair from the table
and stumbled towards the door which swerved and swam before her eyes. Suddenly she could not go on, could not move
another step, but gave in to the whirling darkness.

'No, Doctor—— No——' her voice pleaded urgently, 'you
must be wrong!'

'There's no problem, child. You'll be up and around in no time at all.' He grinned widely. 'And I suspect your Nathan will be dancing in the streets when he hears the news that he's to be presented with a child some months hence.'

She closed her eyes. 'Dear God, oh dear God, what shall I do?'

'You'll get plenty of rest and you'll lie back and enjoy being pregnant, you'll see.' He closed his bag and put a friendly hand on her shoulder. 'Don't worry about Marion—she's a real tartar, always was. You just don't take any of her foolishness, that's all. You told her off at dinner in fine style'—he chuckled —'took the wind right out of the old girl's sails, you did. That needs to happen more often, if I do say so myself.' He paused at the door. 'Now you get some rest and do what you're told. Nathan'll be home in a few days, then everything'll be just fine.' He slipped out and quietly closed the door.

Kristin turned and sobbed uncontrollably into the pillow. Three months pregnant. Three months. How could she have been so stupid? How could she not have known? And what was she to do now? She couldn't stay here, not now. Nathan wouldn't want the child. He didn't really want her—that was certain.

The door from the hallway opened and Marion's tall, straight figure stood, a dark silhouette against the light. Her voice was like stone and her face a fearful mask of hatred.

'So that's how you managed to deceive my son into marriage!' she spat out accusingly. 'I should have guessed how your kind works.' She raised a threatening hand and silenced anything Kristin might have said. 'I want to hear no empty words of explanation from you, girl. Don't even dare to speak to me! Just listen, and listen well. I want you out of here and I want you out tonight. I will not have you under my roof— not for an hour longer. You take yourself and whoever's child you happen to be carrying and get out of here.' Her mouth was a thin, red slash. 'Oh no, you don't think for an instant that I believe it's Nathan's child. I'm no fool. Besides, even if it was his child, that's not Nathan's style. He would demand that you rid yourself of it, so if you want to keep your child, I suggest that you go and go now. By the way,' she added almost casually, 'there's a young man downstairs who says he's from a place called Sitka Landing—perhaps he's your baby's father.

At any rate, his arrival is both coincidental and timely. He can help you pack and remove you from my home. I'll send him up.'

Defeated, humiliated, Kristin lay back against the pillows, unable to fight any more. A tall figure appeared in the doorway and walked cautiously to her bedside.

'Kristin?' his strong, clear voice questioned. 'Kristin, what's happened to you?'

'Luther! Oh, Luther!' She held out a hand to grasp his weakly.

'What's going on? Where's Nathan?' He looked about him, confusion evident in his eyes.

'He's gone—he's in Calgary.' She closed her eyes. 'He doesn't want me any more, Luther. I don't fit in his world.' She sobbed brokenly, not seeing the look of searing rage possess Luther's massive frame.

'I had business in Vancouver,' he said through gritted teeth. 'I came to see how you were doing and to find out when you'd be coming back to Sitka.' He lowered his voice. 'I wanted to know if you and Nathan wanted to go back with me on the *Nova Dawn*. Do you want to come with me now—alone?'

'Yes—oh yes—— Please take me home, Luther. I want to go home.'

She sat on the bluff below the lighthouse, staring out to sea, staring at the islands that lay scattered in the channel, and listening to the sound of the waves breaking on the rocks below her. The wind, tasting of salt, whipped her face and hair. She breathed in the salt air, filling her lungs with the cutting sweetness of it, and for the first time in weeks was almost thankful to be alive.

She had been watching a boat under full sail that had appeared on the horizon nearly an hour ago—a small white dot in the grey, an almost imperceptible part of the line that linked sea and sky. Now it played with the wind, running before it towards one of the outer islands. Kristin watched it unthinkingly, its movements in perfect tune with the wind and the sea. The water was rough today, the seas high. She knew that whoever was handling the boat was indeed a good sailor.

She looked up at the lighthouse—Luther and Alice would

be finished soon. They were moving all her furniture and belongings to the old farmhouse on the other side of the island,
where eventually she would live, once Luther had carried out
the necessary repairs. She had been greeted on her return to
Sitka by the news that the new lightkeeper and his family had
already arrived; her old home was her home no longer. She
had put off the moving of her things for as long as possible,
but today was the day that Alice chose not to be stalled again.
This morning at breakfast, in her matter-of-fact manner, Alice
had told her that she, Kristin, had things to face—life was to
be lived, and there was a child to prepare for. And so the three
of them had come to Sitka Island, although Alice had refused
to let Kristin help with the moving.

Kristin sighed, leaning her cheek on her knees as the sailboat came closer. How good Alice and Luther had been to her
in the past few weeks! She could never have managed without
them; for she had fallen ill with pneumonia on her return
from Victoria and even now was still convalescing. Weak and
delirious, she had tried to explain to them what had happened without talking of Carla's terrible revelations; she knew
they blamed Nathan bitterly for the change in her from a
happy young girl to a disillusioned and defeated woman.

How could she be happy on the island now? She bit her lip,
her grey eyes bleak. Everything had changed. Nathan had come
into her life and had shattered and destroyed all that had ever
mattered to her. He had uprooted her from her home and had
mercilessly led her like a lamb to slaughter—into a family and
a way of life whose rules were so vastly different and so heart-
less and cruel that she could never have hoped to survive.

It was nearly a month since Luther had brought her back
from Victoria, a month that she would prefer to forget. Alice
told her later that Doctor Fraser, the physician who looked
after all the isolated settlements along the Shore, had feared
that she would perhaps lose the baby. But that had not happened. Nevertheless, even when that danger and her fever had
subsided, she had lain in bed, listless and uncommunicative.
After her one attempt to explain to Alice and Luther what
had happened since her marriage, she would talk to no one
about those catastrophic events, her pride preventing her from
sharing how she had been shamed and rejected by Nathan

and his mother. At first she wanted only to die; nothing and no one mattered any more. But gradually the hurt and despair translated themselves into a bitter anger and hatred towards Nathan and Marion that in effect rekindled her will to live. That and the child who was growing within her. She would live for the baby who was to come.

And so she had started to make plans. She had decided to stay with Alice and Luther while Luther worked on the farmhouse, making it habitable for her. She would live there alone, with her unborn child, and learn to forget Nathan altogether. After that? Well, she would decide later. She had to concentrate on surviving now. Later there would be time to go on from there.

The cold wind drew her back from her thoughts and she stood up, shivering in its blast, and made her way carefully up the path to the grassy knoll above. She turned to see the sailboat round the side of the island and head for the inlet. It was obviously someone who knew his way around, probably a friend of the new people in the lighthouse. But something made her stop and look more closely, straining to catch a glimpse of the sailor. Some instinct deep within her caught her attention, made her uneasy. But she dismissed it as quickly as it came and headed for the path which led over the top of the island to the farmhouse. Perhaps Alice and Luther had finished and were waiting there for her. Once she looked back over her shoulder, wondering again who had sailed up the channel to anchor in the inlet; but, seeing no one, she resolutely kept moving.

Alice and Luther weren't at the farmhouse, but at least it was warmer inside. Kristin looked around the place, a little cleaner and tidier than before, but still not feeling like home. A small sob caught in her throat as she put a shaking hand to her forehead. She and Nathan had shared such a happy day here, and through his eyes she had seen the house as it could be—a beautiful and happy place. Now she could only see it as it was: empty, cold and dusty; the porch sagged and the roof leaked. She walked into the living-room, but was no more impressed with things there. She wished Luther and Alice would come. She was so tired, still so very tired. She wondered if she would ever have her old energy back.

The screen door opened and slammed shut. 'Luther?' she called out. There was no answer. 'Is that you, Alice?' Still no answer. She turned from the window and gasped, startled by the sudden appearance of the tall figure who stood in the doorway, frozen into stillness by the fact that it was Nathan who now stood before her. He looked different, changed somehow as he stared darkly down at her.

'So it was you!' she whispered.

His voice as cold and unbending as steel, he said, 'Surprised and happy to see me, my dear wife, after four long weeks of separation?'

She leaned back against the wall and closed her eyes. 'Go away, Nathan—just go away.'

'It seems we might have been through this little routine once before. Is this to be a verbatim re-run of your convincing little scene of two months ago, Kristin?' he asked harshly.

She looked quickly up at him. He was wearing jeans and a heavy sweater, sleeves pushed up above his elbows revealing arms that were still muscled and strong. But the change in him was definite—physically he had lost weight, and the lines that had appeared around his mouth in moments of disdain or anger were now deeply carved. He held himself in check, not moving a muscle, body completely controlled. His eyes revealed a man hardened, a man with a core of ice-cold steel.

Kristin could scarcely believe the evidence of her eyes. This was Nathan—but a Nathan a hundred worlds apart from hers. This was the true Nathan—the one she had not glimpsed until he had taken her away from everything she'd known and loved, until he had made her love him, had possessed her and had shamed her by casting her aside for a woman he had never intended to give up.

'No,' she replied sarcastically, 'this is not to be a re-run. You will, I hope, leave immediately—and alone.'

'Wrong on both counts,' he said to her, with a contempt which made her cringe. 'I'm not leaving here and if I did choose to go anywhere it would not be alone—*you* would be with me, the dear and loyal wife that you are.'

'We're finished, Nathan.'

'Well, I'm not finished, Kristin.' He moved slowly across the room towards her.

'Don't touch me ... don't even come near me! Luther'll be back and he'll——'

He grabbed hold of her wrist. 'Don't threaten me with what Luther or anyone else will do—although I was expecting to find Del's name on your sweet lips rather than Luther's.'

She struggled against his bruising hold, but he held her fast. Suddenly his mouth claimed hers and she felt once again the power he had always had over her. Still she fought against him, fought for her very survival. She could not live with the humiliation of his relationship with Carla. She could not live with a man she had come to hate with all the fire and passion with which she once loved him.

'Kristin, Kristin——' he whispered brokenly, a new note in his voice. He drew back and looked down at her. For an instant she thought she saw a look of total despair and pain, and her heart lurched at the sight of it. But no. She was wrong, she had to be wrong. He was manipulating her, like Marion had done, and she refused to be his victim ever again. She turned her back on him and spat angry, hostile words.

'Get out of here! You don't belong here and you never did. Your kind doesn't belong anywhere.' She heard him draw a sharp breath as if someone had struck him, but she refused to turn around and face him again.

'Kristin ...'

'Don't talk to me, just get out of here. I hate you! I hate you more than you'll ever know. I wish you were in hell!'

'If it's any consolation to you, Kristin,' he replied wearily, 'I am.' He made no move to leave, nor did he attempt to speak again and they stood thus for long moments until she slowly turned around.

'What are you waiting for? I'll never live with you again— never.'

His eyes narrowed. 'Yes, you will, Kristin. You're my wife and that will remain unchanged.' His cold, steel-like control returned. 'Oh yes, at first I intended to let you go. I've lived through four very long weeks when I had every intention of divorcing you.'

'So why didn't you? I can barely stand the sight of you, Nathan.' Her words slashed out at him. 'My hatred for you is that complete.'

He spoke quietly, his voice tight and strained. 'I haven't come here to *ask* you to come back to me, Kristin. I've come to tell you that you will live with me and, hate it all you want to, you will share my bed and be a wife to me again.'

'No, I will not!'

'If I have to carry you out of here by force, then by God I will!' he threatened.

'And what about the child, Nathan?' she cried out. 'What do you want me to do with the baby?' Fear pushed her beyond the edge of caution as she remembered Marion's words. 'Marion said you'd probably make me get rid of the baby. She said ...'

He closed his eyes. 'We keep the child.'

'A child you don't want?' She laughed bitterly. 'You don't really want the child, do you? A baby doesn't fit your scheme of things.'

'Damn you, Kristin!' he rasped. 'What do you think? Does it give you pleasure to torture me like this? What kind of a man do you think I am? Do you think I'm proud that my wife is carrying another man's child—Del Clarke's baby?'

Her eyes widened in disbelief. 'Del's child? You believe that I ...'

'Stop it!' His fist came crashing down on top of the table. 'I know, Kristin. I know all about it. Marion told me. She told me how far along the pregnancy was too. You were pregnant when we got married, weren't you? How fortunate for you that I married you. What a fool I was to be so easily deceived!'

'You believed your mother—knowing what she's like—rather than believing me?' she said incredulously. 'How could you?'

'Deny that you were pregnant when we married.'

'I can't.'

'Exactly.'

'But we—oh, what's the use?' she said wearily. 'It's too late, Nathan.' Tears filled her eyes and her mouth quivered. 'Maybe it was always too late.'

'Listen to me, Kristin, and listen well. I'll learn to live with the fact that you're carrying another man's child. But you—you're mine and you're going to stay with me. You'll be my wife again—in every sense of the word.'

'I won't! I won't go back to Victoria with you.'

'We're not going back. Charles is in charge there now.'

'Where, then?' she demanded, then instantly realised that he intended to settle on Sitka. 'I can't stay here with you,' she said fiercely. 'Not here.'

He reached out, his long fingers touching her slim throat. 'Almost'— he grated, his jaw tightly clenched—'almost I could kill you for what you've done.' Her eyes widened in fear, but he continued, 'Don't fight me and don't push me. Just get your things—you're coming with me now.'

Now she was truly frightened, but she still hesitated. 'Do what I say, Kristin!' he grated.

An angry voice sounded behind him. 'What do you want here?' Nathan swung round and came face to face with Luther, who stood, fists clenched ready to attack. 'You're not welcome here any more, Nathan—get out!'

Nathan expelled his breath with an exasperated hiss. 'It's up to you, Luther, whether you want to welcome me or not. But,' he waved a hand at Kristin, 'she's my purpose for being here. She's my wife and I'm taking her with me.'

'Kristin stays here, with us.'

Nathan's face darkened. 'Don't make me fight for her. Not you, Luther.'

'Well, it's me you're damn well going to have to fight, because she's not going with you.' Luther squared his shoulders. 'And don't let it concern you that it's me you have to fight. It isn't exactly as if you were doing battle with a friend,' he said, sarcastically, emphasising the last word. Nathan didn't move a muscle.

A feeling of dread filled Kristin as she watched the two men face each other; one her husband, the other the man who had been like her own brother ever since she was a child. Nathan's eyes showed no emotion, just a watchful waiting, and suddenly she knew that he was capable of killing in order to have her back. She knew too that Luther would not give up. This had to end—too many people would be hurt if it didn't.

'Stop it, Luther. Please!' she pleaded.

'Stay out of the way, Kristin,' he replied. 'I'll handle this.'

She moved resolutely between them. 'No, I won't stay out of the way!' She swallowed and took a deep breath. She had to stop them before Nathan did something dreadful. 'Don't fight him, Luther. Someone will get hurt.'

Luther put his hands on her shoulders. 'After what he's done to you, you're not going to stay with him.'

Nathan glared at him. 'After what I've done to her? What in hell is that supposed to mean?'

'Be quiet, all of you! Sounds like you're getting ready to start another world war!' Alice stood in the doorway, a carton in her arms. 'That's the last of it, Kristin. Where do you want it?' Not waiting for an answer, she moved across the room and deposited her burden.

So you've come back again, Nathan,' she observed calmly. 'It's getting to be a habit with you, isn't it?' She turned to survey the three people that she cared about most in the world. 'Now listen to me. There'll be no fighting, so pack it in now.' She looked evenly at Kristin. 'This is no way for you to be carrying on. You shouldn't be getting upset. The Doc would skin me for letting you come over here today as it is.' Quickly she shifted her gaze to Nathan. 'Why have you come back?'

'I came for Kristin.'

'She doesn't want to go with you.'

'I'm not taking her away. We're going to stay here where she belongs, where she'll be'—he hesitated—'where I think she'll be happy.'

'I think,' Alice spoke slowly and carefully, 'it might be a very long time before our girl is what you call happy again. Something very bad and very wrong happened to her while she was away and I think, I believe, you're responsible.'

'That's between Kristin and me, Alice. It's something we have to work out between us.'

Almost Kristin detected a note of pleading in his voice. Almost, she thought, he was asking for Alice, at least Alice, to trust him, to understand. But she knew she was wrong. Nathan needed understanding from no one and would ask for nothing from any of them. He had come to claim what was his—his property—his wife—and he would have her despite anything anyone did or said to stop him. As if he could read her thoughts, he said hoarsely, 'No one will stop me, Alice. She's my wife.'

'That doesn't make her a piece of property that you can do with whatever you like, Nathan.'

'I won't hurt her, Alice,' he replied quietly.

'Won't hurt her!' yelled Luther, unable to remain quiet any longer. 'You damn near killed her, and if it means anything to you at all, she almost lost your child because of what happened!'

Nathan turned startled eyes to Kristin, and not for the first time she noticed his thinness, his tiredness, the haunted look in his face. 'I want her to be happy, that's why we're staying here.'

'We want her to be happy too,' Luther said angrily, 'that's why she's staying here and why you're leaving. We don't want you here—you don't belong.' Without warning he lunged forward, his fist lashing out and striking Nathan on the mouth. Nathan had seen the blow coming, Kristin was positive, but he made no move to avoid it. The force of it snapped his head back and drove him against the wall with a sickening thud. He regained his balance but made no attempt to retaliate. He stood perfectly still, staring at Luther, a thin trickle of blood flowing from the corner of his mouth.

Kristin choked back a sob. 'No, please!' she pleaded again. Nathan shifted his gaze to Kristin, then back to Luther. His body, she saw, was like a tightly coiled spring, dangerous but controlled. Strangely enough, he wasn't going to fight Luther, that was obvious. Although he was braced for another of Luther's powerful blows, he wasn't going to strike back, at least not here and not now. She didn't understand.

Nathan expelled a harsh breath and put probing fingers to his already bruised and swelling lip. 'Is that it, Luther?' he asked coldly. 'Or do you have something else in mind?'

'You bastard!' Luther growled, his anger still raging.

'Stop it, Luther!' Alice ordered. 'Go down to the boat. I'll be along in a minute.'

'I'm not leaving her with him.'

'And I'm not going to stand here and watch this kind of foolishness,' Alice retorted. 'Both of you should have more sense. Nothing ever gets settled like this—it only gets worse.' She looked across the room at Kristin's pale face. 'I think you both need to think about Kristin a bit. This isn't good for her. It's her first day out since she was ill. We should get her home.'

'What do you mean, she's been ill?' Nathan demanded sharply.

'She had pneumonia. It would seem that you didn't know about that?' Alice watched his face closely, but he gave no response. 'Look, we'll all go back to the Landing and you two can talk after a hot meal. Let's go.'

Luther stepped in front of her. 'Are you crazy?' he exclaimed. 'He's not coming home with us. He's not putting a foot in our place again.'

Now Alice was angry. 'Step aside, Luther. You may have a few feet on me in height, but that's my house and no son of mine tells me what I can and can't do. Nathan's coming over to the Landing and that's that.' Luther pushed past her and stomped out, slamming the door behind him.

'You coming over with us or on your own?' she asked Nathan.

He looked at Kristin, then replied, 'Kristin and I'll come in my yacht.'

Alice nodded. 'See you both there, then.'

'No, I'm not going anywhere with him,' Kristin exclaimed bitterly. 'I'm coming with you and Luther.'

Alice looked at her levelly. 'Don't behave like a child, Kristin. This isn't the time for it. He's your husband—for now anyway—so meet him halfway and get this whole thing worked out or there'll be nothing but misery for you, believe me.' Then she too turned and shut the door, leaving Kristin feeling deserted and desperate. Her own Alice had abandoned her to the man she hated most in the world.

For long moments they neither moved nor spoke, then Nathan crossed the room towards her, his face strained. She averted her eyes, but gentle fingers under her chin tipped her face up to look at him. Sudden tears stung her eyes and she wiped angrily at them.

'You were ill?' he asked quietly. Still she refused to speak to him. 'Answer me, Kristin.'

Suddenly all her pent-up emotions spilled over and consumed her in the fire of her anger and bitterness. Tears streamed down her face and she lacked the presence of mind to search for the control that fled so suddenly from her.

'Oh, dear God,' he groaned, pulling her to him. Something within her wanted nothing more but to stay cradled, warm and safe in his arms, but something else, stronger and still blazing, within her, hated the weakness she was displaying, hated the very need she had of him. She pushed against him, struggling frantically out of his hold.

'No—no——' she sobbed. 'I don't want you to touch me!' He held on to her and she twisted and pulled against him. 'Let me go. Take your hands off me!'

'Stop it, Kristin. You'll hurt yourself,' he ordered.

She laughed hysterically. 'You don't care about me!'

His hands tightened on her arms and he forced her to look at him. 'I care, Kristin. I came for you, didn't I?'

'That's a different tune, isn't it? Before it was because I was a part of the Raines' property. I was your wife and I did the unthinkable—I left you! Now you say you care. Well, I don't believe you—I'll never believe you again.'

'We need to talk this over sensibly,' he said wearily.

'Oh no—we've talked enough, Nathan.' She flung her words like shards of glass, striking and cutting, hoping to destroy the man before her, as he had destroyed her. 'But in answer to your question—yes, I have been ill. Dr Fraser says that I nearly lost the baby. That would have pleased you, I know, would have made things a little less complicated for you. I got pneumonia right after Luther brought me home.'

'Luther?' he repeated tonelessly.

'Yes, Luther. Did you expect me to say Del?' She pushed on before he could say anything. 'I hate the very sight of you, Nathan—everything you are and stand for. No matter what you do or say nothing will change that. You can make me live with you, but you can't watch me all the time. You'll never know when I intend to leave, and leave I will.' She paused, then added harshly, 'Maybe it'll be with Del after all. That would nearly kill you, wouldn't it, Nathan?'

He stood staring down at her, his eyes searching for an answer to a question that would not take form on his lips. Then he turned and walked across to the door. 'Come on. Alice'll be waiting.' Without looking back at her, he added tightly, 'I can't let you go, Kristin. I tried to—all those weeks, that's what I tried to do. But God help me, I can never let you go.'

'Some day, Nathan,' she vowed bitterly, 'you will have no choice.'

The journey to the Landing was accomplished in almost total silence. The wind was high so they made good time, and despite everything, Kristin found the speed and fine lines of the yacht exhilarating. Once or twice she found herself on the verge of asking Nathan where and when he had purchased the *Stella Marie*, but she caught herself and continued to sit stiffly across from him in the stern. Halfway across he asked her if she shouldn't probably go below, because it would be warmer there, but she refused to respond or move and he didn't push the issue.

Supper at Alice's was no better. Luther had changed and gone out, while Alice was far from her normal chatty self. It was finally Nathan who broke the uncomfortable silence. He cleared his throat, put down his fork, and looked across the table at the plump, kind-faced woman who ate, trying to pretend that nothing out of the ordinary was happening. 'My being here in your house isn't such a good idea, Alice.'

She murmured something in response, but continued with her meal, obviously not giving much weight to his concerns.

'I've driven Luther out—it probably would be better if we left.'

Alice raised an inquisitive eyebrow. 'We?' she asked bluntly.

'Yes, "we"—Kristin and I.'

Alice leaned forward, punctuating the air with her fork. 'Let's settle some of this mess right here and now, Nathan. First of all, you didn't drive Luther out of his home. Luther makes his own decisions. What he thinks he can't live with is his problem—not mine and not yours. Secondly, you aren't taking Kristin anywhere. She stays right here.'

He stared at her in disbelief, dark anger clouding his face. 'She's coming——'

'Be quiet and let me finish,' Alice interrupted. 'All you men are the same, always ready to fight rather than to try and understand.' She got up and started to gather the dirty dishes. 'Can you stand some of my apple pie, you two?'

Kristin sat staring at the patterned tablecloth, the orange flowers melting before her eyes. She hadn't uttered a word since they left the Island and now her heart rose in her throat as she wondered what Nathan's reaction to Alice's pronouncement would be.

'I'm speaking to you as well, Kristin,' Alice said again.

'What?' the girl blushed. 'I'm sorry—no, thank you—I don't want any, thanks.'

Alice carefully cut a good-sized piece for herself, 'Well, I haven't lost my appetite.' She placed it on the table, sat down, and looked seriously into Nathan's eyes. 'I said you aren't taking her anywhere, Nathan, because you can't, not if you really care about her as you say you do.'

Nathan angrily pushed back his chair, stood up and walked across to the window, his hands thrust into his pockets. 'I'm through playing games, Alice,' he replied harshly. 'Because Kristin is my wife she belongs with me. And I intend her to be with me.' He turned around and tossed an icy glance at the older woman. 'Not even you can stop me.'

His ultimatum didn't seem to upset Alice, for she replied in the same calm, even tone. 'It's autumn, Nathan, the weather's turned. There are storms and cold weather coming. This isn't a soft land, as well you know. It's harsh and demands the best from all who live here. Where do you intend to take her?' She waved an impatient hand. 'There's not much time to go anywhere and settle in before winter. She could lose the child. And I'm darned if I'll let you take her to Victoria with you. She came back here a changed girl, not the happy, innocent child I knew. There's a dark side to her now and you, or something you let happen, caused that. Victoria is the last place she needs to be.'

'I told you already that I have no intention of going back there,' he said wearily.

'Where, then?'

'Here—on Sitka Island, in the old farmhouse. I know it's Kristin's now. I'm going to fix it up and we'll live there.'

'That'll take months.'

'No, it won't. It'll take a few weeks to make it liveable in and I can work on the rest during the winter.'

'Well, that doesn't sound too bad,' Alice admitted. 'What do you think, Kristin?'

'I think,' her voice broke and the tears streamed down her face again, 'I think I'm being treated like an object—a piece of property—and I hate you for it, Nathan, even more than before, if that's possible.' She saw the strange darkness fill

Nathan's eyes again. 'Yes, I do hate you, I really do,' she sobbed, her thin hands shaking and gripping the edge of the table for support.

'I believe you, Kristin——' he replied hoarsely, 'I do believe you.'

'And still you want me to go on living with you? What kind of a sham would that make our marriage?'

He turned from her and looked out into the darkness, his strained face reflected on the lighted window pane. 'You didn't always hate me, Kristin,' he whispered.

'That was before—before everything else. Now is what matters, not the past. The past is gone, can't you face that and let it go? Can't you let me go?'

'Never—I'll never let you go, and you must face that.'

'You can't stop me——'

'Be quiet, both of you!' Alice interjected. 'You're travelling in never-ending circles talking this way.' She sighed. 'I care for you both too much to watch you destroy each other, and that's just where you're heading. For heaven's sake put the brakes on.'

Neither of them responded.

'Look, you've got to try to settle this trouble between you. If you walk away now, Kristin, you'll never know if you could have saved your marriage.'

'I don't want to live with a man I hate beyond words, Alice. A man who——' she stopped abruptly.

Nathan swung round and faced her. 'A man who what, Kristin? Finish what you were going to say,' he demanded harshly.

She had almost spoken of his relationship with Carla, but fortunately had stopped herself in time; she had vowed she wouldn't tell anyone about it, so devastating had been her shame. 'Nothing.'

'Damn you, Kristin! Tell me what——'

'Ease off, Nathan,' Alice warned quietly, seeing the frantic look of fear and something else she could not yet define or understand flood the depths of Kristin's eyes. Alice had seen that look before when she had first returned home, when Kristin had not cared whether she lived or died. 'I want you both to stay here, Nathan—until the house is ready.' She raised a hand, anticipating his rejection of her plan. 'No, no more arguing. I've opened the upstairs rooms and they belong to you and Kristin for the next few weeks. All I ask is that you'll give each other a chance. There's already more than enough misery in this world without you adding your broken lives to it.' She smiled gently at them both. 'And here ends my sermon.'

Defeated, Kristin got up from the table and walked slowly towards the backstairs. But Alice's voice stopped her retreat. 'I haven't deserted you, child—no matter what you think. I love you like a daughter, remember that. And you, Nathan,' her voice became a whisper, 'you were family before you left and I pray you'll be family again. But,' she hesitated, her words coming now with great difficulty, 'Luther and I will stop you in any way we can if you try to take Kristin anywhere she doesn't want to go. It's got to be up to her at the end of it all. Remember that, because I mean every word I say. She can't be hurt again, not like she was when Luther brought her home to us four weeks ago.'

There seemed to be nothing more to say. Nathan closed the kitchen door and followed Kristin upstairs. The two rooms were both quite large, occupying the whole second floor, with the exception of a bathroom and shower. The smaller room was furnished with a desk and chairs as well as a single bed, while the other room was obviously a master bedroom. From it a narrow staircase led up to a platform that looked out over the water. Nathan put a hand on the railing.

'It's called a widow's walk, isn't it?'

She nodded, not looking at his face.

'Don't you wish you were in that category?' he asked bitterly.

'I don't wish you dead, Nathan. I only wish you out of my life,' she replied brokenly. 'I can't survive with you the way you are.'

His strong hands gripped her by the shoulders and swung her round to face him. 'The way I am? Just how is that, Kristin?'

She shook her head. 'Never mind, it's no use. Nothing you can say will change anything between us.'

He raked frustrated fingers through his thick hair. 'Dear

God, Kristin—please!' he pleaded. 'Please tell me. I've accepted the fact of your child. What else can I do?'

She gave him a searing glance, all the bitterness of the past weeks evident in her eyes, but she would not speak to him of Carla. Finally his hands dropped to his sides.

'Has the baby moved yet, Kristin?' he asked quietly, placing a gentle hand on her stomach.

Startled, she moved quickly away from him, shaking her head, her voice quivering with emotion. 'No, not yet. Dr Fraser says soon, though.'

For long moments Nathan stared down at her, his blue eyes baffled. Then, moving like an old man, he walked over to the door that led to the other bedroom. He hesitated, his hand on the knob. 'I won't touch you, Kristin,' he said tonelessly, 'not unless you want me to, so you don't have to flinch away from me like a terrified animal. I'll sleep in the other room.' With these words he walked out of the room, closing the door firmly behind him.

CHAPTER TWELVE

THE next two weeks were difficult ones for Kristin, being so near to Nathan and yet feeling so totally separated. She chose to avoid him, spending long hours alone. Luther was rarely home any more, often not even coming home for supper and Kristin missed her easy, comfortable times with him. Nathan himself worked long and hard out on the Island, leaving at dawn each morning and not returning until after dark. The strain and weariness showed in his growing thinness, in the tired lines of his face, and in the haunted look in his eyes. But still Kristin would not give in to him, and could only marvel at Alice's ability to continue on with her life as if everything was normal.

One evening the three of them were sitting in the living-room, Kristin with an open magazine on her lap, her eyes gazing at it sightlessly. 'For the second time, Kristin, what do you say to that?' Alice asked, holding in check any impatience she might be feeling.

'I'm sorry,' Kristin mumbled, 'I guess I wasn't listening.'

'That was obvious, I'd say,' Alice said tartly.

'What did you want?'

'Nathan said that the Island house will be finished in a few days. He's moving the wood stove over tomorrow and then there are just a few jobs to do and it'll be ready. I asked you what you thought of that.' Alice watched Kristin closely.

The girl could also feel Nathan's deep blue eyes focused unblinkingly on her. She blushed, feeling pursued and pressured by them both for a decision she did not want to make. Something in her wanted to give in and go with him, wanted to share the rest of her life with him on the Island, but something else told her to be realistic. He would never be totally hers—always there would be Carla and his belief that she was to have Del's child, not his, to keep them apart.

She avoided his eyes and got up from the table. 'If you'll excuse me, I'm very tired. I think I'll make it an early night.'

She quietly but firmly closed the door behind her and made her way up to her bedroom alone.

But sleep didn't come that easily. For hours she lay in her bed staring at the shadows created on the wall by the full moon, staring until even the shadows faded into blackness. She heard their low-voiced murmurs downstairs, then Nathan's slow footsteps on the stairs. She listened as he paused at her door, waited, then moved on to his own room. She held her breath, hating the treachery within her that desperately wanted him to come to her bed. Finally she closed her eyes and slept.

She was back in the drawing room at Maplewood. Green and gold, a mist shimmering in the morning light outside, the quiet punctuated by distant laughter. Kristin walked slowly into the room, dreading what she somehow knew she would find, her legs tired and protesting, wanting only to turn and run away. The noise grew louder and louder, the sound vibrating in her head. Faces—so many faces—grotesque images with gaping mouths screaming laughter. Mist rising and choking her, making her invisible to everyone—everyone but Carla, who stood by the piano with Nathan. He looked across the room at her, saw her, smiled, then purposefully bent and kissed Carla passionately on the mouth. Pain shot through Kristin, her entire being shattered by the sight of them together. Carla began to walk, holding Nathan's hand, pulling him towards her.

'No ... go away go away, Carla!' Carla finally looming over her, green eyes venomous.

'I told you that you'd just have to live with it.' Carla's thin voice screamed for all to hear, 'Nathan is mine. He will always be mine! *Mine!* Mine! Mine! ...' Carla's hands, long thin fingers with painted nails closing around Kristin's throat, stealing her breath as well as her heart. She fought, fought against the terror that was consuming her and the thin fingers that held so fast——

'No!' a cry, long and despairing, from the very depths of her pain. Then hands, different hands, strong and yet tender, pulling her up from the clutches of her despair; a voice, deep and resonant, bringing her back from the searing madness of it all.

'Kristin—Kristin—you're dreaming, child.'

She opened her eyes. The door between her room and

Nathan's stood open, and the light from his bedroom threw a yellow rectangle across her bed. Nathan, bare-chested and in blue jeans, sat on her bed, holding her tightly, rocking her gently. She stiffened with the realisation of his touch, the closeness of this man who only a few moments before had been with Carla. 'No,' she stammered, shaking her head, as if to clear it. That had been a dream, Nathan had said so. But his love for Carla was no dream, she knew that with agonising certainty. 'You kissed her,' she said brokenly. 'You love her, I know you do.' Finally she could hold back no more, as all the pain and despair of the past weeks burst forth, and she threw herself on the bed and cried openly.

This time he did not try to hold her but instead, with a soothing rhythm, stroked her hair. 'It's all right, Kristin. Cry until there are no more tears. Get rid of it all.' His voice moved about her, enfolded her and held her in its spell. At last she raised her tear-stained face. Alice was standing at the door.

'Does she need me?' Alice asked evenly.

'No,' Nathan replied, looking down at Kristin. 'I'll take care of her. It's all right now. She had a bad dream, but she's going to be all right.'

Alice nodded and quietly closed the door. Kristin heard her footsteps echo on the stairway and then the downstairs door close. They were alone again.

'Tell me about your dream, Kristin,' Nathan asked softly.

'I ... I can't. I can never tell you.'

'What did she do to you, Kristin?'

'Who?'

'Carla.'

She started. Did he know? Was his asking purely a pretence? 'Nothing. I don't want to talk about it.'

'You must talk about it.'

'No—I'm too ashamed.' She lowered her eyes, but he gently tipped her face up to look at his.

'What did she do, Kristin?' he persisted. The tenderness of his touch, the fact that he did not try to hold her, but sat patiently on the edge of the bed, waiting for her to tell him the truth, broke her defences. In a rush of uncontrolled words, she at last told him everything that had happened to her in the days prior to her leaving Maplewood with Luther—Carla's shattering disclosure and Marion's cruel dismissal of her. But still she could not bring herself to deny his charge that Del had fathered her child; the fact that he could believe this of her was too horrifying to be shared.

She finally fell silent. The flood of words and emotion left her exhausted and it had exorcised much of the bitterness and jealousy. For the first time in many days she saw Nathan— her husband—with unclouded vision. She had never seen such anguish in a man's face. Although his shocked blue eyes were trained on hers, she sensed he was not seeing her but others— Carla and Marion. He closed his eyes over the pain that had carved itself in them, and when he spoke, his voice was thick with emotion.

'May God forgive me for what I allowed to happen to you there.' He gathered her into his arms, holding her tightly against his chest. She felt the warmth of him, the rhythm of his heartbeat against her cheek. For a long moment he remained silent. 'Carla and I were lovers, Kristin,' he began slowly, 'once—a long time ago—before I came to Sitka. That was a lifetime ago. I haven't been with her since then. I've been with no other woman since I came to you, Kristin. You've got to believe me.'

'I do,' she replied quietly, relaxing in his arms, silently rejoicing at the meaning of his words—for she knew they were true. But he wasn't finished.

'You're carrying my child, aren't you, Kristin?' he asked in a voice so quiet that at first she wasn't sure he'd spoken. He must have felt the shock that quivered through her frame. She pulled away from him, but his hands rested on her shoulders, preventing her escape.

'Tell me,' he begged.

'Yes, the child is yours. I told you the truth when I said I've known no other man but you.'

His hands fell from her shoulders. He got up from the bed, walked to the window and stood staring out into the darkness. Kristin found herself longing for his return, for the comfort of his arms around her. Surely everything was all right now that they had cleared away the lies about Del, lies that had so nearly destroyed their marriage.

'Nathan?' she began.

'What is it?' he asked bleakly.

'What are you going to do?'

He laughed bitterly. 'That's a very good question. I was just asking myself the same thing.' He came closer to where she lay on the bed. 'I was thinking that——' he hesitated, what he was about to say obviously very difficult for him, 'after everything that's happened, that I've allowed to happen, I have no right to expect you to stay with me.' He reached down and took her hand in his. 'I love you more than my life, Kristin, and yet I've let terrible things happen to you. I've failed you, and I don't deserve to have you with me.' He took a deep breath and said with finality, 'I won't fight your request for a divorce.'

'Nathan, please . . .' she began, frightened now by the change in him.

He bent over her and fluffed her pillow. 'Hush, Kristin, and get some sleep. There'll be no more nightmares—the demons are in the open now.'

'Nathan . . .' she pleaded, holding tightly to his hand. 'I don't want to sleep alone. Don't leave me.'

'You're sure that's what you want?'

'Yes, I'm sure.'

Kristin woke often during the night, but drifted back into an easier sleep, comforted by the presence of Nathan, who held her close in his strong arms, the rhythm of his breathing steady and assuring. Everything would be all right now, she told herself, fully believing it at last.

Kristin stood at the sink, finishing the supper dishes, unconsciously staring at the clock. 'He's really late tonight, Alice.' She turned and looked at the older woman, concern filling her eyes. 'Do you think he's having trouble making the crossing? It's a bit rough out there tonight.' She had fully expected Nathan to return early today—after last night.

Alice too looked worried. 'No, it's not that. He tied up a half hour ago. I saw him come in. I don't know why he would take this long.' She smiled and put an arm around Kristin's slim shoulders. 'Why don't you go down to meet him? I know he'd be glad to see you.'

'I couldn't.'

'And why not?' Alice put her hands on her hips in mock admonition.

Kristin blushed and shrugged. 'I don't know. I . . .'

'Look, girl, he told me this morning about what's been bothering you both.' Kristin gave her a questioning look and Alice continued, 'You've both been victims, and not just of each other, either. But now it's all out in the open and you can heal each other's hurts, child, with no one to interfere or stop you from being honest and open about the love you share.'

'He said he won't fight my request for a divorce, Alice. I think he may want a divorce.'

'That man's done some foolish things, girl, but he's no fool. Divorce? Believe me, that's not what he wants—and definitely not what he needs.' Alice put a comforting arm around Kristin. 'He truly does love you—just as you love him. So never mind the excuses, get your coat on and go on down to the wharf and meet him. The fresh air'll be good for you and the baby.' She touched the girl's face. 'It's good to see that happy blush again.'

Kristin didn't argue further but got her coat and headed down towards the beach. The wind was high and it pushed against her back, as if trying to hurry her along. Because she was tired she thought of the difficult walk back, with the wind in her face. But she smiled to herself. Nathan would be with her. Things were going to be all right now, she was sure of it.

Once she thought she heard someone yelling and she stopped straining to hear, but only the whistling of the wind in the trees and the crash of the waves against the beach filled the air. The night was dark, with clouds scudding across the sky, the light of the moon coming through only at long intervals. Tomorrow would be cold and windy, but perhaps the sun would shine. Then she heard it again—the sound of angry voices, down the beach by the government wharf. She put a tender hand to her waist where the child was growing within her and at first was inclined to turn around and go back to Alice's and wait for Nathan there. But then her eyes widened in fear, not for herself but for Nathan, for her instincts told her that something was wrong, dreadfully wrong, and Nathan was in danger. She started to run towards the sound of voices and in minutes breathlessly rounded the side of the govern-

ment storage shed and came face to face with a circle of men—
angry and taunting, yelling insults at one who lay in the
midst of them, struggling to gain his feet. To her horror she
saw that it was Nathan.

'No!' she screamed, and would have run into their midst
had not someone gripped her arm and with a sweaty hand
covered her mouth. She was dragged back into the shadows,
no one in the circle aware of her presence.

Del Clarke's voice, a low animal growl, spoke in the terrifying darkness. 'Don't mix in this, Kristin. He's getting exactly
what I said he'd get if he stayed in these parts. He won't argue
with my advice again—not after tonight.' He laughed and
added, 'Even Luther approves of this bit of sport.' He took his
hand from her mouth and pointed to Luther's tall figure,
standing straight and still by the *Stella Marie* watching all that
was happening.

'Luther!' she screamed, but again her words were lost in
the wind. She twisted in Del's grip and would have escaped,
but his hand caught her firmly by the hair and yanked her
back against him. 'No,' she whimpered, 'dear God, please stop
them! They'll kill him!'

'They won't, but he'll damn well wish they had by the time
they finish with him.'

Helpless to do anything, she turned her head, not wanting
to see more, but Del's fingers took her roughly by the chin and
twisted her face round towards them. 'You watch, little lady,
it'll do you good. It's time you learned that I mean what I
say. I've been too patient with you. I mean to have you, one
way or another, and you'd better believe that.' She closed her
eyes in sheer horror, but Del swung her round to face him,
then lifted a hand and struck her on the cheek. 'Open your
eyes, girl, and look.'

Nathan was on his knees, his arms protecting his stomach,
his head resting against the wooden boards of the wharf. He no
longer struggled to get up. Suddenly one of Del's friends
stepped forward and kicked him in the side. He moaned and
collapsed into merciful unconsciousness.

Luther's deep voice filled the air. 'No more!' he yelled, the
words drawn out and carried like a cry of pain on the wind.
Del released his hold on Kristin and moved towards his men,

turning to face her once more before leaving.

'If he stays around, I'll kill him. You can tell him that for me. And you,' he sneered, 'I'll come for you when he's gone.' He turned and walked off the wharf, his henchmen following silently behind him, leaving the three of them alone on the wharf.

Luther stared at her with pained eyes. 'Oh God, Kristin, how long have you been there?'

She stood absolutely still, her heart pounding frantically, struggling to make sense of the horrifying things they'd done to Nathan, and the fact that Luther had stood there and watched. 'Oh, Luther,' she whispered brokenly, 'how could you? How could you let them do that to him? He was your friend!'

'That's right. He *was* my friend,' Luther said bitterly. 'I wanted to kill him for what he did to you, Kristin.'

'So you let them do your dirty work for you, is that it?'

'Better them than me, believe me.'

She walked towards Nathan, but Luther stepped in front of her. 'No, leave him.'

She stared at him in wonderment. 'Luther,' she cried, 'he's hurt! He needs help.'

'He doesn't need our help. He can deal with this alone. He's not family.'

The stinging pain in her hand and the growing redness on Luther's face told her she had struck him. But she had no memory of it. She stood staring at her hand and then looked evenly into Luther's face. 'He's my family, Luther,' she replied firmly. 'He's my husband and the father of my child. Now you stand aside, because he has need of me.'

For a moment she thought Luther would try to prevent her from going to Nathan. Then he swore under his breath, stepped aside and let her pass. She knelt beside the motionless form on the wharf, not knowing what to do, at first afraid to touch him. He was so still. For a moment terror shook her slim frame—perhaps they had killed him. He was lying face down on the damp boards. She put out a tentative hand and touched his head; his silky hair was wet and tousled. She tried to roll him over on to his back, straining with effort against his weight.

Luther's gruff voice sounded behind her. 'Stop it! You'll hurt yourself if you try to move him.'

She knew he was right, she couldn't possibly move him—he was just too heavy. Looking up at Luther's unmoving face, she begged, 'Help me, Luther. Please help me!'

He glared back at her. 'I say leave him.'

Anger rose in her throat. 'Damn you! No matter what you believe about him you know he would never have stood by and let such a terrible thing happen to you. And never in a million years would he walk away from you—not if you needed his help.'

Still Luther didn't move. 'I'm not leaving him, Luther,' she reiterated. 'We both need your help now. For God's sake, don't leave him like this!'

Without a word Luther leaned down and rolled Nathan over on his back. Nathan groaned and raised his arms to cover his face, as if to ward off another blow.

'Nathan,' Kristin whispered, 'Nathan, it's me—Kristin. Can you hear me?' His hands fell to his sides.

'Kristin?' he whispered hoarsely, through bruised lips, his eyes still closed.

'Yes . . . it's all right. I'm here with you.' She looked frantically across at Luther, who was kneeling on the wharf beside him. 'What do we do, Luther? How can we get him home?'

Luther shook his head. 'He can't get home. He'd never be able to walk that far. Maybe we should get him aboard the *Stella Marie*. He could stay there tonight.' He looked down at Nathan and thought for a moment. 'No, forget that. Del and his boys are still around. There's no telling what they'd do if they knew he was on the boat. Maybe I can get him up the hill. Go get some water from the *Stella Marie* and I'll try to get him on his feet.' He pointed to the other side of the wharf, 'And hand me his jacket—it's getting colder.'

She did as she was told and within minutes returned with a glass of water and a towel. Luther grabbed the cloth and glass, saying roughly, 'Not for drinking, Kris——' and poured the water over the cloth, wrung it and laid it across Nathan's forehead, then wiped some of the blood from his face. Nathan's eyes flickered open. He tried to speak, but no words escaped his lips, and although he looked into Kristin's eyes, he didn't seem to recognise her.

Luther spoke. 'Come on, man—time to get you on your feet.' Nathan's glassy stare shifted to Luther and something in them indicated recognition.

'Go to hell, Luther,' he whispered bitterly.

'Listen to me, Nathan. If it was up to me I'd leave you lying here. You could make your own way to wherever you choose to go. As it is, Kristin won't leave you and I don't intend for her to get hurt any more than she already has been over the likes of you. So——' he stood up, stretching to full height, 'like it or not, we do this my way.' He bent down, put his hands on the front of Nathan's shirt and pulled him roughly to his feet. Kristin saw Nathan grimace as a wave of pain tore through him. He fought against the faintness that threatened to wash over him and would have fallen but for Luther's strong bulk supporting him in his struggle for balance.

'Take your hands off me, Luther,' he muttered.

'Shut up and do as you're told. It's a long way up the hill to Alice's—you'll never make it alone.'

'That's the only way I'll go, damn you, Luther,' and weak as he was, Nathan fought against Luther's hold on him. Finally Kristin interrupted.

'Leave him, Luther,' she said evenly.

Startled, he looked at her. 'What are you talking about? You said . . .'

'Never mind what I said. He can't take your help, not now—not yet. Let him be.'

Luther stepped back. Nathan stood unsteadily, facing them both. 'Take her with you,' he said through gritted teeth.

'No, I'm staying with you,' she responded firmly.

'I don't need or want your help, Kristin, so get the hell out of here.'

'Do what he says, Kristin,' Luther interjected roughly.

Kristin looked unflinchingly at Luther. 'I know you can make me leave with you, but don't—please don't. I have to stay with him, can't you understand that?' The look in her eyes told him that to force her to leave him now would hurt her more than anything that had happened already.

'All right,' he said helplessly. 'It's your life.' Then he turned and walked away.

The light in the kitchen flickered once or twice, then went out. Alice got up, fetched the oil lamp from the sideboard, lit it, and handed it to Luther. She spoke in a matter-of-fact tone. 'Take it up to Dr Fraser.' The wind screamed mournfully and the rain beat furiously against the windows as Luther left the kitchen, his footsteps falling heavily on the wooden stairs, mimicking the fearful pounding of Kristin's heart. She sat curled up on the couch by the stove, hugging her legs, staring straight ahead into nothingness.

Alice lit another lamp, placed it on the table, then sat down next to Kristin on the couch. 'He'll be all right, Kristin—you've got to believe that.' But her worried tone belied her attempt at reassurance.

Kristin could only sit there, numbly recalling Nathan's agonised struggle up from the wharf. Coming up the hill he had fallen twice, once landing heavily on his side, but still he refused to give in and accept her help, and had managed to get back on his feet and move doggedly on. Finally they had reached Alice's, but the cost to him was immense, pain carving itself on his bruised face and his breath coming in short agonised gasps. He had walked slowly into the kitchen.

Luther had been waiting. 'You're a stubborn fool, Nathan Raines, that's what you are,' he muttered gruffly as he put a supporting arm across the other man's shoulders. Only then did Nathan, his strength spent, close his eyes and lean all his weight against Luther. He let Luther half drag and half carry him up the stairs to the bedroom, while Alice radioed for Dr Fraser.

Now Kristin heard Luther coming back downstairs, Dr Fraser following closely behind him. She got quickly to her feet and went over to the doctor, who took her small hands in his and stared silently down at her for a long, tense moment.

'Doctor?' she questioned, unable to phrase the question that preyed on her mind.

He shook his head and swore under his breath. 'It's a poor business that went on tonight, I can tell you.' He raised his eyes to look sternly at Luther. 'Believe it or not, Nathan's a lucky man—they could have killed him. Somebody's got to stop that bunch. They're a law unto themselves.'

'Never mind all that right now—just tell us how bad it is, Doctor,' Alice said bluntly.

'He's a strong man—he'll recover. Physically he's badly bruised and cut, but there's no internal damage.'

'Thank God!' Alice breathed a sigh of relief. But Kristin sensed something more in the tone of his words, in the tightness with which he held her hands.

'I wish that was all,' he added slowly. No one spoke as they waited in hushed silence. 'Look,' he began self-consciously, 'I don't know what's happened in this family. Except for Nathan, I've known you all a good many years and I care for you a lot.' He waited, then continued, throwing caution to the wind, anger growing in his voice. 'That man up there is being destroyed—and not just by Del Clarke and those outlaws he gathers round him. Whatever it's about he can't fight you any more—he's given up.' He shook his head sadly. 'I'd say he'll be leaving Sitka Landing as soon as he's well enough to move about again—and my guess is that he'll be going alone.' He looked down at Kristin. 'Without you and the baby, Kristin.'

She drew a ragged breath. 'Why? Why do you say that?'

'Because he's convinced that you and Luther both had a hand in what happened to him tonight.'

'No!' she gasped. 'That's impossible! I had nothing to do with it.'

'He didn't say that directly. What he said was that he had no idea how deeply you both hated him, not until tonight, and that he won't and can't fight you any more.'

He released her hands and gently directed her towards the stairs. 'I know I'm not family, Kristin, and I've probably got no right interfering, but what's happening to you both is so useless and wasteful. He's a good man, Kristin, so why don't you go to him? He needs you quite desperately at the present moment, I'd say.'

Blinded by tears, she groped towards the stairs and had placed her foot on the first step when Luther's grim voice stayed her movement. 'I'm not proud of what happened tonight, Kristin. Tell him for me that I'm sorry and ashamed because of what I didn't do,' he gave a half-hearted grin and added, 'And tell him that I'll never regret what I'm about to do.' He turned and walked over to the radio. 'Del Clarke and company are finished in Sitka Landing and any place within a thousand miles of here. The R.C.M.P. will be more than interested in some of the things I have to tell them about our Mr Clarke.'

Kristin slipped into the bedroom and quietly closed the door behind her, the click of the latch echoing in the silence. The lamp stood on the bureau close to the door, throwing off a yellow light, the flame dancing behind the glass. She slowly walked to the bed and gazed down at Nathan's still body. He was resting more peacefully now, his breathing more regular, no longer coming in short gasps. Thinking he was sleeping, she carefully pulled a chair over to the bedside and sat down. His voice startled her.

'What do you want, Kristin?'

'I came to be with you, that's all.'

'Go away.' His words were blunt and toneless and he didn't bother to open his eyes.

'Nathan,' she stammered, 'Dr Fraser told me what you think and it's not true—you're not right about that.'

He opened his eyes and stared at her, not moving a muscle. 'And just what did the good doctor tell you?'

'That you think I had something to do with Del Clarke and his gang and what happened to you tonight.' Her words came with a rush of tears. 'I didn't, you must believe that. I could never——'

'Didn't you?' he interrupted.

'No! I swear to you——'

'Damn you both! Luther said that you wanted me away from here, away from you, and that maybe this way I'd get your message. He stood by and watched it all—he let it happen.' He swallowed and closed his eyes. 'Well, I've got your message, Kristin—I've just had trouble accepting it until now.' She sat very still as he whispered into the darkness. 'The hell of it is that I thought ... that last night we had a chance together. Now I know we haven't.' He cleared his throat and said more loudly. 'I'm leaving tomorrow. I'll make sure that you and the baby are well taken care of—financially at least.'

She got up and walked to the window, knowing that she was

fighting for her very life. Her words dropped into the silence. 'Yes, I think you're right, Nathan. We don't belong together. We cause nothing but heartaches for each other—it's been that way from the beginning.'

Her voice sounded foreign to her own ears, as she watched the rivulets of rain running down the window, the lights down on the wharf melting red in the blackness. All caution fled and she knew that now was her last chance and she must take it. 'And do you know why we don't belong with each other, Nathan? It's because we can't believe in each other. Always something happens and we're more than willing to doubt.' She pressed her warm cheeks against the cold window pane. 'I believed the worst of you with Carla—and let your mother drive me away from you. And you believed that Del and I——' Tears flooded her eyes, the ache in her heart filling her throat. She couldn't go on, knowing that she had lost him, irrevocably. But she had to make him understand. Desperation filled her voice. 'And now you believe that I would condone, actually want those men to do that to you!'

In utter despair she sank slowly to the floor, weeping openly, covering her face with her hands, 'Why can't you see that I love you—that I can't live without you?'

'Kristin——' Nathan called to her faintly from the bed.

She looked up to see him struggling to sit up, a grimace of pain on his face. 'I think you'd better come to me, Kristin, if you don't want to see me fall flat on my face.' He held out his hand to her. 'Please,' he breathed quietly.

She rose and walked towards him as he carefully lowered himself back on to the bed. 'Will you lie with me, Kristin— like last night?'

She hesitated, then took off her shoes and lay down beside him. They lay together for a long time, Kristin cradled in Nathan's arms, but she could not relax, the spectre of his threatened departure looming over her. Finally she spoke, her heart pounding in fear of the answer she might receive. 'Are you leaving me, Nathan?'

He turned to look at her and what she saw in his eyes made her heart leap. 'Oh God, Kristin!' He pulled her closer to him, crushing her with the fervency of his passion. 'I've doubted you when all I should have done was love you. No one's ever loved me that completely and, fool that I am, I found it impossible to believe.' He placed a gentle hand on her breast. 'I can't leave you—I love you more than life itself.' You are my life, Kristin.' He buried his face in her silken hair. 'I want to stay with you for ever—if you'll still have me.'

She did not have to speak, for the joy in her face was answer enough.

Harlequin® Plus

A WORD ABOUT THE AUTHOR

Jan MacLean is a pseudonym for Sandra Field, who is a resident of Nova Scotia, one of Canada's Maritime provinces. Whenever Sandra co-writes a book with her best friend, Jan MacLean is the name she uses.

Born in England, Sandra considers herself a true convert to the Canadian maritime way of life. She has lived in all three Maritime provinces, but it was during her stay on tiny Prince Edward Island, where the beaches are legendary but the winters long, that she first decided to write a book. The local library provided her with a guide for aspiring authors, and she followed its instructions to a tee.

This was no simple job, she recalls now. In fact, a major crisis occurred when she ran out of plot several thousand words short of the mark! But eventually, to the delight of future readers, she completed it. The book was *To Trust My Love* (Romance #1870), published in 1975.

Sandra's many interests, which she likes to weave into her stories, include bird-watching, studying wild flowers and participating in such winter activities as snowshoeing and cross-country skiing. She particularly enjoys classical music, especially that of the Romantic period.